I0637521

SEARCHING FOR A PLACE CALLED HOME

A Novel by Anjana M. Barad, MD

The Anantaram Family
Parents: Ananta & Susheila
Children: T.V Sundaresh; Chirag; T.K. Ramaswamy;
Brunda; Pushpa; Aradhana; Geetha; Shrilata; Pooja

The Srikantayya Family
Parents: Srikantayya & Kamala
Children: Manasa & Vanamali

The Ramaswamy Family
Parents: T.K. Ramaswamy & Vanamali
Children: Murali & Uma

The Hoysala Family
Parents: Natarajan & Parvathi
Children: Sunela; Ratna& Upala (twins); Giri; Manni

The Murthy Family
Parents: Prakash & Ratna
Children: Seetha; Nilkanth; Shiva; Apoorva

PART ONE

Chapter One: Baba. India, March 1940

There was a harsh rap on the door followed by loud honks from rickshaws surrounding the white Ambassador car that parked outside Baba's quiet home, on a hot Sunday afternoon. Baba was startled by the unexpected knock and hurried to put away the meticulously arranged map, Deccan Herald and the pile of letters placed next to his afternoon masala chai and Parle G biscuits. He was not expecting anyone. Maybe it was one of his beloved sisters, he thought, coming to drop off some delicious goodies for the baby. Or perhaps it was a neighbor, although he would have typically known this ahead of time. Vanamali hurried to help, infant in hand, carefully covering her head with her sari dress edge, lest the unexpected visitors peered through the window. She took the biscuits away, but not fast enough from baby Murali, who quickly munched on the cookie with joy. Baba opened his door making sure mother and baby were both safely situated in the bedroom, away from view of strangers.

"Mr. T.K. Ramaswamy, Sir, please confirm that is your good name."

Baba, slightly troubled by the question, nodded while holding back the urge to add more words except "Yes" to his response. He answered obediently.

"You will have to come with us now," said the young police officer timidly, "we have a warrant for your arrest"

"Umm," commented Baba, calmly, looking directly into the young officer's eyes through his round black-rimmed spectacles, "there must be some sort of misunderstanding, there has been no wrong-doing here" he stated, and then paced further into his living room. "Is there something more that I may help you with?"

Officer Reddy took a few steps forward, quickly glancing at the coffee table from where Baba had been reading some papers. He then tracked the layout of the bungalow. It was a comfortable home, clean, with amenities not known to the majority of residents of the town. A radio was in the corner between the living room and kitchen. He had a mahogany dining table a small whicker swing in another corner and a classic Delhi rug defined the living room floor. On the side table next to the radio, Officer Reddy noticed a black and white photograph of a young activist, probably Ramaswamy, embracing another man. Both of the photographed men were smiling, genuinely happy.

"Who is that person with you, in the photograph?" asked the officer.

"That is the honorable Mohandas K. Gandhi," replied Baba. He hurried to change the topic adding, "Can I get you something to drink? Maybe some lemon water?"

"That would be lovely," replied Officer Reddy. "Do you mind if I sit down?"

"All right, go ahead," Baba replied, knowing full-well that he had no desire to entertain this character particularly on a Sunday night. T.K. Ramaswamy quickly called Vanamali out from the room. She promptly made "nimbu-pani", or lemon water and brought this to the coffee table along with some puffed rice and spicy peanut savories. Reddy, who was thirsty and famished from the sweltering humidity of monsoon season, sat down and started to munch. However, the barrage of questions was relentless.

"May I ask you how you know Mohandas Gandhi?" requested the officer.

"Only if I can ask you the same!" retorted Ramaswamy, a bright young lawyer and now public servant.

"Well," replied Reddy, " I really do not known him at all, but I have heard he gives the best speeches."

"Yes, he does", Baba responded, with a kind smile. The officer waited, expecting a response to his original question. "I met him while a law student at Oxford University. Gandhiji is a brilliant man, and most inspiring speaker. He has the ability to motivate a crowd, more than any other human being I know."

Reddy gulped down the lemon sherbet quickly, eagerly quenching his thirst, then wiping the drips from his mouth with the back of his sleeve.

"What is your relationship with Mr. Gandhi?" asked Reddy, with a slightly more authoritative voice than earlier that evening.

Baba took his handkerchief from his pocket and wiped his brow, tired from a mentally exhausting week, and hoping that the officer would leave quickly. Vanamali, rushing behind baby Murali to prevent the infant from disturbing the men, did not achieve what she set out to. Murali, now crawling on the marble floor from bedroom to living room, was giggling while moving away from his mother. Reddy turned to smile at the baby.

"Just like little Lord Krishna!" he exclaimed. While the officer approached Murali, Baba took this momentary distraction and quickly finished the message that he had been writing. He somehow managed to place his little black notebook in between the pages of the Deccan Herald, prior to turning back towards his unwanted guest.

"He's a college visiting lecturer and we try to keep in touch, that's all," Baba finally answered the man.

The officer looked slowly up and down the portage of Mr. Ramaswamy. He was a handsome, tall man, some six feet tall, lean, with a long, fair face and lean nose, a graceful smile and kind eyes. His glasses gave him a scholarly look, but he dressed only in homespun cotton or khadi, stiffly pressed and starched so that it shone with crisp white and beige accents of color. He could not have been more than thirty years old by appearance, but attending college with the Mahatma would suggest his age to be at least forty. This puzzled Reddy.

"Perhaps Gandhiji only gave lectures in Oxford when he was back in India," the officer concluded. He turned his gaze back to his study of Mr. T.K. Ramaswamy. His English was polished, making it somewhat difficult for Reddy to understand all that he was saying. Reddy had only attended Telegu medium schools, and was uncomfortable speaking only English. However, if he wanted to advance in his career, he needed to broaden his expertise and succeed in his duties. He fancied himself as marrying material too. How would he get a good wife unless he was successful in the police force? Pulling his shoulders back and raising his head up straight, he stared at Baba's face and wondered what was his plan. Why would this sophisticated man waste his time with Gandhi and his cause? It certainly would not help in raising his young family.

Reddy imagined living in this setting. For a fraction of a moment he pictured himself married and with a young infant, working and enjoying life. How could he afford this type of living? The only way he could afford his motor-bike now was to accept bribes from local kids caught up in drinking and drug raids, or take some money from the wretched red-light women who would be disgraced if they were written up in public.

"I have been sent to take you into the police station for questioning regarding your role in the movement with Mr. Gandhi," the officer stated firmly. "Please come with me."

"This is nonsense, I cannot be taken for no reason," Baba stated, now beginning to feel irritation at the smug look on the young man's face.

"Mr. Ramaswamy, you will have to follow me to abide by the law. I'm sure you know this."

Baba, sensing the firm tone of Reddy's voice, collected his khadi jacket.

"I just need to explain to my wife where I am going, so that she not become alarmed at this late hour," explained Baba. He proceeded to the bedroom, closed the door behind him, and quickly whispered in Vanamali's ear what had just transpired.

"Vana, you will have to go with Murali to my sister Brunda's house and let her and Dr. Rai know that I have been taken to the station. Let them know right away!" He pushed the rolled up Deccan Herald newspaper in her hands, glancing down its core where the speedily written telegram lay.

"I do not know what is about to happen, so the sooner you go, the better. See if Brunda, or even Parth can watch Murali tonight. And," he paused while turning back to look at his young wife, "Don't let anyone see you leave the house." Leaving Vanamali with a bewildered look on her face, he turned and left, following the officer out of the front door. Moments later, Vanamali grabbed his umbrella from the stand, in preparation for her journey.

Chapter Two: Vanamali

"Little one, come here; follow me," she gently pleaded, tugging the playful infant's fingers away from her plait and setting the buxom boy onto the cool marble floor, so she could straighten her fabric pleats. " Shall we go out for some fun?" she asked the little one, eagerly. "Come on, Murali, let's go on an adventure," she repeated. When he proceeded to play with the tassels decorating her ethnic clothing, not seeming amused by her questioning, she tried again.

"Boppa hoganna naavu?" she asked, with a twinkle in her eye, "Shall we go out for fun?" Murali, this time engaged, giggled and tugged at her dress some more. He followed his mother crawling, into the living room, at times moaning and raising his arms for her to carry him. She was not so thrilled to go out on a monsoon-soaked Sunday evening, with a toddler in her arms, yet the mere suggestion of urgency from her husband worried her. She knew he was a peacekeeper who was untroubled by the trip he was making to the police station. This was a trip he had made many times before, usually self-willed, for the intent of helping another young friend in a particular situation. But police stations scared her. She had trouble with confrontation, and could not usually fake calmness the way her handsome spouse could. She was scared too. The trip to her sister-in-law's bungalow was only a few kilometers, but in the rains she would have typically journeyed in a rickshaw, and at this late hour, she knew these would be hard to find. Plus, the family car which was usually parked in front of her other brother-in-law's house, was nowhere in site. Sundaresh was probably using the car to get around due to a flare up of gout in his knees, an affliction that had never troubled Baba due to his excellent health and walking habit. "Never mind," she thought to herself, time is precious, she'd better get on with it. Hugging Murali on her hip, she left the house from the back door, double bolting it, and glancing around her as she walked away, to ensure no one was watching her.

Murali seemed to enjoy his walk in the rain with his Amma. There was so much to observe, a fiesta for his eyes. He glanced behind his mother, looking back at his house, watching the tiny shed latrine door fade in the distance. He then hugged Amma's shoulder a little closer, so as to peer over her shoulder, giving him a view of the few taller buildings that were cropping up over town. As she turned the corner of her street and veered towards the high street, more small shops and stalls were in sight. They passed a "Qwality" ice cream stand, which excited Murali.

"Ice keem!" he exclaimed, "Mma, ice-keem!" he repeated, turning and looking at his mother, to see if he would get his way.

" NO, my precious" she replied, softly, "We need to reach Brunda Aunty's house quickly now," she explained. "Akka will give you something to nibble on when we arrive." They proceeded, passing several small shops on the way, from newspaper stores, to sweet marts, to the local chemist and drinks stall. Murali, now feeling the fatigue and the humidity, rested his head on his mother's shoulder, as if to nap.

"We are almost there, son", Vanamali explained, feeling the weary head of her little boy in her arms.

"Look at!" she exclaimed, trying to keep Murali engaged just a bit longer, "do you see the bus?" The red cycle rickshaw passed by, fumes sputtering everywhere, and people piling on and stepping off quickly as the vehicle approached the stand.

"Look, look!" the baby exclaimed, acknowledging his mother's attention. He was weary now, eyes droopy as his head bounced back and forth with the undulating movements of his mother's moves, as she picked up the speed of her gait, hurrying to the white mansion that was now in sight.

As Vanamali approached the veranda of her sister-in-law's bungalow, the maidservant was in waiting, with outstretched hands, ready to take baby Murali and dry him off. She was greeted eagerly, with a warm smile from Brunda and butterfly kisses for Murali. Filtered coffee was already prepared, and laid out in the living room. Vanamali, appreciating the hospitality, gave a smile of relief. The fatigue was lifting from her face, and the coffee was refreshing.

"To what do we owe this pleasure?" asked Brunda, pouring herself a cup to give company. "Where's Chickanna?" she asked. Brunda was younger than her brother Baba, but since she had three brothers and Baba was only the second eldest child, she and the siblings preferred to call him "little brother," or "Chick-Anna". Just like all of her other siblings, she called Baba this with the greatest affection, doting over him for they loved him so much. He was the sweetest, and gentlest of the family. Vanamali turned to make sure Murali was settled in. Indeed, cousins Parth and Preethi, Brunda's children, were already playing with Murali, doting on him and following his every little crawl. She turned to address Brunda. "Where is Dr. Rai?" she asked.

"He is just washing his face. He will be down any moment," she explained. Vanamali sipped on her coffee, anxiety slowly weighing on her weary mind as she thought about her husband, from whom there was no news in the last two hours. Dr. Rai's voice was heard coming down the curved staircase.

"Namaskara ,Vanamalamma!" he exclaimed joyfully, "Where is Chickanna?" Arvind Rai, although elder to Baba, also enjoyed referring to Ramaswamy affectionately as, "little brother." Vanamali carefully explained her situation: the police officer's unexpected visit, the questioning and Baba's subsequent trip to the station. She stood up now, remembering the newspaper and message in the center of the paper that Baba insisted be shown to the doctor. Rai first glanced at the notebook, eyeballing the detail. He observed the date, the headlines, then turned to the center where the white notepaper was placed. He took the paper and proceeded to the coffee table, beckoning his wife and sister-in-law to follow him. They sat, staring at the paper in front of them. Vanamali's face was ashen white. Dr. Rai looked at her, with kind eyes. He stared at the paper again, following each letter carefully.

TELEGRAM GANDHI NOW. TIME IS RUNNING OUT. SPEAK TO NEHRU SAAB. TAKE ACTION IMMEDIATELY. I DO NOT KNOW WHEN I WILL BE COMING HOME. RAI- THE TIME IS NOW.

"I do not understand!" cried Vanamali, eyes filling up with tears. "What does he mean by this? What am I to do? Why have they taken him?"

Chapter Three: Hardball

"We wish to know what is your involvement with Gandhiji and what are your group's plans within Hyderabad?" questioned the officer. He paused, and stared directly into Baba's eyes, watching his facial expressions and eager to see if he would flinch, blink or look away. Baba pondered for a moment.

"Should I educate these policemen and try to make them understand the cause, or fake innocence?" He thought to himself. He slowly took his handkerchief out of his breast pocket and cleaned his spectacles methodically. He looked at the officer.

"It's getting a bit late, no?" asked Baba, looking at the young officer. "Perhaps you desire to go home to your family and eat a hot dinner." Officer Reddy, growing a little weary now, paced the interrogation room for a few moments and then faced Ramaswamy again.

"Look," he said firmly, " I know that you also need to get home to your family," Reddy sighed, "but I have been asked to question you in conjunction to the Shah Jahan and Osmania College protest riots last week. What do you know about them?"

Baba smiled pleasantly, looked directly at the officer and slowly proceeded to answer this question.

"I did hear of the unrest on campus last week," he admitted, "but I do not know what spurred so much chaos. I for one deplore commotion. I do recall that I was heading home from my office, by foot, when I saw police cars and heard sirens heading in the direction of the college. Unfortunately, I know nothing of the events that later unfolded. Could you enlighten me, officer?" he requested.

"Listen, a few students were held in conjunction with the riots. The British gentry were so frightened that their Colonel Brumley took a holiday back to England, unpaid. The British fear the political uprising is coming from the local professors, who may be invoking the youngsters. One of the law students admitted that he was being fed information and provoked to act in quiet protests, yet rather than quelling the disturbance, the professor apparently fueled him into a skirmish. You seem like a reasonable man, with a family, surely you do not wish young lives to be affected this way?"

Baba took out his white handkerchief again and wiped his brow.

"Forgive me!" he exclaimed, " I do not tolerate much heat The humidity this time of year is rather like a steam bath for me. My wife worries that I develop a ruddy complexion much like a beetroot!" Baba looked at the officer as if to judge his mood. Reddy smiled, the frown on his forehead relaxing, and took a seat opposite Baba, facing him across the exam table. He sipped on his masala tea that had become slightly lukewarm from sitting out on the table unattended. It didn't matter much to Reddy, who had grown accustomed to cold meals and many cups of overcooked chai. It was better than nothing, he thought. He looked up at Baba, raised his eyebrows, and awaited a response.

"My thoughts and prayers are with the students who are pulleys in the arms of the politicians."

"Yes, but do you know anything about this? The teachers, students or politicians?" Reddy inquired, beginning to show his impatience.

"I know that you would probably know more about the politicians and their ways, more than an ordinary civil servant like myself," said Ramaswamy. "I'm just trying to raise a family, earn my keep, and keep my head!" he added, with a smile.

"Ok, yes, I do see that you have a young family", Reddy responded, softening his voice and slowing his pace. "But, don't you want your wife to feel safe and your son to grow up as part of a thriving community? This is what we seek. I'm just a local police officer, assigned to your neighborhood. I was notified that you were a person of interest in the riot at Osmania College. I would like to understand why your name came up if you are just an ordinary claims agent?"

Baba pondered, removed his spectacles again and cleaned them, breathing on the glass lenses then wiping them clean. He wished he had been able to speak to his brother-in-law Dr. Rai to seek advice. Did he know yet that Baba was at the station? What should he do? If he detailed the officer, and the officer was not an honest man, then a travesty would occur. If, however, he risked revealing the plan but the officer was honest, then lives could be saved and his homeland could be a better place in the future. If only he had a sign or some way of knowing what was the best course of action. He worried about Vanamali and baby Murali. Did they reach Rai's house safely? Had Vana given Dr. Rai the message? Would they risk coming to the station? If only he knew what to do next.

Baba closed his eyes for a moment, thinking about the officer's entrance into his home and how officer Reddy had picked up the photo in his living room. Baba was remembering his friend and mentor, Gandhi. It was only ten years prior that Baba had marched alongside Gandhi during the infamous Salt March. It was a privilege walking alongside the Mahatma, pride and unity the central focus of the nonviolent protest of British taxation. Though weary after the first ten miles, the young men of the Satyagraha movement felt bonded and committed to the mission to create an Independent India. Baba remembered how energized the men had felt when they arrived at Dandi in Navsari, Gujarat, and made salt. Later, he and Gandhiji marched on to Dhanasara. Mahatma was captured by police a day prior to reaching the Dhanasara Salt Works. Baba recollected the anguish people felt, but how they had all plodded on, eager to finish what they had set out to do. Sure enough, the police and British forces were waiting for the protestors in full force, at Dhanasara. Baba, who had crouched down by the lake to look at the shoreline and see the salt, was behind some of the other men who were already harvesting salt with glee. It seemed perfect, a unified front, collecting salt for their nation. Pride resounded as further Satyagraha supporters joined in. Baba took the help of a local farmer, entering his humble abode so that he could mend his spectacles. The pair of eyeglasses was damaged during the long journey. He used cloth and tape to fix the corners, and soon he could see easily again. He marched back outside to the shoreline, only to bear witness to thousands of people being pulled away brutally by the police officers. Some eighty thousand people were jailed that day, for standing up for their rights. Baba shook his head in silent disgust nauseated that brutality could still preside in spite of civil behavior. He still was in disbelief that the young farmer and his children had been jailed simply because of their participation in the March. Baba had wanted, just at that wavering moment, when the to strike the policeman.

"How could anyone take a child away from his mother?" he had thought. Yet the officers had been relentless, ridiculing the farmers and jeering at the poor, while the British men divided the crowd harshly.

Baba traveled that night, to the local prison, in the hope that his legal background would assist the prisoners in being released. It had taken two full weeks to release most of the captives, even though there had really not been any legal reason to imprison the masses. Gandhiji still was not released, for one full year. On his release, Baba and some of the Mahatma's closest men had received him. The framed photograph that was displayed on Baba's foyer table was of this very reunion of activists and friends. It was a gift to Baba from Dr. Rai, his brother-in-law. Yet now, a decade later, he was in prison without fair reason, interminably questioning if the day of independence would ever come.

Baba continued to dream about the decade that had passed, and about all the elements that had shaped his personality. "Stay focused," he whispered to himself, trying to keep his mind calm, void of anger, but centered on the common purpose.

Chapter Four: Vanamali's story

Tirumakudalu, November 1930

How she loved the village! Fresh air, plenty of lake water, scenic walks and beautiful creatures! But most of all, she loved to swim. It was an escape she looked forward to every day. She would leave school, run home and, if the weather permitted and no chores were expected at that time, she would take a scenic adventure. Vanamali would wrap her scarf from her "langa-downy" maxi-dress in a dhoti fashion, threading the material through her legs, so that the maxi skirt now looked like a pair of modern genie pants. Then, tying her plaits across her head like a German maiden, she prepared herself for the swim. She was quite precocious for her age, when it came to doing things like this. She had already given her school notebook to her elder sister, Manasa, to take home. She was free! Oh, the joys of simple pleasures. The air felt light and the grasses and plants gave the afternoon air a fragrant scent. As she dove into the water, the thoughts in her head seemed to disappear and she imagined she was a mermaid, always in the water, beautiful and rare, like a pearl in an oyster. The water was cool, but she enjoyed the freshness and started off in a front crawl, moving like a fish. She had about a mile of swimming to do, but this did not intimidate her. She could have chosen to walk home with her friends, but she preferred her solitude and adventure. There was nowhere else in the world that she imagined she would find so much joy and peace.

A half kilometer into her swim, she took a breathe out from the water, and glanced towards a cliff edge and riverbank in site. Opting for a short break, she swam to the shore, and propped herself up on the grey boulder. She sighed, looking up at the sun beaming down. She tidied up her plait, squeezing the drops of water from the plait that was weighing her down. It was amazingly serene. A panoramic view of the lake revealed there was no one in sight. Her sister Manasa would have been so frightened of this scenario. Only too often their mother had threatened them of the woes of a single timid girl alone in the woods.

"What could become of you?" or "How do you think you will find a life partner, if you are always out alone? What will people think?" she would say. Lucky for Vanamali, she was the younger sibling, still years from the search for her mate, and still young enough to enjoy these simple freedoms without being upbraided at home. She smiled, naughtily, at the thought of Manasa, already having reached home, starting her chores while being lectured to by mother in the kitchen.

"What did you learn in school today?" she would ask, "did you talk to the professor about the mathematics assignment?" and just when Manasa would begin to respond, the topic would swiftly change to, "wipe the table, come to the kitchen and help me with the coconut shredding," or even more mundane, "cut and squeeze these limes and mangoes for the pickle preparation." It was never ending. What made things worse was the constant barrage of negative comments or stories from their mother, that made the girls feel that being a girl was a curse.

Vanamali dipped her toes into the water, enjoying her solitude and smiling at her coyness in spite of being alone. She thought of a life without gender rules, where she could be free to swim or play sports at her leisure, and not be sentenced to a life in the confines of a kitchen, or separated by gender when guests were visiting. "Such a strange world!" she thought to herself. A world where despite democratic values and renowned universities, a woman's life could be determined by the color of her skin or her family's wealth and bank balance. She would never get married, she thought to herself, as she tossed a few pebbles into the water and watched the rippling of the waves and bounces it created. Marriage was surely for idiots, she reckoned. Who in their right mind would want a life sentence of making meals and servicing her husband? Why did the man get to go out on the town, travel the world if he may, and then return to a hot meal and the comfort of home? Why could she not have all those things? No, marriage was not her cup of tea. She would train herself for a better life. She could compete to become the first female swimmer from India! Yes, she would love that! Or, perhaps she would go to college and become somebody famous. Maybe a judge or lawyer, like her father.

She felt her mind wandering into that dark place it sometimes traveled, gloomy and dense. She quickly changed her thoughts, turning her gaze onto the birds that had come to play at the riverbank, chirping sprightly as they fluttered from leaf to blossom, enjoying their freedom and lapping up the sun. Vanamali stood up, shook her maxi skirt a bit, and then proceeded to prance around as if she were a bird, playing with her friends, fluttering in and out of branches and petals, no cares in the world. She laughed, and sang and imagined herself to be a flapper, like she had read about in the papers, with shorter dresses and tassels on the skirting, shaking lightly with every dance move and enjoying every beat. She giggled at the expression of her older sister. "If she were to see me prancing around at this moment I would never hear the end of it!" she thought. "Ah yes, this is the life!" With advances in clothing, transportation, employment, and even music, she could not imagine being left behind in the home when there was so much happening outside. She twirled and spun, singing to her hearts desire. Only a few moments had passed, yet Vanamali felt rejuvenated. She took a slow, cleansing breath and prepared for the second leg of her journey home.

Vanamali reached the sickle-shaped riverbank by her home, fairly smoothly. She came ashore, squeezed the excess water out of her drenched maxi-skirt and pulled her slippers from her belt, where she had secured them. As she threw her slippers to the ground and stooped a little to wear them, she heard a whistle coming from the west edge of the bank. Funny, she thought, she usually made this trip in solitude. It was not the time for the farmer to make his rounds, nor was she on the north end of the riverbank where her friends and she would sometimes play. She turned to look at where the sound was coming from, but saw nothing.

"It's time to get home," she thought to herself. She walked quickly towards the mainland, through a hiking path that had been made over the years, a welcome shortcut on her weary way home.

"Pew, pew!" the whistling sound came again.

She was bewildered now, not a person in sight yet the whistle was unnerving her. Should she run, or hide? Her heart beat faster and she could feel herself trembling a little. Luckily, she was not too far from home now. Vanamali picked up her pace a little. She turned the corner by the banyan tree and knew home was in sight. She was tired and hungry, but mostly distracted now by the whistling that she was not accustomed to. Finally, she saw the concrete wall of her backyard, separating the common hiking trail from private property. It would usually take most people another ten minutes to walk the perimeter of the home, arriving at the double door that was the entrance into the atrium, then the actual home. But Vanamali was smarter than that. She had traveled this route far to many times to not know the shortcuts. All she needed to do was climb the back wall, then walk across the compound to her home. As she reached up to find a grip to climb the wall, She heard footsteps and whistling again.

"Pew, pew!" the sound echoed. "Hello, there! Can you help me?" She was continuing to feel rather uncomfortable now, not being able to see a visage of a person, yet hearing sounds and footsteps approaching.

"Who goes there?" she shouted, trying to sound tough, yet trembling inside.

"Excuse me, my lady," replied a calm voice, the shadow now approaching. The tall, lean young man came closer to her, finally a few feet away from Vanamali's view. "I mean not to frighten you, but I was hoping that you can help me?" he asked. Vanamali nodded her head in consent, studying the young man's face and trying to come up with her own version of the truth. "I am not from around here," he said, " and I fear that I am lost. I am trying to get to High Court Judge Shrikantayya's residence," he explained.

"How did you get lost in the woods?" she asked, interrogating the handsome man further, and buying some time to determine whether he was the trustworthy type.

Baba looked closely at her beautiful face, and glanced into her kind eyes.

"Well," he replied, "I was asked to deliver these documents from my office directly to Judge Srikantayya. These papers are from the company where I work and they specifically requested these documents to be hand delivered. I was too proud to tell my boss that I have never been to this house. I grabbed the envelope and left anyway. I just started there a month ago. I am trying to impress them!" he disclosed. "But, I am lost. I had no idea the woods were so dense yet close by to Tirumakudalu."

Vanamali shrugged her shoulders in that tomboyish way that her mother deplored. The weariness drifted from her face, and now she was happy. She would be happy to escort Baba to the judge, maybe even score some brownie points for the gesture!

"Follow me!" she gestured, waving her left arm and beckoning Baba to follow.

"Do you know the judge?" he questioned, not sure what to believe on seeing the beautiful girl dripping with water and grinning with mischief.

"Sure! Can you give me a lift?" she requested the man. She was looking at the wall she wished to climb.

"You want me to follow you over the wall?" he said in disbelief.

"Yes".

"But, are you going to take me to the judge?"

"Yes, certainly!"

"Well, how do I know that you are taking me there?" Baba added.

"I guess you will have to trust me!" she responded cheekily.

Baba paused, and tugged on her as she hoisted herself over the wall.

"Are you sure you know the judge?" he repeated, wearily.

"Why of course!" she replied.

"What is your relationship with him?" Ramaswamy now demanded. Vanamali peered down at Baba, who was waiting for a response before climbing up the wall. She smiled, enjoying the moment, and eager for it to continue.

"Ok, I will put you out of your misery" she stated. "Judge Srikantayya is my FATHER!"

They chuckled together, weary smiles on their faces as they jumped off of the wall on the other side. Baba and Vanamali began to talk to each other, introducing themselves to one another and actually finding the conversation to flow effortlessly.

"My name is Vanamali. I took the scenic route home from school. I attend tenth grade at the girl's school across the other side of the river." She added some color to her description of town, knowing that Baba was new there. "And what about you? What is your name?" she asked.

"I am T.K. Ramaswamy, but everyone calls me Baba, even my friends. It's a term that has stuck with me. I am not so sure I even recall my full name!" he laughed.

As Vanamali approached her back door, she saw her sister Manasa from the parapet.

"Hi, Akka!" she exclaimed. Manasa waved her sister inside quickly.

"Mum is waiting for you" she replied. "What took you so long?" she questioned, glancing at the handsome young man beside her sister.

Vanamali ran inside and requested the young Ramaswamy to sit in the living room, where she would return. She hurried upstairs to her room changed her clothes after a quick bath. After washing up and powdering herself with Pond's sandalwood powder, she skipped downstairs and greeted her guest. Her mother saw her and scurried towards her.

"What is all of this? Whom did you bring home?" asked Kamala curiously, inspecting her daughter from top to bottom and studying her expressions.

"His name is T. K. Ramaswamy and he is sent here on business", she stated. "He was recently hired by an insurance company whom father knows, and was asked to bring some documents for father to sign."

"Oh," sighed her mother, acknowledging her daughter's detailed explanation. "Well, make him some filter coffee then," she demanded, "He must be rather tired and hungry." Grinning, Vanamali began to prepare the best filter coffee they had, while Manasa, an expert in the kitchen, started to fry crispy peanut bites and other savory treats for the welcome guest.

"So, where were you so long, anyway?" Manasa asked, smiling at her sister suspiciously from the corner of her eye.

"I did not really realize it was getting late," Vanamali responded. "I was following my usual swimming routine when I stopped at the halfway point to rest, and probably took a little longer there. But, on swimming back and reaching the riverbank, I actually picked up the pace. It was only ten minutes later that I suspected I had company, and sure enough then I met Mr. Ramaswamy. We did not take long returning, once we knew we were both safe," she replied.

Manasa smiled broadly and handed her sister the silver tray on which she then placed the savory treats, hot crunchy chips and sweet dish, then steel cups with aerating cups underneath each, and the coffee filter pot. She signaled her sister to proceed into the living room and then followed. Baba was appreciative. Hungry and weary from his travels, such hospitality was a symbol of kind nature and 'khatirdari' or, taking care of guests, since guests were considered next to God. Vanamali set the serving tray down on the coffee table in front of Baba. She wasn't sure if Manasa would want to serve, so she paused for a moment awaiting a sign from her sister. But Manasa patiently waited for Vanamali to serve the handsome guest, clearly observing the chemistry already obvious between the youngsters. Their mother finally came in to the living room to supervise and greet the young man.

"Namaskara," she greeted, folding the palms of her hands in the traditional welcome pose and bowing her head humbly. "From where did you come?" she asked.

"I came from Himayatnagar" Baba replied, taking the steel cup of fresh- brewed filter coffee from Vanamali. "I live there with my family, and have recently started employment with Railway Insurance Company". Mother nodded approvingly, then glared at her two daughters who had neglected to offer any sugar in Baba's coffee.

"Yaynee neeevu," she critiqued, " Saccray bayca kellaybedwene?" she asked. "Shouldn't you have asked whether he takes sugar?" Vanamali and Manasa giggled spontaneously at each other, which then quickly turned into belly laughter as the young man joined in. Mother was embarrassed, not expecting Baba to join in. "Sorry", she apologized. "My girls are just learning the art of hospitality," she explained, "forgive them, they neglected to offer you sugar." She was very thoughtful that way, never wanting any guest to feel unwelcome or in the dark. Surely this stranger was Telegu-speaking and didn't catch her Kannada words.

"I love sugar!" replied Baba, enjoying the scene. "Mooroo-Nallakku cubes codree" he requested in Kannada, addressing both girls who were still in splits. The three women's heads turned to glare at Baba's face, in astonishment.

"Kannada baratha nimge?" they asked, "Do you understand Kannada?"

"Of course, it's my mother-tongue!" The entire living room was now rumbling with the scene, laughter and surprises making for a sweet end of the day. They all relaxed, formality was gone, and they sat together for coffee.

After snacks, Vanamali and Manasa both offered their guest more treats, making sure to let him know he was very welcome to stay. Their mother, feeling more comfortable, invited Baba to stay for dinner. He declined, politely, citing some urgent work in the office the following day and stressing the importance of completing his tasks and meeting his deadlines.

"I'm an intern you see," he paused, to sip his coffee, "and I just do not want to give anyone the opportunity to criticize my work. It's important to work hard and make a lasting impression on one's first employment", he preached. Manasa nodded in agreement, and quickly started to inquire about his work in Tirumakudalu.

"Well, you see, judge Srikantayya is one of my boss's clients, from a long time, apparently. I was asked to come to town to review his claims, and settle them if agreeable. If not, then I was to take down information, and arrange a meeting with my boss later this week. I know your father to be a very busy barrister, so I thought I would come quickly to Tirumakudalu to meet him." He happily explained the details of his work, and was eager for their reply.

"Where is the good Sir?" Baba asked.

Mrs. Srikantayya looked up at Baba, and replied, quietly.

"He is constantly busy with his legal work and High Court cases. He often goes several weeks without coming home. He does have a townhouse in the city, which is helpful. But sadly," she hesitated, wondering whether this was too much information for the innocent young man, "he is really married to his work. I have become accustomed to raising my girls as a single parent since he is rarely present."

Baba gulped the last few drops of the delicious filter coffee, popped a small peanut wafer into his mouth and swallowed it down. He was a patient man and an honorable one. In his young life, he too had become accustomed to parents in absentia, and growing up too soon. He was already burdened with responsibilities above his age and was handling six possessive sisters and their spouses, plus worrying about his father's income and future upcoming retirement plans. With the changing tide of the current democracy and Indian pride, he did not fear hard work. In fact, he believed in Emerson's words, that employment was nature's physician and man's true medicine. Baba did not shun Mrs. Shrikantayya. Rather, he was empathetic. He wanted to make a difference in the world in whatever way he could and respected diligence in all who possessed it. Looking up at Vanamali's mother, who was still standing next to him, waiting to see if he would respond, he gently grasped her hand and with a soft clasp, he stated soothingly,

" You inspire all youngsters like myself to seize the opportunities lying at their feet. If you can raise two children singlehandedly, in spite of your current circumstances, then what can the next generation do?" he asked, rhetorically. "I am touched that you would honor me with such personal information, and I say in no uncertain terms that I will respect your wishes and support you with anything I have." He turned to address Manasa and Vanamali, who were gazing admiringly at his kind words, "Now, where can I find your father?" he asked, with a boyish smile on his face, "It looks like he owes my employer money."

Chapter Five: Judge Srikantayya. April 1931

The Judge set down his gavel and majestically arose from his chair. He was pleased with himself, having conducted a difficult trial. The case had finally concluded, and now he could close his court room and call it a night. As he hung the robes on the hook and peered over his desk, he noticed a few papers and documents that must have arrived by post that afternoon, while he was in session. One of the envelopes was stamped, "Important. First Class." Shrikantayya carefully opened the letter with his paper knife. It was an almond colored piece of paper, thick and textured. The top left corner bore a gold emblem that appeared to show the side profile of a swimmer racing in the water. Shrikantayya started to read the letter, which was addressed to he and his wife:

Honorable Judge Srikantayya and Mrs. Srikantayya,

It is with great happiness that I wish to inform you that your daughter Vanamali has been selected to represent the state of Andra Pradesh in the National India Games, in the division of freestyle swimming. This great honor comes with request of additional paperwork and documents, which are listed in the enclosed papers. Kindly complete them, making sure to include Vanamali's signature of consent. Further information will follow accordingly.

Congratulations and Jai Hind!

Sincerely,

Bhagat Kapoor, National Team India developer

The judge set the letter down on the table, and brushed his fingers through his thick hair.

"Why did she not tell me about this?" Shrikantayya thought to himself, feeling more blighted at the lack of knowing. He looked around the perimeter of his chambers, as if searching for an answer. It had been a few weeks since he had seen his daughters. Life was too busy, he thought. He had papers to write and meetings to attend. Of course, there were always the obligatory dinners and socialite gatherings that Srikantayya had to participate in, for climbing the ladder. The politicians wanted to meet to find out the judge's viewpoint on so many things. He enjoyed the collegiality of other lawyers and judges that he met. So, going to his daughter's school conferences or events seemed remedial. Indeed, he had traded off these duties to his diligent wife many a time, but never heard any word from her about Vanamali participating at National level. Plus, too, she was at marriageable age for their family standards, and swimming wasn't a typically acceptable sport for girls to perform once they had reached womanhood. He was frustrated, and tired. Shrikantayya stood up and reached for his raincoat and umbrella. He gathered his belongings, tucked the letter inside his document folder and set out the door.

An hour later, Srikantayya was still in town, exiting the local coffee house where he had eaten his typical light snack and drunk his beloved Mysore style filtered coffee. The sun was beginning to set, and colleagues and passers-by were heading home. As he peered in the windows of a new shopping area in town, he heard his name from behind. He made an about turn, always rather paranoid, and somewhat fearful. But, what caught his attention was not what he had expected.

"Shri, Shri, come with me! Let's go out on the town and have ourselves some fun!" It was one of his workmates, by the name Shravan Gowda. A handsome young man, approximately a decade younger than Shri, he was finely dressed in Western attire, and was surrounded in each arm, by two beautiful fair ladies, also, expertly dressed. The girls looked like air -hostesses, dressed in skirts and blouses with neck scarves. Indeed, they stood out like peacocks in this quiet village town. Shravan had a fine mustache and wore a hat, the brim of which shadowed his face. He was also heavily perfumed with cologne, which his companions seemed to like.

"Oh, hello there, Shravan. What brings you back into town? Weren't you finished with your case hours ago?" The judge, always a sharp observer, would not let this slip by him. Being the senior of the two men, he felt it important to show that his subordinates' actions were not going unaware, even if off-duty. But Shravan, who was familiar with the burly, authoritarian presence of the judge, was not intimidated.

"Shri, why don't you join us? It's practically suppertime and you must be famished. Please, come along!"

"Well, I should be going home to the wife and kids. It's been a while, what with the hectic work we put into the last case, and I should talk to Kamala." Shri sounded hesitant, as if he was waiting to be urged on. He looked down at his pouch, and then at his watch. It was half past eight already. By the time he caught the train home, the family would have probably finished dinner.

He looked up at Shravan, and grinned. Shravan, equally adept at catching people's body language, was quick to respond.

"Shri, you look like you need a drink and some warm food. Just come with us for an hour, then we will see you on your way." Obliging, and rather happy to have the company, he followed along.

It was eleven thirty at night when Shrikantayya looked at his watch again, glassy eyes and a heavy head still clouding his judgment.

"Where have you brought me?" he asked Shravan, who looked like a black beam in the distance, as Shri gazed forward. He could recall having a few drinks, then eating some good food. But, unlike before when he had shared a few drinks between friends, this was the first time he remembered ever passing out for a moment.

"Well, you knocked back a few before dinner, so I think it finally went to your head! Never mind, we have to take our leave, so the ladies and I will take you back to your residence home. Shall we?" Shri was still in a daze and a heavy nausea began to weigh him down. He quickly paid the bill, and proceeded to stand up. But he could not. He felt queasy and tilted in a stupor. Shravan and Sadhana came to his aid, placing both her hands around him and raising him up gently. She took her friend's help to carry his weight between them both, and then called for their driver.

Shravan and his lady friends lifted the judge out of the car. They took their driver's help to carry the sturdy man into his apartment. He gave the two women the key from his jacket pocket, barely able to hold a grip to the bunch. As they entered his apartment, the girls helped Shri settle on his bed, removing his shoes so that he could finally rest. He tried to fight his sleep, raising his eyebrows to help lift his leaded lids, but the urge to close them was too strong. Within minutes, the judge was in a deep sleep. The women, however, did not rush to leave. Sheila, who had taken a fancy to the fine German crystal decanter and glass on the buffet table, poured herself a drink.

"Hey, you should not do that, we were not invited to stay," Sadhana whispered urgently.

"Oh, do not worry so much," Sheila replied casually, "It's not as if he is alert enough to notice. It's just a short one anyway." She grinned looking down at her drink and then tossing back the shot in its entirety. Her curiosity did not stop. Sheila walked around the prim apartment, opening cupboards and doors and peering in. There was another bedroom that was set adjacent to the main one. Sheila entered it and, seeing the beautiful bedspread laid out in majestic fashion, she did not resist the urge to touch it. It was velvety to touch and had silk sheets underneath. Exuberant, she assessed, for an assigned office apartment, yet perhaps acceptable given the Judge's stature in the city, and indeed state. As Sheila nosed around, she reflected on how strange it was that Shri did not have any touch of family living in it. Certainly she did not expect family photographs on the wall, but she thought perhaps, a few personal belongings would be acceptable. Maybe a toothbrush and soap in the bathroom, or some kitchen supplies. Yet, there was no trace of a female's touch here. "Hmm", she pondered, "perhaps the legal life is a dull one. No time for play or home. Just work, work, work!"

Just then Sadhana entered and pulled her friend outside. "I'm leaving. Are you coming?"

With a nod and a last look around the apartment, the girls left the Judge to his deep slumber.

Chapter Six: The State Championship

"Amma, come on, we need to go!" Vanamali pleaded. Manasa was already outside, holding a jute bag with her sister's extra clothes in as well as a water bottle and tiffin box. Amma, who was stalling while silently hoping her husband would arrive home, finally gave up and followed her children out the door. She was heavy hearted, upset that her last words with Shrikantayya were oppositional, as he had upbraided his wife, proclaiming her a bad influence on her children for allowing the girls to participate in sports.

"But they are good at it!" she had cried.

"Perhaps if there were no other outlet, there would be reason and motivation. But, our girls are approaching marriageable age and they should not be labeled tomboys. They are from a successful family, with all of the luxuries most others dream of. Why do you encourage them so?" Shri had asked.

"Because they are good at it. And also," she paused, looking her husband straight in the eye, "They look up to you. They see you conquering your cases, and they assume they can conquer the world! They see it as a challenge. Plus, Vanamali is actually the best in her school. Why don't you come watch her some time?" She wanted to say more, but held her tongue back, not wanting to exhaust herself fighting her unpredictable husband. She watched, apprehensively, as Shri paced the bedroom, thinking of the perfect retort. After a few long moments, Shri spoke.

"I am not happy about this choice you have given the girls. You should be teaching the children how to cook and clean, not get filthy in the water!" He paused again, this time looking at his wife's distraught face, weighing down her petite frame. Indeed, he was a giant in front of her, intimidating to anyone if size were the only factor. "My kids will not be permitted to fail in anything! " he added sharply. "Tell her to go to this event, and tell her to win. But, after this competition, she will not be allowed to enter others. And don't expect me to watch the spectacle." So saying, he turned and marched out of the front door fiercely, barely noticing the two trembling teenagers perched up on the mango tree outside the home. It didn't take more than a minute for Vanamali and Manasa to run to their mother's side. The children hugged her, wiping her face and holding her tight.

"Amma, it's fine. We don't have to go if father doesn't want us to. We'll do whatever you say."

"No, no. Don't say anything!" Kamala croaked, her voice raspy from fighting more tears. "We will attend Vana's swimming competition. She deserves that and so does our family! We are going to enjoy these rare moments. Look at me. How proud I am today. I do not even know swimming yet my daughter is the hopeful to win! We must rejoice and not look back to old fashioned ways." The girls kissed their mother, took her bags and headed out the door for a second time.

She had played over the scene a hundred times in her head. Why did she have to constantly manage her beloved children on her own? What was lacking in her that she had this predicament. Kamala closed the house, locking the front door and gate, and, wiping away a silent tear she followed her children out of their neighborhood.

Chapter Seven: The Uprising. Himayatnagar, 1940

"Call to Order!!!" rapped the gavel on the podium. They were in the basement of the cricket stadium's general manager's office, on a rainy Sunday night in town. Shiv Prasanna, best friend to Baba, had called for the meeting, eager to have great minds come together to discuss a plan for their young and hopefully bright futures. There had been several such meetings around town, which Baba had obediently ignored on the advice of his mother, who wanted her good son to have nothing to do with a crowd of "hooligans and loafers" desiring some entertainment. However, Baba had agreed to attend this particular meeting on request of his friend, Shiv Prasanna, whose elder brother was spearheading the campaign for Gandhi's "passive resistance". He was uncertain what to believe in politics, and was just truly beginning to form his own opinions on the freedom struggle and Indian independence. In fact, he was rather confused on his political stance. When he was younger, his parents encouraged Baba to attend English speaking medium schools for senior school and then college. He enjoyed this thoroughly and could not help but feel a little distinguished in a crowd when Kannada- English, or even English-Hindi translation was required. There was something so refined about the British and their ways. Even though the British were privately despised by the locals Baba did not believe them to be completely foul. He liked the properness and formality that the Brits displayed. Currently, world war two was underway, and this only served to send a chill down Baba's spine, for he despised the war.

"Hopefully this meeting is a quick one," he thought to himself, hurrying to take a seat close to the back of the room where he was less visible. This way, he thought, he would probably not be called to give his opinion or show his agreements. He began to get lost in his thoughts of Baby Murali at home with Vanamali, who would be awaiting his return for family dinner.

The room was rather more crowded than expected, with adult men filling the meeting hall from front to back. There was a makeshift desk on the stage with three chairs aligned, awaiting guests. The average age of the men attending was about twenty-two, but a few slightly older members were present who seemed to be coordinating the function. The men were spirited, chatty and eager to air their views on the political climate afflicting India at this time. Baba recognized a few of the faces as classmates from college, or neighboring boys. Finally, the last of the attendees had taken his seat, and the meeting was initiated. The speaker made an announcement that future meetings may have to be held in a different location, due to British officers or policemen suspecting unrest. Then, Colonel Virender Singh was introduced to speak on behalf of the members presiding.

" Greetings everyone. I am Colonel V. Singh, squadron leader for the elite Ashoka Force, special operations division, based in Mumbai. My roots are in Hyderabad, however, since my family is settled here. I returned this week on break since my nephew is getting married this weekend. " He paused, smiling proudly and scanning the room. " Prasanna asked me to call this meeting when I informed him via telegram of upcoming events in Mumbai, Delhi and Kashmir. You see, all is not what it seems. At this present time there are a lot of changes within our beloved nation that are about to occur. Some are good, but most are bad. We are gathered today to discuss possible consequences of said actions if nothing is done, versus a call to act, to draw the attention away from hostility, but towards passive resistance.

Last week, I myself was involved in an exchange with British officers who were upset by the young M.K Gandhi and his words. Gandhiji stated, in his address outside of Parliament,

"The weak can never forgive. Forgiveness is an attribute of the strong."

This evoked hostile comments from the British Gentry, who took our Mahatma's kind, true words and turned them into an attack on Indians, citing that they were our rulers, and we, under Gandhiji's baton, are creating unrest through insult. I fear that the Brits will try to destroy Gandhiji and I am coming here to tell you that we as a nation cannot allow this. Now is the time to act. Will you help me fight for freedom and lead with Mahatma's will? We gain our strength in numbers. We should march to the Capitol and protest against occupation by the British. We should stand up for justice by uncovering the current crooked governments attempt to sell out their nation. Will you fight for freedom through peaceful, passive resistance?"

The room went from pin drop silence to a crescendo of whispers that then turned into questions and arguments. Prasanna had to use his gavel again to quell the crowd. Many heads were shaking in disbelief, while other colleagues and friends were discussing the possibilities calmly. Then, a few young men approached the podium, and, seizing the microphone for themselves, began dividing the crowd with doubt and pessimism.

"Where you will be employed when your current boss fires you for your connections with the mission? What will you tell your fathers or wives? Are you out of your minds? This is simply too risky. The time is not ripe to wage a war on the British. There are armies and politicians for that. Colonel Saab, you are wasting your time. Go back to your squadron."

Another member, slightly more timid in appearance but with a calm demeanor, took the microphone from his enraged friend, and beckoned the friend to take a seat. Looking at Prasanna, and acknowledging that it was his turn to speak, began with these few simple words,

"Friends, I request you to take a seat, and simply listen first to the facts being presented before you. None of us here is unreasonable. Indeed, most of us have come tonight because we wish for peace yet desire a unified voice that represents us. We also wish for a safe place called home, a place that our families and loved ones will enjoy. I never would have believed in the past, that I would be standing here right now waging a non-violent war on the colonialists. Yet, here I am waiting for safety, waiting for India to be free of the Brits, and still waiting for a united front for my beloved India. Progress is dependent on intellectual growth. How many residents of Himayatnagar are educated? In fact, how many of Hyderabad's entire population are educated? Not many. You're looking right now at the future of our home, and that future is dependent on you. If you cannot stand strong for your nation, who will?"

Pausing, poetically, and looking to the stage side wings for the approval of Prasanna and Colonel Saab, he returned his gaze on the captive audience. Smiling and tracking the faces of the audience, he ended with these words:

" I am requesting your allegiance to the Independence Movement, and the movement for Passive Resistance, spearheaded by Gandhiji already. The movement is underway in several of our states, but you may not have heard anything about the mission due to a request for extreme secrecy. We cannot trust most anyone at this time. There are cops whose allegiance is to the British, and others who take bribes from anyone for the better price. If you really want to see our movement in effect, we need your support. We need strength in numbers. We need intelligence. We need a plan. Indeed, we are running out of time. I am not going to put anyone on the spot. That is not my intention. However, I will be placing a sign up sheet on the paper next to the exit door. If you have it in you to fight for India's freedom through non-violent passive resistance, then please sign up. I remind you again that Gandhiji needs your support. We need you. Please think wisely, before you exit."

Ashwant Rao made his way to the side of the podium, but remained on the stage, preferring this height to view the crowd. He was hopeful, yet realistic as he witnessed the exodus of at least twenty young men, shuffling their chairs and quickly scurrying out of the door, heads down to avoid eye contact. Ashwant turned to look at Prasanna and Colonel Singh, both of whom seemed unaffected by the exodus. He relaxed his shoulders, realizing that this was expected, and sat back down on a chair. He closed his eyes in quite meditation, realizing that letting his emotions cloud his mind was wasteful at this moment.

As the doubtful young men exited, Baba was left sitting in the back row of the hall, central view to Prasanna, Ashwant Rao and the Colonel. They looked at him, acknowledging his friendship.

"Come on over here and take a look at this!" exclaimed Prasanna, beckoning Baba onto the stage. Baba got up quickly and followed the order. When he made his way to the right of Ashwant, he noticed that the men were studying an old map of Hyderabad and the neighboring towns.

"What are you studying?" Baba asked curiously.

"Here we have a map of our town and it's surrounding. Colonel Singh was filling us in on what he thinks may happen this week." The Colonel turned to face Baba and began detailing him on the Uprising that he was suspicious was about to occur.

"But, where is this uprising planned for?" asked Baba, a bit bewildered at the prospect of upcoming unrest.

"Osmania College," replied Colonel Singh, confidently.

"How can you be so sure?" Baba pressed on.

"Well, the facts are fairly clear," the Colonel answered. " My British sergeant was overheard telling his colleagues that they absolutely could not take a vacation or trip away from Hyderabad within the next fortnight. I was approaching the sergeant to discuss my upcoming family wedding leave, and the Brit, rather than condescend my request, was all too eager to grant it. I don't think he wants me around, since I would have been an obstacle.

I fear that some of the Brits have planted fake college students at Osmania, to attend meetings and political party rallies. They have created a following rather quickly. This group is putty in the Brits' arms, since it appears to be doting on the words of the Brit spies. Little to the group's knowledge, these spies are simply there to create a divide, start a rally and then succumb to the terror of British force the moment they become unruly. The student's rallies have all been peaceful, yet the Brits, I feel, wish them to blunder so that they can swarm in with police officers and troops, and create uproar. Then, all the British would need to do is blame the young students and their political views for the turmoil and take forceful action. I think this would scare Gandhiji into retracting into a quiet corner, since actions of violence and trauma to youths are two of his fears. Then, the Brits would have won."

Baba paused, reflectively. "My brother is a professor at Osmania," he stated, with a slightly worried look on his face. "Are the students and teachers going to get a fair warning of the upcoming events? What should I do? What are you all planning on doing?"

Colonel Singh turned to Baba, raising his eyebrows in concern.

" I think it is time for all present today to act. I do not know whether a forewarning is beneficial, since policemen will turn to us as the protestors. But, I think we should do something. Are you ready to join us Ramaswamy? Can you make contact with your brother to warn him or discuss the situation?"

Baba sighed. He worried about his new baby, and his young wife. He worried about his job responsibilities and getting into trouble. Indeed, he had a clean record and did not want to mar this. But, he agreed, no action is as telling as action. And, he longed for a better country for his young family. He wanted to do something he and his family would be proud of. Indeed, his family were disappointed that he chose not to continue postgraduate studies at Oxford University, due to his own family discouraging his time abroad. Baba was persuaded to stay in

Himayatnagar. His parents and sisters had cited fear of unrest with the war, and also requested that he be the man around the home, for his family as well as his six sisters. Indeed, his elder brother-in-law Vinaya had died in the devastating Spanish Influenza that took the lives of thousands. Sadly, he had not returned from Oxford, but had expired at his prime, a young newlywed taken by influenza. His younger sisters did not want any harm to come to Baba. Consenting, Baba had agreed to stay on in India. He was deeply disappointed with himself. He needed a sense of purpose. What should he do?

Prasanna moved towards his best friend and, placing a hand on his shoulder, patted him gingerly on the back.

"Rama, I think you can do this. You are the best person to represent us, and the most intelligent. We need you to stand with us." Looking at Baba straight in the eye, he smiled gently, acknowledging the struggle going on within Baba's head. Baba pondered, and, looking at the palmar creases on his cupped hands and muttering a few prayer words to him self, he pleaded with himself, toying with the thoughts of changing India, versus fear of death or imminent danger. He began to gently chant, muttering the empowering words of the poet Tulsidas's Hanuman Chalisa in his prayers:

"Oh Hanuman, you are the great hero, you are endowed with valor, your body is as strong as Indra's Vajra. You are the destroyer of vile intellect, and you are the companion of one whose intellect is pure. Oh great one, please guide me. Let me take my men across the tempestuous oceans and save our motherland! Oh great devotee of Shiva, your aura and majesty is great and is revered by the whole world. Surely you can help my plight! Please guide me."

"I will rise to this challenge on one condition," he commanded "I will not engage in wrongdoing, thievery or mischief. I believe that we, as responsible law-abiding citizens, have a duty towards justice, peace and tolerance. I do follow Gandhi's principles, to seek peace in a nonviolent manner, but I fear the political climate we live in. If you all are unable to truly follow Mahatma's principles then please let me know now, so that I can move on. Otherwise, yes, I will follow you."

Chapter Eight: Osmania College, 1940

T.V Sundaresh stood in the teacher's common room, sipping his madras-style coffee while looking at the morning headline news in Deccan Herald. "Funny", he thought to himself, why had his younger brother tried to call him that morning? It was a regular working day and surely Baba would have been busy tending to his toddler or getting ready for work. Instead of engaging him in a coffee morning, T.V had opted to hurry out the door, citing the importance of getting to the college early that morning to prepare for his most important lecture of the semester, which was scheduled for later that day. Admittedly, this was rather improper, but T.V. was known to be rather bull-headed when it came to his own affairs. He had rushed out the door, leaving the phone receiver in the hands of his wife, who was chatting to Baba about the upcoming 'Gowri-Ganesha' religious festivities. Sundaresh had hurriedly requested Baba and Vanamali to come home that weekend for the religious service and then family feast.

"Murali will love it Chickanna," Sarojini added, noting that the sweet modaka delicacies that were being prepared, plus the lavish dinner, would be reason to not miss the family feast.

"Thanks, Akka," Baba replied, quickly cutting the conversation and putting down the phone. Baba grabbed his khadi cotton jacket, umbrella and wallet, and hurried out of his home. He cycled to Osmania College campus, reaching ten minutes later. He then entered confidently, searching for the teacher's lounge. At first, he did not see anyone whom he recognized. Classes were well underway, since it was now ten o'clock in the morning. As he turned to leave the lounge he saw his brother running into the lounge again, brushing up against Baba who was not in plain view. T.V turned to apologize, only then realizing that it was his own Baba who stood at the entrance.

"What an earth are you doing here?" T.V asked, jokingly adding, "Coming to earn another degree? Planning to switch careers? Maybe a teaching degree to add to your hat?" he chuckled, somewhat condescendingly, although T.V. was known for his dry sense of humor.

"Actually," Baba replied, gently pulling Sundaresh further into the room, " I need to talk to you privately about some urgent news. It affects you, so please listen." T.V. was taken off guard a little. He looked at his watch, worrying about being on time to his lecture, and despising lack of punctuality. It was all right, he thought, he still had at least fifteen minutes prior to the start of his lesson.

"Sure, Baba," T.V said, patiently. Baba proceeded to quickly and methodically outline the events of yesterday night's basement meeting. T.V. had already been invited to attend that meeting, but had declined due to not feeling too well. He was, however, a staunch Gandhian, and marveled in his legal abilities and political activism. In fact, his scheduled infamous lecture was about taking a stand and doing something that you believe in.

"Don't talk about making a difference," he would say to his class, "Be the difference. Make a change. Stand up for justice." Baba explained how he had agreed to be a part of the peaceful civil rights movement, wanting change for his country but in a nonviolent manner. T.V. was only too thrilled with this knowledge and applauded his young brother for joining the movement.

"But, that's not all," Baba responded, a sense of urgency and fear creeping up in his gentle voice. "There is going to be an uprising on campus today, created by the British and the crooked police members who have apparently planted some spies within the campus. The traitors have influenced some of your college students. My sources from the movement have informed me there will be riots on campus tonight, when some students are going to be peacefully protesting and rallying for freedom and democracy. I fear people will get hurt and many may be jailed if they are found to be associated with the rallies. It is the British people's way of gagging Gandhiji. They want Gandhiji to notice that they will fight with force the very citizens who are capable of making positive change - young intellectuals. It is for this reason that I joined the freedom movement. I fear the consequences of inaction more than I do fighting for freedom. But I am worried about your upcoming lecture and campus presence. I think we should go home." T.V listened carefully to Baba's words. He was conflicted. In a way, he wanted to drop everything and join the movement in full swing, an anti-establishment philosophy. He believed in freedom and independence from the British Commonwealth. But, he was fearful of injury and riots. He was a mere eighteen years old when he was enlisted to fight for the Commonwealth in World War One. The war had been unkind to him. An innocent adolescent, happy and mischievous, he had been protected from the harsh world outside of his Himayatnagar home. Enlisting was a service of courage looked proudly upon by his middleclass parents, who wished the best for T.V. They felt that the service would open up doors for him. He would return from the war mature, and possibly honored, and could then go on to Law School as planned.

But times were harsh. He suffered badly in battle, both emotionally and physically. The War at Passchendaele had claimed several of his best friends and classmates, leaving him alone and weak. Although he survived, it was not without a battle with gastroenteritis, dehydration and burns. He was only forty-two now, but had suffered some hearing loss already. He could never sleep through the night since returning. They called it a "stress reaction," yet there were no counselors or medications that were provided to him. His parents also became scared of his jumpy, irritable nature and moodiness that was notable since his return. Indeed, his moodiness had almost cost him his marriage, if it were not for a doting wife and loving siblings who patiently waited for T.V to gain strength and get back to doing things he cared deeply about. He also worried about the next generation. At forty-two, he was old enough to have grandchildren, and elders were inquiring as to whether T.V had "a medical problem" that caused he and his wife to not have children yet. Sarojini, his beautiful wife, had supported T.V. through medical visits, particularly when he was made aware that he was likely the cause of the infertility problem, not Sarojini. They could have adopted, but he did not want to. He wanted his own biological children. He loved his young brother Ramaswamy, but was a bit jealous that he had conceived of a beautiful boy without any apparent issue. He was scared. What should he do? He decided to ask Baba what to do. Baba, appreciating the confidence placed in him by T.V. replied with a very detailed plan.

"I think since your infamous lecture is scheduled for eleven o'clock in the morning, you should stay on schedule and give the lecture. But, I would like you to interject some suggestions within the class, so that the young students who may be involved in the rallies tonight would perhaps get the gist of things to come. They could make a backup plan."

But what if the British spies are attending my lecture?" he asked. Baba thought about this carefully.

"Do you have a student attendance sheet, that we could review now? Maybe we can determine whom we might now, versus those who are new or unfamiliar?" T.V liked this idea a lot. It made sense. As he made his way to the back of the teachers' lounge to the filing cabinet, he glanced at his wristwatch. It was already five minutes till eleven. His lecture was supposed to start in just five minutes. He swiftly opened the filing cabinet and grabbed the folder labeled "Student Roster, Legal Terms 101," and pushing the cabinet shut, he rushed to Baba's side.

"I have a better idea," he said, looking at Baba directly.

" You're coming to class with me." T.V handed Baba the folder, and the men made their way out of the lounge and down through the Law Quad to the last entrance to the lecture hall. Sundaresh beckoned Baba to sit to the side of the stage, and introduced him as a guest advisor. Feeling a surge of energy and confidence rise within him, he stood at the front of the lecture hall stage, and tracked the captive audience in front of him. The room was full occupancy, with even a few senior students standing in the back, to listen again to a lecturer whom they greatly admired. Baba took a few moments to read the list of students on the roster list. Most of the names seemed pretty normal, he thought. There were no atypical names, no add-ons or deletes. Most of the students were incoming freshman, except the seniors who were allowed to audit favorite classes out of respect. He then slowly looked around the auditorium to see if anyone appeared different or was acting strangely. No one stood out. This could mean either T.V's class was unaffected, or that the spies were really good at camouflage. He kept on going over the last part of yesterday's meeting, the details given to him by his friends Prasanna, Ashwant Rao and Colonel Singh. He tried to imagine that he were a Brit, or a spy, and wondered how he would behave. He racked his brain. Nothing. No clues. No leads. No suspicious behavior. Trying to calm his mind, he looked up at T.V. who was nodding at a few students and smiling. He decided that the best plan would be to sit back and enjoy his brother's lecture, a welcome treat to those who loved words and goals. He sat back in his seat, closed the manila folder, and folded his arms, as the lecture began.

Chapter Nine: The Rally

T.V. decided to head back home after a successful lecture to a packed student body. He left the university with Baba who was eager to leave the campus. In celebratory mode, T.V. suggested that they swing by the local tiffin room cafe for snack and coffee.

"Sounds like a good idea," said Baba, who was rather famished. The waitress took time to seat the men and take their orders, but eventually their hot spicy lentil soup and dumplings arrived, with tamarind rice and saffron sweet dish on the side. The aroma took over their senses and the men quickly indulged, squeezing fresh lime on the rice and savoring their meals. Later, a pot of filter coffee arrived along with the customary local steel tumblers and aerating cups. Baba and T.V. really enjoyed their hot afternoon coffee break and, tummies full, they left content towards home. Life was great, Baba thought, as he reflected on the morning's events. He had thoroughly enjoyed his brother's riveting lecture and his company at the restaurant. "It's a wonderful day!" Baba summed up, reviewing his day. He had avoided involvement in the Osmania rally and this alone was a tremendous feat. Now the only remaining tasks was for both men to reach home safely, have a home cooked meal, play with Murali and then get back to campus alone, to meet up with Prasanna and company. He was ready. He felt recharged today, from being with college students and had reflected on the political situation and task at hand. He reasoned with himself regarding getting involved with the freedom movement, but really could not see a down side to involvement at this time. "How can a man be guilty just by saying a few words?" he thought. He was eloquent, calm, and the protest would be nonviolent in nature.

Ten minutes later the men turned the corner to T.V's home street. He parted with T.V. at that time, without a fuss. It was about four o'clock now, and he still had about a twenty minutes walk home. Feeling that the walk would provide him some exciting visual stimulation, he continued by foot. He took a few paces and felt as if something was missing. He could not recall this area in the morning. Was he lost? As he paused to retrace his steps mentally, a light bulb flickered in his brain. "You came by bicycle, dummy!!" Baba reminded himself. He quickly made an about turn, and began to walk swiftly back towards Osmania college.

By a quarter to five in the afternoon, Baba was within the college campus again. He quickly rushed to the teacher's room, outside of which his bicycle was parked. He unchained his bicycle and walked it toward the college entrance. He was just about to mount his bike and cycle off towards home, when he heard a marching sound, with singing to the footsteps. He actually saw a large group of college students all marching quickly towards to central Law Quadrangle area. Baba decided to follow along towards the back of the group, wheeling his cycle along. As the crowd came to a halt, he looked around the crowd. An eerie sense of misplacement overcame him, as he observed the youth around him. He looked carefully at the faces of the students, trying to make out which of them were in attendance at his brother's lecture. A hum of chants seemed to be echoing louder and louder in the crowd. Baba could not discern what was being said. He propped his bicycle up against one of the pillars marking the Law Library entrance. Baba gently made his way closer to the front of the student body. A burly yet handsome young law student leapt onto the top steps, entry way to the Debate Room. He was popular, Baba could imagine, looking at the student clap hands, grin, and lock shoulders with friends and fellow students, many of whom seemed younger than he. After a few nods of approval, and cheers from the crowd, the young man echoed the chant loudly, for all to reiterate.

"SATYAM, SHIVAM, SUNDARAM!!" Shekhar bellowed. "SATYAM, SHIVAM, SUNDARAM!!" he again echoed. "Let me here you say it!" he commanded. The crowd readily obliged, repeating the mantra, "satyam, shivam, sundaram," again and again until they were in unison. "TRUTH, GOD ALMIGHTY, and THE BEAUTIFUL will prevail," Shekhar again echoed, to the applause of his student body. "We need to come together tonight to declare a peaceful war on injustice and civil oppression. We need to come together to fight for freedom. We need to come together to fight for an independent nation that stands as one!"

He continued, his words now gaining momentum as further students, some teachers and administrators had now joined the growing crowd in the Law Quad.

"In the words of the infamous Netaji Kekre, we must remember that the greatest crime is to compromise with injustice and wrong."

Janaki, a young political science classmate of Shekhar's now approached the stage, and mounted it easily with the help of her friends. With a few smiles and waves, she greeted her captive audience. She took the microphone from Shekhar, who nodded approvingly.

"SATYAM SHIVAM SUNDARAM! SATYAM SHIVAM SUNDARAM", she also bellowed, raising her right fist into the air and pounding the air like a hammer on a nail. "We have to fight for truth, trust in the lord, and a beautiful nation. We need to press on for the truth and see if it takes us to the path of freedom. I believe it will." She smiled again as the crowd again cheered her on, and needed to be quieted down for her words to be audible. "M.K. Gandhi said recently in a speech about the Brits who occupy our nation and the politicians who deplete it, the following pearls:-

"First they ignore you, then they laugh at you, then they fight you, then you win". The crowd embraced MKG's words, which were now held up in banners, by other student leaders, all wearing now black armbands on their left arms.

"First they ignore you, then they laugh at you, then they fight you, then you win!" the crowd chanted,

"FIRST THEY IGNORE YOU, THEN THEY LAUGH AT YOU, THEN THEY FIGHT YOU, THEN YOU WIN!"

The student chants became louder and louder, till almost a rumble like a mini earthquake was felt by all around. The afternoon heat seemed to rise causing a few humid drops come down from the skies. A few students wiped their brows of sweat, while others grabbed lemon water to sip on. The chants continued. Janaki then calmed the crowd with a few gesticulations, palm facing down in a gentle slow movement. The students settled down and listened to her words again.

"We are fortunate to be young and alive during a time of tremendous change. We are lucky to bear witness to the ability of only one man, who like ourselves, was a law student. We are fortunate to have brains and physical ability. We are lucky to know better than to react violently to violence. Gandhiji preaches nonviolence. He preaches equality. He preaches peace. He sets an example for us youth. He believes in a better nation, a better world. He believes in a unified nation, not owned by other countries. Do you believe in you? I do. I know we can be the change. We can be the example. The time to act is NOW. Do not wait quietly in the corner for others to make change. Do not be weak or shy. In M.K.G's famous words, I quote, "The weak can never forgive. Forgiveness is the attribute of the strong." So, let us not be weak. Let us not give in. Let us stand together as one, and join M.K.G in the Freedom Fight. And always remember this: do not give in to weakness. Do not resort to violence."

By now, the college Dean, department heads and hostel leaders from the various campus dorms had made their way to the quadrangle, in search for Shekhar and the student body. They were not interested in what the kids had to say, but were hassled by a phone call that had come from the local police station, whose officer had stated that he was sending a team down to the campus since they were just informed of a rally that could go bad. All the Dean wanted to do was to go home to his family, and enjoy the weekend. It was Friday, and a great weekend lay ahead for him. But the officer had insisted that trouble was on the horizon, so

Dean Reddy rushed towards the Law Quad, pushing his way through the mass of students and finding Janaki and Shekhar, hands locked in a fist, chanting something. "SATYAM SHIVAM SUNDARAM, SATYAM SHIVAM SUNDARAM!!" again the crowd repeated. The sweltering heat reached dew point and now drops of rain came pelting down. Most of the students were unprepared for this, but seemed to enjoy the rain, since it was cooling.

Janaki and Shekhar discussed a plan to rally to Himayatnagar's City Hall, in similar protest of the current political climate. As the Dean began attempting to break up the crowd, and waved off several attempts to reason with them, two darker students in khaki pants and white cotton shirts, who seemed unfamiliar to most other students, were invited onto the stage by the student leaders.

"We are lucky to have with us Asif and Amir, two recent law grad students who were in Mumbai last week. They would like to say a few pearls", cried Shekhar. Asif took the microphone and began to chant a few words. He looked a bit different-older perhaps than the average age of the other students, and unfamiliar. His face was weathered, almost scarred. Perhaps, Baba thought, he had had smallpox as a child, a common childhood illness in India. Or was he a burn victim? Baba could not quite make it out from where he stood. Asif paused, looking around the quadrangle as if searching for someone.

"Do you want freedom?" he yelled, awaiting a response. Again he cried, "DO YOU WANT FREEDOM?" The crowd yelled a response this time, loud and clear,

"YES WE DO!"

"HOW ARE WE GONNA GET IT?" Asif asked. The crowd did not respond yet. They were waiting for a prompt or a sign. "We need to fight for freedom. Are you with us? Are you going to lead with me or just bury your heads? Are you going to forge a great future for the next generation?" Then Amir took the microphone, and had Asif hold up a large sign that they had made by hand.

"AN EYE FOR AN EYE MAKES THE WHOLE WORLD BLIND!"

"AN EYE FOR AN EYE MAKES THE WHOLE WORLD BLIND!" the crowd repeated after him. The student leaders led the way, as the rain downpour, Dean of the college, and now the buzz of police officials, forced the crowd to disperse. The mob followed the student leaders peacefully, in line, towards the campus entrance. Along the way they continued to chant, "An eye for an eye makes the whole world blind." The kids seemed to be enjoying their words and companionship and were unaffected by the now heavy monsoon rains that drenched their attire. Baba thought this would be a perfect time to exit. He marched out of the campus, walked around the street block then got into a cycle rickshaw that took him home. If only he had realized that he had left his bicycle behind, chained to the pillar of the Law Library.

Chapter Ten: Tirumakudalu. The Wedding, 1935

Vanamali thought she could never be happier that she was at that very moment. Dressed in a pure lotus colored baby soft pink sari, with silver (zhari) threads throughout it, she looked like the young goddess Lakshmi. She was radiant. A beauty herself, she had never realized her attributes, since she had that tomboyish nature and loved to run or swim rather than prance or skip. Her mother had never encouraged her to be fanciful.

When she was a little girl, mother would sing her nursery rhymes in her bedroom, trying to take command of the English language herself, so as to teach her children to be worldly.

"What are little girls made of? What are little girls made of? Sugar and spice and all things nice, that's what little girls are made of!" Her mother would chant. But then, one night, Manasa, already ten years old and developing a very practical demeanor, questioned her Mum with these words.

"Amma, how does this make sense? Really, do all girls smell of sugar and spice? Do you? Who invents these rhymes anyway? They are foolish!!"

"Ayyo, Rani, don't think about it too much!" she replied, eager to tuck the girls in bed and get back to her cross-stitching project. "It's just a sweet nursery rhyme, for sweet girls, that's all!"

Manasa felt irritated by this exchange. Developing a rather argumentative tongue, she turned to her sister and teased her.

"Vanamali, do you think you smell of sugar and spice? I bet after all the swimming you do daily, so rather smell of fish and seaweed!!"

Vanamali began to tear up, upset by her elder sister's comments and eager to dream sweetly of all wonderful things like down feathers, rose petals, and the comforts of a cozy home. She missed her father, and was troubled by his extensive time away. The only way she could bring comfort to herself was to cuddle her blanket, and clasp her "Punya Cote" story book to her chest, thinking of the kind mother who would not sacrifice her children, and loving her mother all the more for her loving guidance without her Dad's support.

"Manu, I love that rhyme, what's your problem?" she screamed, getting red in the face and trying to grab her mother's hand.

"Nothing Vana," Manu replied, adding,"I don't like stupid nursery rhymes that lie about children and their future and set you up for false dreams. Where's father? Where's mother's knight in shining armor, saving his damsel and playing with his children? It's all a pack of lies."

Manasa sank back into her side of their bed, feeling also upset, but realizing she had said too much. Her younger sister was a mere eight years old, far too young to have the burden of worrying about father's whereabouts. Manu decided to give her sister a hug, lovingly, and change the topic. "Mum," she pleaded, "Can you make some mango pickle this weekend? I want to eat it with yoghurt rice. I want this so badly!"

Vanamali, lost in her sweet childhood memories, had stopped combing her hair, and was in a fixed gaze at her musical jewelry box that lay on the dressing table countertop. Manu rushed in, "Vanamali, the muhurtham is approaching. We need to get you fully ready and proceed to the hall, like, NOW!"

Manu herself was looking gorgeous that morning, adorned in a teal blue Mysore silk sari that was also covered in zhari. The color suited her well. She was a little darker compared to Vanamali, and her face was a nice round shape. Vanamali, in contrast, had a beautifully lean, long face, with high cheekbones and chiseled angles. Her eyebrows were naturally well arched without any for tweezing or plucking. She also had her father's longer nose, giving her an aristocratic profile, elegant and sophisticated. Her neck was long, like a swan's. Her hair was tied in a bun, with extra hair braided and dressed around the bun. Final touches were added with white jasmine flowers pinned to her hair. Manu brought in a pink colored pin, which, rather than using to pin her sari, she placed it atop of Vanamali's bun, so that she looked like a classic Tahitian bride, or Bharatanatyam dancer. She was stunning. With a peck on the cheek from her big sister, she left to the main hall.

Their mother was ready and waiting at the front of the hall, where the altar had been arranged. It, too, was adorned with fragrant flowers, and the hall looked beautiful. It was time to start the bride's service followed by attending outside the hall for the arrival of the groom. The groom's party could already be heard outside, but the girls' mother was cool as a cucumber. She was not troubled by her husband's late arrival. In fact, she was so accustomed to running the show on her own, that she requested the priest to begin.

"It's a girls' pooja anyway", she stated, "The Judge will come when his work is complete. Let's not keep our groom waiting."

Ten minutes later Kamala Amma and Manasa walked to the groom's family outside, holding a silver plate in hand. Baba was looking like a prince, in stiff white raw silk pants and fresh pearly white kurtha with gold details and buttons. He was wearing the groom's patka (turban), also in white and gold, and was already garlanded with roses from home. He dismounted the horse on which he sat, and the band changed their tune from trumpets and processional music, to traditional instrumental shennai. The girls' mother Kamala took yellow haldi powder and red vermillion powder from the arati plate and placed it on Baba's forehead and neck. Then, she dressed him with a small lotus pink rose that she pinned on his lapel area. Manasa then was instructed to shake a few drops of fragrant perfume on his head from the beautiful silver dispenser, and then feed Baba some Indian sweetmeat. That was the fun part, Manu felt. In the last few months of Vanamali and Baba's engagement, when the families had had the time to get to know each other, she discovered Baba's affinity for Indian sweets. He had a real sweet tooth! She placed a milk pebble-shaped delicacy in his mouth, and then five other aunts proceeded to do the same, feeding Baba naan katthai, pista burfi, ladoos, and finally, his all time favorite, Kalakhand. The wedding ceremonies were going well, and smiling faces could be seen all around the hall.

As Vanamali and Baba took their seats on the special floor cushions, hand made for the occasion, they faced each other and smiled. They were truly happy. Mrs. Shrikantayya sat next to her daughter, while Baba's parents, Ananta and Susheila, sat on either side of him. Just as the priest was about to ask the obvious question, "where is Judge Srikantayya?" the wedding party turned to see the judge running in, looking rather important in his black barrister garb.

"I wonder why Dad did not change yet?" Manu thought. The judge acknowledged his wife, removed his black robes, and, removing his shoes he sat next to Vanamali, to her right. He patted his hair down and took a deep, cleansing breath. The hall was quite full now, as eager guests were awaiting the stages of the ceremony. After a brief one hour, the priest requested the parents to leave since the ceremony of giving away the bride, or 'kanya daan' was complete. Now the couple would have to take their seven circles around the sacred fire, together as one. They were very happy.

The last circle around the fire was now over, the wedding necklace was tied, and the priest requested the extended family to approach the mandap. Next was the garlanding ceremony, followed by throwing of rice confetti. The story goes, that whoever was able to throw the rice first, and then garlanded the other first, would win the title of boss and keeper of the home. "Well," Vanamali thought for a moment, "This is going to be interesting. How can I possibly throw rice on Baba first? He's about three-quarter foot taller than me!!" She didn't have time to ponder, but Manu had a better plan. She whispered to her sister to try to back away from the garland, so that she could avoid being garlanded first. This seemed to work, since Baba was taken off guard and, pausing to regain his composure after some chuckles,

Vanamali swiftly tossed the flower garland over her new husband's head, winning that game! But Baba's six sisters had better plans for the next round.

Srilatha, who was probably the closest to Chickanna, and the most petite, had snuck in a small wooden stool to her side of the family crowd. Geetha, who was holding the rice grains confetti tray, quickly signaled her brother to grasp a handful of rice from the platter, while Brunda cheekily distracted Vanamali by feeding her a special Dharwad sweet. Immediately the audience roared with belly laughter as they witnessed Baba gently dropping two handfuls of dry rice onto his young bride's head.

"Yay!" he yelled, "I won!!"

"Hey now Bhava," Manu retorted respectfully, "Don't be so sure. Now you are actually equals! Don't you remember that my sister just won the garlanding game!" Joyfully, the families hugged each other, while the priest, anxious for the ceremonies to be completed before the inauspicious time period, hurried the new couple back to the altar floor, to sit down and finish their wedding chants.

"Hello husband!" Vani whispered endearingly into Baba's ear.

"Hello wifey!" he responded. They held each other's hands and, already tied to each other (sari pulloo tied to Baba's shallya) they willed the ceremonies on, eager to eat lunch and then go home and start their new life together.

Chapter Eleven: Himayatnagar Police station, 1940

Mr. Ramaswamy turned to look at Officer Reddy, who was standing with one leg propped upon the chair facing Baba. He leaned in. Baba knew his time was running out. He needed to give some answers to the police officer, but he really had never planned on being arrested. He thought of what he would do behind bars, when the freedom movement needed a lot more work before truly effecting a change in policy. These thoughts weighed heavily on Baba, who always held himself to a high moral ground and was a born leader. Just as officer Reddy began to speak there was a loud rap on the exam room door. Another, more senior-appearing officer marched in. The two officers moved further away from Baba, and Rao, the senior man, whispered some words into Reddy's ear. Then, Rao approached Baba.

"Good evening Mr. Ramaswamy," he addressed Baba respectfully.

"Hello Sir," Baba answered.

"Mr. Ramaswamy, I need to ask you a few more questions and give you an opportunity to give us some detailed feedback regarding recent events." The officer was straightforward, and kinder in style than the junior officer.

"It is getting rather late, and I'm sure that you are eager to head back home," Rao stated. "I wanted to ask you if you could explain your involvement in the Osmania College Riots."

"Well officer," Baba replied, "I fear you will be disappointed when I tell you that I was not involved at all." Rao seemed a little suspicious of this answer, but he did not let this deter him from his interrogation.

"Why were you on campus of Osmania last Wednesday?"

"I had gone to visit my brother T.V. who is a law professor at Osmania. I had called him in the morning to meet up for coffee and breakfast at my sister's home, but T.V. was rushing out the door to campus. So, I just decided to meet him at the college. I had gone for that reason. We had our coffee and chat, and after a bit, I left. It's a very simple explanation," Baba said, logically.

"What was the nature of your visit?" Rao probed.

Baba, a bit surprised by the question, was prepared.

"I like discussing my questions with T.V. He is my mentor," he stated adding, "Sundaresh is like a father to me. He is my elder. I have six doting sisters, one brother who recently expired, and aging parents. So, T.V. is the only male family member role model that I have. I discuss everything with him. I am a young married man with a young family and I find myself needing advice or approval for a lot of the decisions that I need to make. T.V. is able to guide me. He is a good man."

"But I still would appreciate if you tell me what you both discussed," explained Rao.

Baba obliged him, and slowly and methodically detailed the coffee in the teacher's lounge, T.V's Law Lecture, the snacks they ate for lunch and the walk back. He explained how he absent-mindedly had forgotten his bike, then returned to Osmania College to get his bicycle. He then candidly admitted that he became engulfed in the student march, and, listening to the students he lost his focus and began to listen to the student speakers.

"The weather turned wet and students tried to disperse, so I followed the crowd yet again," Baba explained. "I actually left the campus, and was happy to be away from the mob. I had made it about two blocks and had just turned the corner to the High Street, when I realized that I had left my bicycle chained to the Law Library pillar. I felt stupid for having forgotten my bicycle twice in one day, and I did not want to be the subject of one of my family members' jokes, so I headed back to the college to get my bicycle. When I arrived at the Law Quad, I saw my bike and rushed to get it. I then retraced my path back towards the main entrance of the college. As I approached the archway, I saw my brother T.V, leaning up against the sidewall and splinting in pain. I inquired what had happened, wrapping my arm around his shoulder and helping him to the bench within the campus walls. T.V explained to me that the rally had indeed become unruly when some police officers came on campus and started to use unnecessary force to shove the youngsters backward.

"The force was completely unnecessary," Baba explained. "Students were simply chanting slogans such as "an eye for an eye makes the whole world blind," or " Satyam Shivam Sundaram!" but the officers actually beat them into retaliation. T.V. deplores violence or conflict, but if there's one thing he cannot tolerate, it is physical abuse of children. So, he raised his voice, beckoned the

Dean to join him, and forcefully pushed the two policemen down to the ground. By this time, I am not sure quite how, but sticks and sprays were being used and people were scattered everywhere. Then, a jeep full of British gentry arrived on the scene, sirens firing and bellowing voices from hand speakers.

"You are commanded to immediately cease violent protests or risk physical action being taken against you!" Student leaders Janaki and Shekhar locked arms together to form a wall and decided to stand on the stage that they had spoken on earlier. They requested a few moments to speak peacefully to the army members and policemen, but they were denied this. The scene became ugly. My heart was beating fast since I feared that T.V. would not withstand the chaos, crowd and violence underway. So, I grabbed my dear brother, made him sit on my bicycle seat, wrapped his arms around my waist, and I took off through the back of the college campus, past the teacher's lounge and out through the medical college entrance. I did stop in the medical clinic so that T.V. could be examined properly, and lay down on the examine room table. This was a good decision. The resident doctor on duty was very thorough and advised us to have T.V rest a while at the hospital. I was a bit apprehensive to leave him in the hospital knowing that riots were starting up outside, but it seemed like to right thing to do.

I left the campus and headed for home. I did not look back to see what was happening at the riots. This was not due to fear, but more due to wanting to return home to my Vanamali, and my sister, and inform them of what was happening."

Officers Rao and Reddy seemed to be content with the detailed recount of recent events that Baba had given to them.

They both paced up and down the room, slowly, until Rao decided to step outside the room. He returned moments later with Baba's family- Vanamali, toddler in tow, and Dr. Rai, in accompaniment. Baba was relieved to see his family at this late hour. Murali reached out his arms, signaling his father to hold him, which Baba did, happily. Vanamali gazed at her husband, trying to read his face for answers to her many questions. She wanted to talk freely with him, but, realizing that the police officers had still not released Baba from their charge, she remained mute, and waited patiently for others to speak.

Eventually, the officers broke the silence with words of comfort. "Go ahead, talk to your family", they ordered Baba. Baba addressed Vanamali and his brother-in-law, softly.

"Oh my, so sorry that you were troubled to late at night. I hope it was not too much of a bother." Dr. Rai however, simply smiled and shook his head.

"Not at all Chickanna, you know we would never leave you here! Unless you like it, of course!" They chuckled together, and Murali, who had been bouncing a little on his father's lap, began to giggle also, turning to look at his Uncle and wondering if they were engaging Murali in a joke. Murali started to clap his hands and smile. Vanamali, whose legs were achy from the long walk, and late hour, peered over the men to scope the room and see if there was a bench or other chair to sit on. Unfortunately, there was not.

"What is all of this nonsense!" she addressed her spouse, "what is happening? Are you not allowed to return home yet?" she asked, despondently. Officer Rao interjected,

"Actually, ma'am, you can help us with that," he stated. "Mr. Ramaswamy has just given us a detailed recount of the events of his day and night yesterday. I would, however, like to ask you what your involvement was?"

Vanamali laughed spontaneously, startled by the question. "I don't understand why you ask me!" she replied.

"We simply wish to know everything that you know about the Osmania Uprising and local Freedom movement."

Vanamali looked at her husband, searching for any clue or advice as to what to say or do. Baba was rather fatigued by now, and failed to see any benefit of playing blind man's buff at this point. He looked at Vanamali, and then at Dr. Rai, and simply shrugged his shoulders. He knew they would not speak of the telegram or the actual resistance movement plan. They had trained themselves right from the get go to never speak of it in public. But they had never imagined themselves to be captive in a police station. Rai was the first to break the silence.

"Officers, why have you still detained my brother-in-law? Under what jurisdiction can you do that? Have you allowed Baba legal representation? It is getting rather late and we need to get home. Baby Murali is exhausted, as are we."

Rao, the senior official, started to pace again but addressed the doctor.

"Sir, I understand that everyone here is exhausted, as are we, but there is something missing in this puzzle and we need the missing pieces. If you can help us complete the puzzle, we will gladly let you go. If not, then I'm afraid you will all need to stay."

"Don't be ridiculous!" Rai exclaimed, shocked at the officers' suggestion. "You have no reason to keep us all here, and you are not even giving us any explanations. Who is your boss? I would like to speak with him!"

Reddy, clearly ticked off by this last exchange, barely took a moment to respond. He walked towards Dr. Rai and stared him down firmly.

"You do not know whom you are dealing with!" he yelled, waving a pointed finger in Rai's face, angrily. "We asked you all to give us information regarding the Osmania rally that turned into riots. We requested your input regarding any knowledge of upcoming resistance movement activities. None of you has given us this information. What do you believe is the right thing to do?" Reddy exclaimed, marching back towards officer Rao noisily. Rao had used this time to ponder over what his next move would be. To him, this was one giant chess game being played out. Who would be killed, who was the pawn, and who first would state "Check-mate!" With a slight smile on his face, Rao opened his mouth to speak, but was interrupted by a junior officer calling the boss out to receive a phone call.

"Ok, where were we?" he questioned rhetorically, on his return. "Ah yes," he reflected, the reminder having come to his mind, "I am afraid that you will all have to spend the night in the station. We are concerned with the information, or lack thereof, that has been presented. I have concerns that further skirmishes may occur from other rallies around town turning riotous. The safest place for you all is here, truly. Officer Rao will show you your cell."

Vanamali, who had been weary but calm the entire day, finally broke down.

"I need to go home. I need to take Murali to bed. What is all of this? Are you out of your mind?" She turned back to looks at her husband as a frustrated and tired expression consumed her. "Should I call my father?"

Chapter Twelve: Srikantayya's Achilles Heel

Vanamali sat with her baby, hugging him close to her, consoling his tears of fatigue as well as her own. "Don't cry my little prince, don't cry." As she held him close to nurse, a surge of dark thoughts brewed in her mind. "Why can't we be just a regular, peaceful family? Why do I have to fear imprisonment or riots? Why can't my son be put first, rather than the mission?"

She was tired, and the frustration of leaving her child was enough to provoke anger in any new mother. She had tried, as well, to capture the attention of her beloved Baba, in the way the two had met. But he was constantly preoccupied with the movement, and she felt ignored at times, but unable to talk about this. Vana had self-reflected, wondering whether she was mentally unsound that these darker thoughts engulfed her mind in sudden dark moments. Baba had noticed her dwelling on things, and moving slowly sometimes in the kitchen. Rather than ask her privately, he had resorted to cajoling her in front of Brunda, her sister-in-law. Brunda, loving and kind, responded with a little teasing, something that Vana had never taken well to. She now felt as if she were on the wrong side of the fence.

Murali was now sound asleep. Vana opened her Godrej bureau and removed the woolen blanket that Baba had purchased while on a trip to Delhi. It was warm and plush, with a silk edging that Vana herself had sewn on. She placed it over the infant, and continued to watch him, observing gently the ebb and flow of his breaths. Five minutes later, she had fallen asleep next to her son. A little later, she arose from the bed, realizing she had left the Godrej cupboard wide-open. Her heart was quickly racing and her countenance flushed. She studied the cupboard closely, scanning the compartments up and down, and making sure her inventory was intact. She found her wedding sari, and made sure the blouse was in place. She then unlocked the inbuilt safe, and reviewed its contents. Her Maharani drop earrings were present, as was her ruby and emerald choker. But, she couldn't find her wedding amulets, specially crafted from her grandmother to her. She was now tearful, and listless. She sat back down on her platform bed, lying down next to Murali. "How can I live with myself? How clumsy I have been", she thought to herself. "Somebody must have come in and stolen from me while I was sleeping…", she sighed to herself, still frantic from what she believed to be a trespasser. She sat on the edge of the bed and quietly wept, rocking her body gently back and forth as if to comfort her self.

She was a teenager again, heading back to her childhood home, having returned after what was her final swim meet. She was victorious, having brought home the state championship title, and she was glowing. It felt like she was in her prime, and she had a sense of grandeur.

"I finally did it, Amma," she had joyfully expressed to her mother, "I won! Dad will be proud of me now!"

"Rani, don't say that! We are both very proud of you. You are good at many things; you don't need to hang on to this success only! Enjoy the moment!" her mother praised, sweetly.

As the Srikantayya women approached the house, Kamala noticed the door ajar. It frightened her, since, being the only adult in the house most of the time, she feared strangers. Kamala found the spare keys that were hidden behind a makeshift cubbyhole in the garden wall.

"Ahh, it's still here, that's good!" she exclaimed. Tucking the key on her sari waistband, she entered her home. There was a men's sports coat on the back of her dining chair, which surprised her.

"Appa probably bought a jacket," she said to Manasa, who was also viewing the scene. Kamala looked around, and seeing nothing else out of place, decided to take a deep breathe, and carry on her duties.

"Hurry, children, help me prepare dinner!" she called out to the girls. Manasa was quick to respond, washing her face and then tying her long scarf around her waist and then knotting it in the back so that she could help her mother with kitchen preparation. Vanamali, however, was still glowing in the light of sheer joy from her win in the pool, and was walking around the house and humming tunes.

"Vana, hurry and put your trophy away, and come here to help us!" Kamala beckoned her elder daughter to give Vana the keys to the Godrej so that she may put away her trophy and come down to earth again. So doing, the children rushed to the cupboard and unlocked it.

"Let me do it, I'm the responsible one!" Manasa touted.

"Oh, hush, you're not supposed to self-praise, you know- it's not ladylike!" Vanamali replied. The girls wrapped the golden trophy with a cotton towel, and decided to open the upper safe, where the jewels lay. The trophy was only palm size, so would easily fit in the cubby and would be better off out of site. Manasa reached up to feel the sides of the cubby, making sure it would fit. Indeed, her mother's jewels usually took up most of the space, so she would need to be careful in placement. But, to her surprise, the cubby was empty.

"Vana, get the step stool and help me up. I need to look into the cubby." The girls climbed up together on the small stool and peered into the cubby. To their astonishment, it was empty. No jewels, no money, no trophies. The cry for their Amma was almost in unison. Kamala, who was in earshot distance, heading to check on her girls with the Godrej key, rushed in.

"WHAT HAPPENED?" Amma screamed, fearing an injury or even an animal intruder from the forest. The girls began talking all at once, making their cries incoherent. Finally, Kamala herself stood on the step stool and peered into the compartment. It was empty. Not one piece of fine jewels or even a rupee bill remained. It was disbelief that overtook Kamala's mind.

"Are you toying with me?" she asked her children. "I need the truth NOW! Who took all of the safe contents? Vanamali, Manasa, are you playing around?"

The children, now panic stricken, hugged their mother, fearing that something grave was in progress.

"We just came to put the trophy away, Amma. But when we opened the Godrej there was nothing to be found in the safe. What is happening, Amma? Who do you think did this?" Manasa pleaded, frustrated and fearful. Vanamali, however, was mute. Her rush of emotions had overflown, from the high of the championship title to now the low of defeat. She was spent. She was angry. She and her sister watched in horror as their mother, typically exuding confidence and poise, shriveled into a childlike ball, hand to her head, sobbing and broken down.

"Why? Why is he doing this to me?" the girls heard their mother muttering as she rocked back and forth on the floor. "What did I ever do to him to deserve this? Who is protecting me?" Kamala cried.

"Amma, let's file a police complaint. Surely they can find who stole our things?" Manasa asked, hopeful.

"No, dear, that won't be necessary. I'm sure we can find out the culprit on our own. We don't need to involve the police department. Once you let them into your house they find a way to keep on nosing around. I think we will have this sorted out in no time," Kamala said quietly, composing her self once more. She paced the room, studying every angle and corner, surveying the loss, and looking for clues. There was nothing out of place, except for the missing articles of jewelry and black money. The children helped their mother, searching the room until no corner was unturned. Finally, weary and low, Vanamali grabbed her mother's hands and placed them on her face. Soothingly, she consoled Kamala. "Amma, let's leave this room and prepare for dinner. If we keep staying in here, we will only feel depressed. All your beautiful jewels are gone, except one."

"What are you talking about? I don't see any more jewels left in the Godrej. What do you mean?" Kamala asked.

"Oh. Well, the one jewel left is you, Amma!" Vanamali replied. Kamala stood up, took both of her children in her arms, and embraced them fondly.

"What would I do without you two?" she cried, softly stroking the girls' silky hair before leading them in to the kitchen for dinner.

Kamala turned around to hold the doorknob shut, but worried about the Godrej again, she decided to return to the scene and lock up. She peered into the bureau, feeling the corners of the dark metal shelves with her fingers. There was nothing. The lower shelves had Kamala's wedding saris and her husband's special ethnic wear. The last appeared empty. The silver prayer idols and lanterns had been taken, leaving nothing behind but the white cloth on which the items had been laid out. Kamala sighed, thinking of the number of prayer services she had performed with her parents and in-laws' blessings, carefully arranging the idols and making the candlewicks to light.

"Who would want these personal things? Who would come all the way to my little country home, to steal my silver? Surely they could find some wealthy couple in the city who have many articles of value?" she pondered, distressed over her losses. As her fingers ran through the very last upper shelf in the Godrej, she felt something cold against her tiny fingers. She pulled on it, nestling the object out from in-between her middle and index fingers. It was a brass key, relatively small as if for a front door rather than a gate or compound lock. It was slightly bigger than a cupboard key, and definitely not one that belonged to her. Her frustration only welted up further, as her interrogative mind began to conjure up formulas for how and why she had been robbed. Her inner fear was that someone was watching her, realizing she was essentially a single mother, with husband far away. In the early years she was never hassled since people recognized her powerful husband and left her alone, respectfully but also out of fear. But now, with Shrikantayya nowhere in sight, and her young girls' beauty gathering attention, maybe she was being watched? But the key did not make sense…

Kamala turned it over and over in her hand, then, stretching the key ring from her waist cummerbund in her hand, she placed it in the loop and attached it to her sari. She left the room quietly, closing the door behind her and rushing to join her children in the kitchen.

Chapter Thirteen: The town home

"Amma, look who is here? It's Appa! You didn't say he was coming home for the weekend!" Manasa yelled, rushing in the house from the front yard, where she was collecting her clothes hanging on the line. "Hi Appa, welcome home! How has court been? Have you had any fascinating cases or just mundane boring criminal ones?" she joyfully asked, greeting her father and taking his bag into the home.

"Oh, rather good cases, Manu; I should have to tell you about them after dinner. But for now, call your mother, I have much to discuss." But Kamala did not rush out of the kitchen on the request. Instead, she continued about her duties of cooking dinner and preparing for her busy week ahead. After about ten minutes, Kamala laid the table and called the family for dinner.

"Now she emerges, just like a crocodile, ready to snap!" the judge joked at the table, children on either side. Kamala stared at her husband, taking in his face, one she hadn't set eyes on in several months. "Are you going to address me, or are crocodiles mute?" he snidely remarked.

"I've been very busy running the house, and words beseech me," Kamala responded.

"Yes. Well, you're lucky I came today. It was a sudden stroke of genius. The lawyers in my case approached me in my chambers and came up with a good bargain, thus closing the case quickly without much fuss. So, I'm free. There's so much happening in the city this weekend but I thought it best to return home. Haven't seen the children in a while now. They have grown so much!"

"I'm surprised you noticed!" she attacked, blushing from her tongue yet not shying away from the discussion. Srikantayya looked sternly at his petite wife, studying her from top to bottom in a way that sent chills down her spine. It was effective. She dropped the conversation and served her husband on the silver dinner plates that the children had set out.

"Beautiful presentation and delicious food. Thank you Kamala," the judge expressed. "How comes the silver plates?" he added. The surge of emotions proved almost too much to handle as Kamala started to retort. She stuttered, and then held her tongue, looking at her girls and deciding to hold back. A few minutes later, the plates were empty and everyone had taken their second rounds.

"Amma, is it okay if I go up to read? I have some homework that I want to review," Vanamali asked.

Shri, who was quick to react, spoke purposely, interrupting Kamala.

"That is up to me to decide. I am your father. Why don't you show me your work? I would like to see what Mysore schools are teaching nowadays." Vana looked rather perplexed, not enjoying the dent in her routine, and frustrated at her father's interruption. She quietly rushed upstairs. Manasa excused herself from the table, but continued to assist her mother, cleaning the table and putting away the dishes.

When Kamala continued to work in silence, Shri, now blood bubbling beneath his skin, broke out. "Pour me a drink, would you?"

"You know, drinking is not good for you," Kamala spoke, now addressing him face to face. "It can cause liver sickness, it is dangerous. Not to mention the diseased mind it can cause."

"Oh, stop that nonsense. It's only one drink. Where have you hidden my decanter anyway? That was a gift from the Mysore Maharaja. Why have you not displayed it?"

"Because it's useless. I do not drink and we never have male visitors over. And, too, you're never home to entertain. Why do I need a decanter out? It only collects dust."

"You are a strange piece of work," Shrikantayya now added, "I don't know any other women who hides royal presents! Are you mad or do you like living like a hermit?"

Kamala was now holding back tears, years of longing for her husband's attention coming to the surface.

"If I do not show any wealth it's because you never give any to me! Shame on you! Why do you insist on treating your family this way? Perhaps I'm not modern enough for you, but what about the children? What have they done to suffer like this? I'm basically raising them solo and you cannot even send anything for their upkeep? You're lucky I have maintained your respect with your parents. If they even came to know about your alter life they would be mortified!"

Kamala was now facing Shri with the drink he had requested, hand trembling as she held out the glass with whiskey. Shri grabbed the drink from his wife's hand, an uncomfortable pause suffocating the room. He gulped the drink down his thick throat, savoring the warmth it provided and giving in to its control. To Kamala's astonishment, he did not react verbally to her words, choosing instead to ignore his wife, as if she were a fly on the wall. As he poured himself another peg, Kamala broke the silence.

"Say something would you? Can't you talk? You spend all day judging others in your fancy suits and big words, yet now you are speechless?" She continued, hoping to provoke a reaction. He remained silent, cold as a cucumber, hypnotized by his whiskey and ignorant to Kamala's heart. Yet she continued.

"I went into the city to find you last week, when you refused to return the messages sent. I tried so hard to contact you after the robbery. We were so scared Shri. Where were you? The girls and I had cried, we had felt violated, all of our possessions gone... But you didn't even show concern. So I traveled in to town when the children were in school, with the assistance of the neighbor's servant. You were in session, busy with a long trial. Your personal assistant was also off on holiday so I had to inquire with the other judge's assistant as to where your city accommodations were. He gave me an address quite different from where I had been sending you letters. It was a new development in the city, a new town home. I figured something was up when you would never return home, but I knew that you had an allotted work apartment. But this was entirely a different thing. This was a luxury home! I entered the building but rather than being greeted with kind smiles, the doorman looked at me as if I was the maidservant. I continued up one floor to the address, hurrying so that I could make it before being turned away. You can imagine my surprise when the assigned key did not fit in the lock. I tried about five times before giving up. Finally, out of frustration, I took the key bunch from my waist and sifted through the chain. In a last minute stroke of madness I tried this key." Kamala now was brandishing the larger key that she had found in the Godrej that was broken into. Shri now turned his gaze to his wife, squinting through the side of his peripheral vision to study the key. "This key fit the new town home. This one. How can you do this?"

"What nonsense do you speak of?" Shri said, brushing her off.

"When all of my special possessions were stolen from the safe, there was nothing left in the Godrej besides this strange key that seemed to belong to nothing? How is it that it fits your town home? Is there something you need to tell me?"

"Stop rambling on, woman. Two events don't make a case. Now what are you accusing me of?"

"You know who stole from me? You do otherwise why is this key here?" Kamala spewed out, the words crocking from her strained voice. "I think something strange is going on here and you are the culprit. Who else would stand mute when their wife has been robbed?"

Srikantayya paced the room, looking around the length of the room as he pondered his next retort.

"Give me the key!" he finally ordered Kamala.

"Fine, I don't want it!" she shouted, throwing it at his feet.

The judge picked up there key, a stern look shadowing his portly face.

"How do you know I didn't put the key in the Godrej myself? How can you be sure the town home was acquired on suspicious premises? How can you be sure of anything? Why is it so strange that the state judge acquires a town home? Must everything with you be clouded with pessimism? If I was busy in a case, you never doubted me before. Just because of a house robbery, rather than look for the culprit you accuse your husband?" Ever ready, the judge smiled coyly as he contemplated his win. But Kamala was quick with the joust.

"My diamond jewels were on the nightstand, Shri. WHOM did you steal my jewels for? Your supposed to stand up for justice, but you alone are the criminal here!" Kamala turned to wipe the tears from her eyes that burned like fire on her ruddy cheeks. As she stooped to pick up her hair that had separated from her plait, Shri clutched his crystal glass and tilted it to his mouth. Sipping the last drops of whiskey from the third glass poured he savored the fire that burned within his throat from the warmth of the fluid and lifted his chin further. Now empty, he raised the glass, studying the angles of the crystals that decorated the base.

"I do too much for you anyway! You should be lucky to be married to me! Quit your complaining woman." So saying, the gargantuan man threw the glass at Kamala. The glass chips cut her arm and right cheek, as she had turned slightly. The tears rolled down even further. Shri rushed out of his house barely noticing his younger daughter Vana, who was sitting in the kitchen, sobbing, and full view of the scene.

The judge was back in his court, ruling his jurisdiction, and taking back his pride that had momentarily been swallowed a week prior.

"You're done! Guilty as charged! The gavel came down, the small, silky smooth hammer diminutive in the burly giant hands of Shrikantayya. He started to collect his papers, neatly smoothing the edges of the documents so that they would easily compress in his folder.

"Please, your Honor, please listen to me one more time. I have something to say," the farmer pleaded, wriggling out of the officer's arm hook that held him back. Srikantayya frowned on the man, similarly knitting his brows and peering down through his glasses at his courtroom staff.

"The case is over, you may follow the officer to the holding room."

"But sir, you do not know what actually happened. I did not steal from the minister's house. I went to his home to return to him a men's watch that was found farm kitchen. I do not know how it was in the kitchen, but Lakshmi, the kitchen cook recognized it and asked me to return it. Since it was later in the night she herself was scared to go out alone. I took the responsibility, but when I came to the minister's home, he arrested me. He told you this was a family heirloom and that I had stolen it from him. This is simply not true. I please ask you to disregard what he had told you. He then concocted a deep story stating that I have been stealing from him for months. Please, your honor, I have no lawyer, but I know who I am, and I request your consideration." The judge laid down his gavel, the weight of his own hand slumping carelessly on the desk. He wanted to believe the farmer, studying his face for a moment and seeing honesty in his eyes. But, he was a logical man, and was taught to follow the law and the facts. There had been no documents or evidence submitted to support the farmer's claim. It was already six o'clock in the evening. Session should be over. He looked at the courtroom doors in a gaze. As the pleading of the farmer dulled out, the judge's attention drifted to a red flicker behind the window. There was a shadow of a woman whose face was invisible through the tempered glass door slit, but who waved at Shri. He smiled, and waved the farmer out of the room. "Case is closed. If you wish to appeal, you may find yourself a solicitor and file a complaint."

"But, your honor, I have no means to do that on my own. Please, sir." His cries were drowned out by the gavel again, and the sound of the wooden chair legs screeching as the giant frame of the judge emerged from his seat and walked out of the room. He opened the chambers door and placed his stack of legal papers, tucked under his armpit, on the mahogany desk. He removed his robes, and, per usual routine, approached his decanter to pour himself a drink. But, to his surprise, it was already poured, waiting for him. "Hello, there, your honor!" the voice came from behind him. He turned, startled, to see Sheila, the air stewardess, approaching from the bathroom in the corner of his chambers. I waved at you from behind your courtroom door! Did you see me? I've missed you. Do you like the drink I poured you?" she gleefully said.

"It's delicious, thank you." He placed the glass down after taking a few sips. " You're a welcome sight! What brings you in to town, tonight?" Sheila approached the judge, smoothly and calmly placing her arms around Shri's neck before choosing her words.

"You do!" She gazed at Shri, who was smiling now. He touched her face, his fingers now smoothing her cheeks and then ears. The back of his hand touched her diamond earrings. "You suit these well. You are a bright and sparkling part of my life, Sheila, just like the earrings. You are dazzling!" The couple was heard laughing and chatting, as the office around them closed down for the night.

Chapter Fourteen: The Resistance, August 1940

Baba entered Dr. Rai's compound, turning the lever to the divider wall door and stepping in. He approached his sister's front door, and knocked gently. He was surprised to be greeted by Rai himself, who quickly explained that it was a late Sunday night and the household was sleeping so he stood waiting for Baba. The men took off, by foot, to the back of the compound, then hopped on Dr. Rai's moped and sped away.

They reached Rai's Mysore Soap Factory within ten minutes and stepped down the factory stairs to its basement level, where more of the "Quit India" members had already assembled. Prasanna was working on typing small pamphlets to distribute at the various college campuses. Suparna, a recently graduated law student, was writing what appeared to be a newsletter that would be mailed or hand delivered to various friends and colleagues within the community. Then there was the Colonel himself, who, surprisingly present in spite of the family wedding, was focused on looking at a large map of Hyderabad and surroundings. He studied it carefully, noting down a few pointers, or asking questions to those around him.

"Where would you start a riot?" he blurted out loudly, looking at Baba who had just entered the scene. "Do you mean, if I were a Brit, where would I instigate a riot?" Baba clarified.

"Yah, that's correct! " replied Colonel Singh.

"Um, let me think about that," he replied. He had never been trained to think like a criminal! It was sort of exciting, he thought to himself, analyzing movements, motives and maps for the movement. He wanted to feel a sort of guilt towards his involvement with the movement, thinking this would keep him "on the straight and narrow", as the Brits would say. But, he actually felt drawn to the movement. His mind was constantly preoccupied of late with ideas of how to, where to, and when to act. He felt important, and admired his friends who had placed so much of their trust in Baba, and were very optimistic that as a group, they could change the political tide to their advantage. As he pondered, he gazed at Colonel Singh's uniform. Such pride, such honor, he thought, as he studied the fatigues and all of the glory it brought. A thought suddenly occurred to him, and he blurted out, "Maybe the British Army Barracks or British Embassy?"

"Oh", exclaimed Suparna, who had been diligently working but had been listening intently to the discussion, "That's a great idea. It makes sense. Let's take the protest directly to the squatters!!"

Prasanna approached Baba, and, handing him a cup of chai, he also commented.

"I think that is a wonderful idea, Baba. You're definitely onto something. Although I admit I'm a bit apprehensive approaching the enemy directly on their territory, I think the idea is stellar. It shows that we want to exchange words, but is simply targeted, void of confusing messages or implications. It also will go down in the newspapers and radio broadcasts very well. It shows that we want to talk, and are not afraid of confrontation. Let's work on this."

Baba's mind was ticking now, imagining the protest march reaching the British Consulate office and gathering enough attention to create public waves. The group swiftly began to work, like poets epically crafting their work with their muse in front of them. Each member seemed to easily communicate ideas and exchange information, while another began to design their next pamphlet to distribute. No one was lethargic, in spite of the dawn hour. By six o'clock in the morning the last of the pamphlets was complete, and Colonel Singh discussed the next meeting venue, which would be the last, prior to the upcoming protest march. They decided on a few code words that could be used in the event that spy activities or the presence of unwanted strangers was felt. "The Albatross Approaches", was what Dr. Rai came up with, which received a few head nods from the team. Baba liked it, but then added,

" How about we call the mission Punya Cote?" The other members nodded in agreement, liking the comparison of the children's story to the freedom mission, and having a group sense that saying, "Punya Cote" in an urgent moment would not attract unnecessary attention.

Rai and Baba left the factory, as did the rest of the group. Rai dropped off Baba to his home, and then returned to his residence just in time for morning coffee and breakfast.

Chapter Fifteen: Geetha Sastry

Geetha was the middle sister of beloved Baba, or Chickanna as his doting sisters addressed him. She was a gentle soul, not really bothered by the events around her. She was a newlywed, but her husband, a lawyer by the name of Vinayaka Sastry, was practicing his hand in politics and as a consequence, always seemed to have pressing work or engagements to attend outside of the house. This put a tremendous cloud on Geetha's psyche, and she found herself preoccupied with her thoughts and worries, alone in the house most of the time. While her elder brothers were engrossed in their freedom struggle or factory supervision, she was left to tend to her young household. She was an early bird, so dinner preparations were usually complete by midmorning and she twiddled her thumbs thinking of things to do. Her elder sister Brunda was skilled in the kitchen, and no one could top her in making delicious savory and sweet delicacies. Aradhana was a talented seamstress or knitter, so everyone in the family who had any fixing work would trouble her and she would oblige with pleasure. Young Pooja was not married yet, only eighteen years old and planning on a home economics degree. Yet, she too, seemed to attract attention for advice on home organization, letter writing and nutrition, much to Geetha's envy. Although she adored her family, she felt like the odd one out. She wished she loved the homely life, but she did not. She felt encapsulated, imprisoned. She wished she had the attention of her peers, but she did not. She wished her husband would spend more time with her, like most newlyweds would, but he did not. She craved something to keep her mind busy and her heart content. She had even suggested to her husband that she would like to attend college, but he had denied her that dream, instead demanding that she be present in the home to entertain colleagues and guests that he may be bringing home on short notice. Even Vanamali had more fun than she. Vanamali had a toddler to entertain her and Baba even allowed Vanamali to participate in some of his peace protest marches and activist work. How sad her own life was, she thought.

When Officer Rao had knocked on her door earlier that morning, she was reluctant to let him in, and a little nervous. Her husband was not home, and she did not like officials and policemen when she was alone in the house. She felt nervous. Officer Rao was pleasant. When Geetha offered him lemon water or coffee, he eagerly consented, thrilled to be treated with such hospitality. It was a hot afternoon already, yet his work was far from done. He had piles of folders on his desk that needed his review, yet the moment he had reached his office, the captain had ordered Rao to immediately go to Geetha's house to interrogate her.

"There is a lead," he was told. "You need to gently extract the information, and quickly. We do not have time for an uprising. Let's nip this in the bud."

Geetha brought the lemon sherbet water and snacks, setting the tray on the table and pouring the coffee decoction with fresh steamed milk.

"Thank you," Rao responded.

"If I may officer," Geetha asked, "To what do I owe this visit?"

"Mrs. Geetha, I am here to ask you a few questions about your brother. I thought you would not object," he added, " In fact, it was your good husband that advised me to come here. You see, Mr. Ramaswamy is being interrogated in conjunction with the Osmania riots. Can you shed some light on this?"

Geetha was taken aback. She was not expecting this visit, nor was she aware that her own husband had sent the officer over. She was feeling angry and hurt, yet tried hard to separate her head from her heart.

"He's a politician," she kept thinking to herself, "These things are to be expected." As she consoled herself in her mind, officer Rao gulped down the delicious coffee and proceeded to ask Geetha the same question again.

"I do not know anything that he is doing that is wrong, officer, so I am afraid that I cannot help you."

"All right," the officer replied, " at least can you tell me when was the last time you saw him or spoke to him?"

"Er," she pondered, " Well, he was with us last weekend for Sunday brunch and then I went over to spend time with baby Murali. Baba was busy with his work but was in the home. I do not recall if he had other events planned. We were talking more about Brunda's new arrival, so we really did not have time to discuss boring work details."

The officer paced slowly, scanning the room and then turning around to face Geetha.

"Did Mrs. Rai have a boy or a girl?" he asked.

"Oh, a baby girl. They are going to officially name her Sripriya but I already started to call her Preethi. She's as fair as milk and has the cutest dimples!"

The officer smiled, interested in the small details and eager to make Geetha feel comfortable. He gazed at Geetha's young face, looking at her gesticulations, expressions and excitement on discussing baby Preethi. She was barely twenty-one, he thought, and full of life. She must be thoroughly bored at home alone. He wondered about her relationship with Vinayaka Sastry, her politician husband, who appeared to be much older than her, and much more weathered. They seemed more like father and daughter, lest husband and wife. And, why would Sastry sir have sent police men to interrogate his own wife? If Geetha was his wife, Rao thought, he would never allow such an interrogation unless he himself was present.

"All is not what it seems," he thought to himself. Perhaps they were not well suited for each other. Perhaps, Rao had dishonest motives for this marriage.

Geetha looked up from her cup of coffee, and noticed how the officer was daydreaming. She didn't know what to make of this, but decided to use this moment to her advantage.

"Officer, I do not wish to offend you, but if your questioning is done, I request you to leave. You see, I have pressing work to do before the upcoming Deepawali festivities, and I do need to rush to the market before the rains begin."

The officer consented, and politely took his leave. Geetha, feeling a little more mature after this unwanted encounter, put on her raincoat and rushed out of the door, locking the door behind her.

Chapter Sixteen: Incarcerated

Baba sat on the small bench that was placed in the holding cell, gazing at his sandals. He always prided himself in his shiny, polished shoes. It bothered him tremendously that now, his shoes were coated with the black dust that was so well known to coat the mucus membranes of Indians even when they had showered, and even when they were hygienic. He took his handkerchief from his breast pocket, and wiped his shoes down. Vanamali, seeing him cleaning his shoes, peered at her own slippers and smiled. She had the grey-black dust on her toes, slippers and heels, as well as mud on her shoe soles from the long walk in the rain. Yet, Vanamali differed from Baba tremendously when it came to things like dirt. She loved to get "down and dirty", since it reminded her of her childhood in the village, swimming when she chose to, and dancing in the mud soil and rain when nobody was looking. She had different beliefs when it came to dirt. "A little bit of mud is good for a child," she had attempted to tell her husband just last week, after bringing in baby Murali from the gardens in the neighborhood. Indeed, she never recalled a day when she was ever really sick. She attributed this to the clean air in the village, but also to her carefree play outside. Baba, on the other hand, had grown up in the city and was always advised by his parents to stay "clean and bright, like a distinguished gentleman', words, that to this day, he continued to preach.

"A child will get pneumonia from wet hair and respiratory diseases from play in the mud!" he would respond to his wife, who would despondently take the baby for a bedtime bath but disagree quietly. But, when Baba handed Vanamali the handkerchief, she consented, knowing that she was wiser to choose her battles than to wage war at home. She slowly and methodically cleaned her leather slippers then kept the handkerchief for herself, tucked in her saree as a reminder to wash it whenever they would be released to home.

Baba, seeing his wife and recognizing how fatigued she was, started to address Vanamali. "What do you think will happen now, Vana?" he gently asked. Vanamali, eager for some conversation, turned to face her husband.

"I'm not sure dear," she replied, "But I hope my father will hear about this and get us released."

They stared into each other's eyes and wondered about this moment and its implications.

A few hours had passed by when a young man was brought into the cell. He sported a stylish brimmed hat and small brown neck scarf. He wore his hair without brushing or tying, and had oiled his long strands down a little. What set him apart from the other young prisoners was that he had grown a small chin beard, or goatee. His jawline was angular, so the effect was rather striking. He was pushed into the cell, hands tied behind his back, the thrust causing the man to stumble at Baba's feet. The hat fell from his head, revealing a bruised left cheek and eye. The young man squinted from the corner of his eye, peering up to Baba, and nodding apologetically.

"Sorry, sir, I couldn't predict that one". Baba stood up and helped the man steady himself. The prison guard sneered, and locked the door behind them.

"Don't mention," Baba replied kindly. "Your good name?" Baba inquired.

The man smiled, and looked around the room. He seemed to be studying Baba and the cell, trying to ascertain whether to speak or stay quiet. After a momentary pause, he responded.

"I am Harmeet Singh, and I am being held here on no particular charge at all. You see, I head up a student organization called "Awaaz" and we direct protests to challenge the British occupants. However, the government seems to have taken a disliking to me, and have incarcerated me under no particular grounds. I have no lawyer, and no money, so for now, I will lead things from this tiny cell." He was confident, talking as though fighting with powerful enemies was an everyday occurrence for him. "I like your khadi cotton attire," Harmeet added, "I assume you are a Gandhian?" he asked.

"Well, yes, we are. I have been an avid supporter since the South African uprising. But, I do not think we can talk about this in detail here. All I can say is that I believe in a free India, and I am going to raise my voice in support of an Independent India, free of British colonialists rule."

Harmeet listened, politely, smiling at Baba, whose mere countenance commanded respect and kindness. After some whisperings of Baba's plight, and why he was imprisoned,

Harmeet spoke again. "Baba, I respect your vision but not your methods."

Baba raised his eyebrows, slightly taken aback. He leaned back slightly, catching Vanamali's attention as he listened. Harmeet continued, softly whispering and carefully choosing his words, to avoid drawing unnecessary attention from the prison guards.

"Kya, mey Hindi ya Urdu mein baath karsaktha hoon?" he asked. "May I speak with you in Hindi or Urdu?" The men agreed, thinking that the guards would have poor ability to decipher these poetic, yet non-regional tongues. "I have followed the papers of the passive resistance movement a lot over the last three years. In fact, when my hometown suffered vandalism at the hands of the colonialists, I found myself questioning my faith. I did not know whether I could accomplish anything in the movement towards freedom, with my meager connections and finances. My family had been violated, in that we were forced from our home by greedy landowners, who couldn't even pronounce the name of our village. My father, a farmer, had by his own right succeeded in our neighborhood. He had gained respect from the other villagers by managing his crops and his profits very well, and soon a small hut home had become a brick and mortar house. The other farmers relied on my father to guide them. We were celebrating the successful harvest, and enjoying how remote we were from other political factions or "civilization." There was a massive celebration and my father, who had been appointed by the villagers, to be the head of the neighborhood council, was openly sharing the joy. My sister Meenakshi, or Mini as I call her, was to be engaged to our neighbor's son, who was heading off to the city to train in the army. Money was tight, but the friendship that the fathers had for each other, with mutual respect and adoration, provided a sense that everything would somehow be all right. Mini was thrilled. As the sweets were being shared and we boys danced bhangra to the music, the Britons came. They made us stop what we were doing. The women were nervous. Mini contemplated running into the house but she didn't want her party to end, so she continued to sit in the throng of children, hoping the festivities would continue. A rather prominent looking official, by the name of Colonel Geoffrey, approached my parents, and asked them, rather curtly, what was the occasion for such noise. My father explained that the friends and neighbors were celebrating his daughter's engagement to Raja, who was expected to have a bright future in the Indian Army someday. The official laughed at them, pointing at the poor families and children and commenting on their poverty.

"You don't have permission from us to host any party tonight," the Colonel said, "so I command you to break up the party and return to your homes." The Brits didn't stop at that. When my startled parents respectfully approached the officers and asked to please continue the function, the officers jeered at them and lectured them on the new ordinance requiring permission prior to any outdoor event, and even taxing the locals for using the premises.

"But, good sir, we have been living in this hamlet for generations and have never been required to pay for celebrating in the streets", my father had said. "We cannot afford more taxes, we are mere farmers, living from day to day. Please, allow us this night to celebrate our children." But the officer did not stop. My father was kind to invite the officers to stay for dinner. But they laughed in his face. They peered around at the woks full of chickpea curry and lentils and spat on the food, sneering.

"You monkeys don't even know what real food is. Serve pork or beef, not this dung."

Colonel Geoffrey by now had beckoned his soldiers to circle the locals, and after taking a few swigs from his breast pocket flask, he threw the liquor down, tossed a cigarette onto it, and signaled his men to action. Within minute flames engulfed the common ground. But, the bastard did not cease his tyranny. The farmers and their families had done nothing to provoke the men, yet the Colonel's ego ruled that night. He locked the compound to the village, and let innocent victims die. At the end of the night, twenty innocent villagers had been killed. Why does one not fight against such atrocities?

So you see, Baba sir, I do NOT believe in non-violence. I believe that we need to take justice in our own hands, and right the wrongs our nation has suffered. If they can burn us, why can we not stand up against them?"

Baba paused, listening carefully and observing his new cellmate closely. Harmeet wore a frown, knotting his eyebrows giving him the appearance of an older gentleman, not the student that he was. He couldn't have been more than twenty-four years of age, yet he had the passion and conviction of someone much older. He was now slightly flushed in the face, and appeared to be agitated, tapping his right foot in restless fashion, on the cement floor. Vanamali, ever so gently, nudged her husband in the arm, trying to get his attention.

"Ask him what happened to his family," she said in Kannada, imagining the scenes in her head. Baba did just this, and within a few minutes Baba realized the man's story.

"She died. She's gone. My darling Mini is gone. She was heading inside the home when her friend informed her that her fiancé was among the villagers at the center of the atrium, where the fire had been lit. She went running against the crowd only to find him covered in a blanket of fire. As she tried to stop the flames from their burning rage, the officer pulled her away in an attempt to claim her for himself. She resisted, and within minutes she was being thrown into the tower of flames as the drunken officer galloped off in the dark. If only I could have saved her. But I was rescuing my parents. I did not know what was happening at the atrium center. I could have saved her."

Harmeet wept silently, sobbing into his cupped hands then wiping away the tears. He stood up, and paced the room, charged with anger. "I can die for this country. I will fight for the lives of the innocent. I am not going to take this quietly. Forgive me, Baba, but what exactly is passive resistance? How can it possibly cure the evils of this world? As days pass on we are just getting trampled upon. I am not going to allow that to happen."

Baba grabbed Harmeet's hand, showing him the bench to sit back on. He felt compassion for the young man, but deeply disagreed with the man. He wanted to take him under his wing and teach him the principals of Gandhiji, but he also feared the man's anger. After a few words of condolence and empathy, Baba spoke his mind.

"Harmeet, you have been scarred at a young age, suffering what no man should know, that being the loss of their sibling. Your compass is your anger. But, you should think of the greater good. If the British people see your anger, they will convict you, and punish you with death by implicating you in some conspiracy theory, based on your behavior. Then, this will contribute to the colonialists supporting their claim that India needs rule. Yes, they put us down. Yes, they treat us like animals. But, if they create an animalistic society by fueling anger and anti-establishment groups, they will punish us and never feel sorry for it." He looked at Harmeet, observing his demeanor. He was pleased the man was listening.

" I suggest we allow Gandhi principals, because we cannot rightfully be killed for that. We are not having angry outbursts, killing or physically attacking anyone. We are simply speaking our mind. Yes, it will take longer, but I truly believe this is the right path and will lead us to the end result eventually. Be patient, great things take time and effort. Keep your faith, and believe in the good of humanity. This, I feel, is the path to justice."

"Keep my faith?" Harmeet echoed. I don't know how to do that. I shaved my beard for my fight, and I won't go down silently. My voice will be heard, along with those of all the other innocent victims. This is my faith. I believe in the free voice of the nation, and to invite all people to take a stand." He stood up and began pacing, peering momentarily out of the prison gate to see if any guard was eavesdropping.

"Why, it was only eleven years ago that my uncle was slain for his role in protecting India. He vowed to vindicate the honor of Lala Lajpat Rai and joined the HSRA. I can only respect a man who stands up and shouts. I will do the same. I will fight for my India. Inquilab Zindabad! (Long live the revolution!)"

"Are you a part of the HSRA?" Baba inquired, whispering under his breath.

"Yes, I am. My entire existing family has active members. I am proud to fight for India's Independence Movement. I will keep going".

Baba, deeply concerned, looked at Harmeet in the eyes. He peered up from his round tortoise-shell rimmed glasses, and held both of Harmeet's hands in his own. Baba was only about a decade or so older than Harmeet, yet seemed so mature in comparison.

"If your entire family is part of the freedom movement through the HSRA, then you are targets for their violence. You must play it safe, or fear for your own life. How many members of your family are you willing to lose? What legacy will you be leaving your loved ones if there is no existing future generation? Think about that, and shape your future. Please be careful. If you think about it, we are all on the same side, against the British. Be strong, but don't raise arms. Please be careful."

Harmeet smiled, shook Baba's hand, and adjusted his hat. He pondered the words, but somehow the fury within him continued to play in his mind. He thought about his family's struggle and move from town to village, then finally settling on the farmland of his uncle, and forging a life of normalcy. He dwelled on the loss of his beloved sister, and thought about how different life would be if she were still in the picture.

An hour later Vana was asleep in the corner of the cell, head leaned back on the wall. Baba was rocking Murali in his arms, pacing the cell floor to avoid waking his infant and wife simultaneously. He gazed at his son, who had finally fallen asleep thumb still placed in his mouth. As Baba approached the small bench and began to sit down, the prison door creaked open, startling the young family and Harmeet.

"Come with me!" the harsh voice bellowed, beckoning to Harmeet to follow the guard. The young man arose, wearily, blinking a few times to focus upon the man at the door more clearly. "The warden wants to see you", the guard repeated, taking his stick now, and tapping Harmeet's back.

"Officer, that won't be necessary, as you can see, he is following you," Baba explained, concerned for the young student's safety, and trying to reason with the guard.

"You do not need to come in-between this situation, Baba sahib" the guard replied, respectfully addressing Baba. He looked at Baba, then turned his gaze again to Harmeet, and hardened his countenance. He was now glaring sternly at Harmeet, and he cracked the stick again, on Harmeet's back. Harmeet winced in pain, but refused to make a sound or complain.

"Please, sir, do not do this. He was cooperating, so where was the need for this brutality?" Baba questioned, upset visibly at what he was witnessing, and worried too, for the young man.

"Arre, Saab, do you even know who you are defending? This is a very dangerous man, wanted in many states for his actions. We were just holding him here till we found out which region had the most right over him. We will now ship him off to Howra, where he will be punished for his crimes. He is nothing more than an antiestablishment terrorist. Don't let his charms fool you."

"But officer, he was here, consenting to your commands, Why the hostility? This is not correct."

"He is a dangerous fellow, mark my words. I'm sure he didn't tell you about all the things he has plotted", the guard reiterated.

Baba, concerned for the man's welfare, pressed on. "Surely you do not believe everything you hear from your bosses? There's a world of injustices out there, they cannot be all pinned on one young student. Please help this man; he has suffered. He needs support, not condemnation."

Harmeet, hearing Baba's plea, turned and smiled, acknowledging Baba's support. The guard simply shook his head, and continued to pull the man out of the cell. As the men bade farewell, Baba sat back down on the bench, a weary look on his tired face. Vanamali, now awake and handling her infant, gazed at her husband, listening to his words.

"He's not going to make it, is he?" she asked. Baba simply stared back, frustrated in another brilliant young life being taken away from society.

Chapter Seventeen: A lifeline

Murali was sleeping soundly in his father's arms, now, both parents trading off every few minutes until he fell back asleep. He was a good baby that way - never any fuss or crankiness in spite of his curious age. The lack of proper light in the holding cell was now beginning to wear on the young family. After another hour had elapsed a junior officer walked in.

"You may leave to your home now" he instructed.

"How come all of a sudden? Who called? What were you told?" Baba questioned the man, directly.

"I don't have that information, sir," he responded respectfully, "but my boss called the station and told me to let you go."

"So, are we out on bail, or are we out free totally? What exactly were we being held for anyway?"

The officer paused, tired now at one o'clock at night, and turned to smile, gazing at baby Murali. "All that I have been told Sir, is that you and your wife are all set, and that you should go home and get a good night's sleep. Also, you should get the baby settled. I do not know what is in store for you tomorrow. If I were you, I would contact the chief in the morning."

By now, Vanamali had already collected her belongings, and baby on one hip and purse in the other, she arose, beckoning

Baba to no longer question the junior officer but instead head home.

When the couple reached home, they thanked the rickshaw driver and, stepping carefully out of the vehicle, they walked into their home compound. Baba reached for the keys, opened his front door, and went inside after Vana and Murali were in. He was troubled, restless. Baba could not sleep. Vana and Murali had already taken a quick bath and settled into bed, but Baba could not find peace. He kept on going over the events of the evening and earlier that week, the political rally at Osmania College, the meeting with Dr. Rai and the Resistance, and the recent newspaper articles on Gandhi and the uprising. He had hoped to hear some news by now from his fellow resistance members but no one had called or dropped him a telegram. What was he to make of all of this? Maybe he was just fatigued. There were even moments of despair, worrying internally that his family reputation would be scarred while others' would secretly be unsupportive, in their attempts to climb the political rungs. Times were tough as it was, but to have a police record made matters ten-fold worse. He also wondered why not one of his friends had stepped in to help yet? Was he missing something? Had something happened that he was unaware of? As he pondered this and tried to think positive, he went to the bathroom to wash his face. He splashed the warm soft water onto his face and massaged in the luxurious Mysore sandal soap that his brother-in-law had given him, freshly milled from his factory. As he carefully turned the taps off and turned to reach for his face cloth, something shiny caught his eye. It was attached to his bathroom window. As he opened the metal hook and pushed the window slightly ajar, he noticed that there appeared to be a small handwritten note, written in crayon on the back of a waxy paper bread wrapper. Opening it, he read,

" Punya Cote. Six o'clock, October Eighteenth."

Chapter Eighteen: The mole

The Ramaswamy family awoke leisurely the next morning, still fatigued from the previous late night. Baba, after a morning shower, prayer rituals and south Indian coffee, detailed his wife on what important work had to be addressed this day. He explained that time was of essence, and getting to his brother -in - law Rai, or at least Prasanna or the Colonel, was vital. Vana did not need much explanation; she was very understanding when it came to Baba's work and the Freedom Movement with which he was so passionately involved. She was hoping for a more peaceful, uneventful day, but was happy that Baba at this moment was not insisting on her presence with the scurrying around that morning. Grabbing his umbrella and wallet, he took off. Vana contemplated whether she should start preparing the day's meals ahead of time, do laundry, housecleaning, or just go back to bed, Murali at her side. She opted for the latter, snuggling all warm and cozy next to her baby and falling quickly back into a deep slumber.

Baba arrived at Rai's residence quickly, since he had chosen to ride his bicycle that morning, rather than his usual path, by foot. He was anxious, eager to meet up with his family members and have updates on the movement.
When Brunda eagerly greeted her brother, hugs and pecks were exchanged. Even a few tears were seen rolling down Brunda's

cheeks, which her Chickanna quickly wiped away with his kerchief.

"Why the misty eyes?" he gently questioned his sister.

"Oh my goodness, Anna, you have no idea how we have worried. Why did they take you? Why did baby Murali and Vanamali also have to be kept at the station? I do not feel this is right. Is something happening more than I know? Pray do tell me, since my postpartum hormones on this brain just cannot handle the stress!"

"Brunda, dearest, there is nothing to be worried about. We have done no wrong. But, I am eager to speak to your good husband. I think he knows more than I do."

A few minutes later Dr. Rai was heard coming down the curved staircase. He looked regal, wearing his recently acquired Moghlai mozjdi slippers and fresh cotton kurtha with pajamas. He greeted Baba with love and compassion, patting him gently on the back and walking him to the kitchen table where they sat down for coffee. "So, you must be having a lot of questions for me right now? Rai asked.

"Yes, Indeed I do".

"Where should I begin?"

"From the beginning. I need to understand what we are dealing with."

"Baba, you need to listen to me carefully, since I need your full awareness and input. Let me begin on the Osmania College riots day. I believe you took T.V. to the Osmania Hospital and then left from the back of the campus, to home. Is that correct?" Dr. Rai inquired.

"Yes. I rushed out from the back campus after ensuring T.V. was safe. All I could think of at that time was getting home to Vana and Murali. I did not even consider the bicycle I had left behind!"

"Right. Well, the story unfolds from that point forward. T.V. was sicker than he looked and started to speak unintelligible words, muttering forth words of anguish and nonsense. The nurses did not initially pay heed to his words, but after observing his eloquent words, one of them listened in. While cleaning his wounds she heard over and over again about Punya Cote and the mission. T.V. kept on repeating words of pain followed by smirks of confidence and gestures of a plan, a warehouse, a march, and about freedom. The junior nurse Jyothi, who was known to have connections with the police force, had been pulled over for questioning when the police visited later that night. Although she was eager to please the young officers, she unfortunately gave up unnecessary information, much to the disappointment of T.V. who was coming around by then, just mildly sedated by some anesthesia and pain medications given to ease his painful wound. She told the young officer Shetty about T.V.'s words of a "freedom movement" and a warehouse. It didn't take long for Shetty to then quietly inform the police force and then bring you in for questioning. You see, they have been waiting for leads in this matter, and all too eager to bust any honest freedom movement. The British had the strong hold on the cops on one end, but the politicians had them on the other. They had been waiting for weeks to find an honest link to take the blame. Initially, they placed their hopes on the college students at Osmania, but when the rally essentially failed to place one team at fault, the next thing had to be found. Then came you; even better than a young college student. An articulate lawyer would serve as a welcome distraction from the politicians and British gentry. Shetty decided, I believe, to send in Rao to question you rather than do it himself, since he didn't wish to bring any unwanted attention to Osmania just yet.

He had seen you earlier at Osmania. He had noticed, you, (indeed, your good looks make it hard to be inconspicuous) but he still wondered how everything would transpire. I think he was taking a long shot, because T.V. denies saying anything of substance to the nurse, and the officer had no way of knowing anything about our freedom struggle plans. I think things simply just unfolded, in a random way."

Dr. Rai began to doodle with his pencil on a writing pad that lay within his newspaper on the kitchen table.

" I don't think there is any possible way that the nurse or the officer can know about Punya Cote, besides it being a child's fable. But, I just am not sure whether the officer will investigate you and then bring search warrants for the warehouse, etcetera."

Baba paused, quite shocked by the information already detailed thus far.

"I thought I had been quite discrete," he professed, apologetically, "I had no idea we would still be investigated based on a few of T.V.'s ramblings. I am sorry. What should we do now? How much do they know?"

"Well, that's the million pound question, I suppose," the doctor replied. "From the police taking you into questioning, then Vana coming over to talk to me, followed by the police still bringing her in, we just do not know what the cops have in store for us. I think you could be a seed. Meaning, they are trying to use you to get the entire picture. I think this is why they let you free."

"But, I don't think it is that simple. Vana's dad, High Court Judge Srikantayya was responsible for the policemen letting us go. That seems plain and simple to me. The question I have for you is how much do the cops really know or are they guessing? Did they see the warehouse? Do you think anyone in our mission has been compromised? Maybe the police have threatened some of our members into submission?"

He thought and paced. The men exchanged a few looks.

" I think we need a plan A and also a plan B. A would be in the event that the police do not appear to have any knowledge of our movement itinerary. Plan B would be if they were to know something more- a second set of plans that can be carried out without repeating explanations. Kind of like a flowing river; we need to let this run its course but in the most natural way possible."

"Have you met these police officers before?" Baba asked. " I mean, Shetty, Rao and Reddy- how do they seem to know you?"

Dr. Rai stood up to reach for the codbelle snacks and puffed rice that his wife had served the men.

" Yes, I met them recently. I don't know what to make of them. Sometimes I think they are a bunch of monkeys, and other times I actually believe they mean well. Perhaps they are not corrupt and do seek out the truth. But, I just do not understand what they are up to at this time. Something is not right. I do smell a rat, as they say!"

Baba turned to look at his brother-in-law. A very fine gentleman he was, always neatly dressed, crisp and fine, with the most fashionable of attire from around the world. He was privileged but educated too, a favorable combination in today's India. Yes, India, a democracy of culture and religion, color and caste, was changing and the tide was favorable if you were both educated and in the right caste.

Baba, on the other hand, had the education, good looks and Brahmin caste, but he was not born to wealth. Actually, his father had lost his inherited money close to retirement, and, having nine children, struggled with making ends meet. The girls were married off quickly, but the three boys including Baba were pushed to both be top of their class and earn some money on the side to pay for all of these weddings. But, Baba never complained. He was no stranger to hard work and he actually admitted to Vana that he loved working and meeting people.

"What is the point of these fine linens and marble floors if we do not have a purpose?" he had been heard lecturing his young bride Vana many a time after marriage. Baba looked like a movie star, but not the aristocratic or nouveau riche type, but rather the poor professorial type. He suited this role well, with fair looks and Gandhi-style spectacles, atop a chiseled lean face and khadi cotton shirt, pajama and vest.

The men were troubled deeply as to what they now needed to do to figure out what the police and politicians were planning. The other mission members had not come to know about any other upcoming events. The planned protest march would still happen, according to Rai, but there was some fear voiced from the lack of communication between the members in the last few days. Prasanna, Janaki and Colonel Singh had not spoken to the doctor and Baba feared that if he were to approach them the police, already on his tail, would arrest them too. Then came the issue of Vana and Murali. Baba just could not figure out why the police had arrested them too? He struggled with various mental scenarios. Maybe it was to threaten Baba and cause him to back down.

Then he pondered whether his father-in-law Judge Srikantayya was perhaps being threatened or blackmailed. "Do you believe the police are trying to blackmail or buy the favors of my father-in-law?" he asked his brother-in-law.

"It is definitely a possibility. Did the good Judge know that you were involved with the movement?" Baba paused, wanting to discuss the tenuous relationship Vana had with her father, but hesitated. What would become of her status, if her sister-in-law came to know that Judge Srikantayya was never around to raise his girls? Rumor had it that the Judge had a mistress in the city, with whom he lived, and he had been spotted on many occasions drinking heavily at professional events and parties, with mistress on his shoulder and flirting with another on his other side. Baba was always so thoughtful, never wanting to caste doubt or resentment within his family, but working hard to strengthen family bonds. Finally, thinking of the bigger picture and running out of time, he conceded.

"Rai, Vana's father-in-law is not what he seems. He is a brilliant man, well educated, an amazing barrister and a commanding man. But," he paused, looking at his brother-in-law and wondering if he was engaged in truth and non-judgment, "he really led a double life. He was not involved in Vana and Manasa's upbringing."

"Well, he was busy earning for his family and making a name, I'm sure," Dr. Rai added.

"Yes, true, but it was more than that. There was a distance; he seemed to never want to return home to Tirumakudlu. He loved the city and what it had to offer. So, knowing his nature as I do now, I fear that he may have been influenced. Whether he truly is the gentleman he plays in daily life remains to be seen. He is an enigma, and knows well how to play the game, if you know what I mean."

Dr. Rai pondered, observing Baba closely and digesting the information just given. "Are you telling me that he may be on the wrong side of the Freedom movement?" he asked.

"I'm saying that he may not be on any side of the movement, just playing to his own interests at any given moment. I would not put it past him. He is not the level-headed judge off of the bench that he is in his courtroom."

"Okay, so let me review what I am hearing. You were taken into custody, held with Vana and Murali, for twelve hours or so. We came to know of this when Vana gave us a heads up, and then met you at the Station. We do not know if anyone in our freedom movement has been compromised, but I do not have reason to think so. You were held for questioning, and only informed of the uprising in Osmania and the following few issues. You were not told why you were being held. You were only interrogated since your bicycle was found at the college campus after the riots. After answering questions, they still did not let you go. Then, Vana is imprisoned with you, even though she has little connection to the current uprising. Then, a few other officers entered the interrogation room and proceeded to probe you both further. They did not reveal anything more as to why you were there. They simply seemed interested in your involvement with potential upcoming freedom protest marches or speeches. They did not inquire about me, T.V. or the other members. They did not hurry to let a mother and child go. Finally, when we all arrived, they reluctantly conceded to let your family go home, probably after talking to Judge Srikantayya. At this point, the only new information you have is that a riot may occur later this week, and the police are scared about it and the media onslaught following the riots. I have only one more bit of information that may be news to you."

Baba looked up, processing the account story just detailed by Dr. Rai, curious and fatigued at the same time. He leaned in to pour himself some more coffee and grabbed a handful of spicy peanuts to munch on. Dr. Rai continued,

"Your sister Geetha visited me early this morning for a few minutes. She was flustered and in a hurry to return home. She told me that the police had visited her and interrogated her a couple days ago about your involvement in the freedom movement. When I asked her why they would do that, since it seemed so unusual, she informed me that her husband was involved with a lot of political rallies this month, and was trying to appear important. I think he is trying to frame your involvement in the movement intentionally, so that he can rise up in his political career by discovering such resistance movement behavior. I think he is the mole."

Chapter Nineteen: A Family Matter

Baba sat at the foot of his bed and slowly took off his shoes, massaging his feet slowly. Vana, who had just put Murali to sleep, entered the room. She noticed the dazed expression on her husband's face. "What did Dr. Rai say?" she asked.
Baba recounted the entire story, not missing the minute details of Geetha's involvement and the possible framing conspiracy invented by yet another brother-in-law trying to climb up the political ladder. They looked at each other desperately, wondering how to navigate the troubled waters, surfing the family matters and emerging strong.

"We should not forget our primary purpose and Gandhian principles of freedom from oppression, independence, non-judgment. This is what we chose to do, to teach our children a better way to live, and leave a better neighborhood for our children. I am not sure how to do all of this now, but we must not lose focus. I will not rest until I see that Hyderabad is safe from the British, and safe from the scoundrel politicians and crooked police officers."

Vana, listening intently, responded. "My father can surely help us?" she questioned, knowing his word had clout.

"Vana, there may be a time that we will need to use your father as a lifeline, but now is not that time. Also, there is the issue of his influence. Do you know whether your father preferred a certain political party? Do you imagine that he may be favoring or helping one? I know he is a great man, but I do not know if he is being influenced. With the political climate right now, I know that all politicians would be trying to win his support. I just do not know whether he would concede. What do you think of this, Vana?"

"The truth is plain and simple if you ask me," she responded quickly. "You see, around the time my father was an upcoming judge in Mysore, the B.J.P. members from Hyderabad came to pay him a visit. I must have been just nine years old, but I remember the scene like it was yesterday. These strange men gathered in my mother's house, and would not leave. They lapped up her hospitality from afternoon tea, to snacks and then dinner. Father was initially reluctant to make conversation, but then after some refreshments one of the politicians poured Dad some whiskey. "From Scotland," he touted. Father drank it up happily, relaxing his countenance and unwinding with the men. Slowly, his worries about the early morning court case and papers needing to be filed had been forgotten and the drinking night continued. Before the night was over, the men were talking deals and sponsorships, and the Judge just listened and smiled. Even though he did not openly commit to being biased, it was obvious he was now keeping the company of some bad influences. I do not believe he is "bought off" or "controlled", indeed, he is too smart for that. However, I think he knows how to play the political game so well, that he may be engaging these Brits and cops, for his own humor. I would not put it past him. Particularly after mother had him choose between her and the mistress, he just became more and more heartless. He's probably playing with all of these baboons."

"So, where does that leave us? What should we do now?" Baba asked.

"I think we should head back to jail," Vana replied, raising her eyebrows and shrugging her shoulders as she gestured to her husband her own frustrations.

"That's insane!" Baba replied, fear setting in. "What of our baby? Both parents in jail and what will become of Murali?"

"Baba, do not let fear rule you. The police cannot keep us for long. But, they cannot object to us being confined if T.V. or Dr. Rai recommended it. The way I see it, if we are imprisoned, it may help focus the members' attention back on the freedom struggle and away from the past riots. This is what we need. They need to hold some of us to feel they are winning and that our mission is compromised. If not, then we will continue, fully watched every second, and nothing will ever happen in our favor."

Baba got up to go to the bathroom, and get ready for bed. They had a lot to ponder. Tomorrow would be yet another day. "Let's sit on this till tomorrow," he said.

Chapter Twenty: The Plot

A scrumptious breakfast awaited Baba the following morning. Potato curry with fried puffed bread, his favorite meal lay hot and ready on the breakfast table as he came down the steps toward the kitchen. Vana had also made sweet treats of almond halwa and sweet saffron rice, as if to fatten her husband up before the day was done. They ate together for a few minutes, while Murali played with the maidservant, who was cleaning his room. Then, Murali too joined in the feast, enjoying the hot unleavened bread and potato, his favorite vegetable. After morning coffee, the family sat together and planned their day.

"I'll take Murali over to Brunda's house. He loves it over there, and with the new baby and Parth, he has tons of company. What do you think of this idea?" Baba questioned Vana. She thought for a few moments before nodding approvingly.

"Yes, I was thinking of the same scenario. Murali loves playing with Parth and Brunda and now with little Preethi there, he will be engaged for hours. I think this will keep his mind preoccupied and off of anxiety about us not being with him." Baba walked over to the bedroom where the maidservant was cleaning, and told her to hurry up and finish since he had work to do. When the maidservant had left, the family closed up the house, drew the curtains, turned off the lights and double locked the front and back doors. They left, with Murali's small suitcase, off to the Rai house.

"Good day to get imprisoned!" Dr. Rai chuckled, arms raised to hold Murali while Baba and Vana entered the home. Brunda came running towards her nephew, grabbed his pinky finger and walked him up to the nursery to see their newborn. The cousins cooed at each other and Murali crawled around the nursery, playing with the toy train and soft toys on the floor. Brunda left the children in the presence of the maidservant, who seemed to be enjoying watching the children together. When she returned to the kitchen, the mood was more somber.

"I don't think this will be a very long affair," Dr. Rai comforted Vana, who was clearly having second thoughts about the upcoming imprisonment. "I do not know what the community will think of all of this," Vana commented. Baba turned to face his wife, looking first at Rai as he did so, and smiling softly.

"It does not matter what the world thinks, since we are fighting ignorance and it's an uneven battle. What matters is what we know, which is that without timely action India risks being owned by Great Britain forever, or risks war with the border states. I do not know even whether the police chief may turn us away, since we were released once before. But, I have to believe that the government will want us behind bars, since it will make them seem more effective. In the meantime, Colonel Singh, Prasanna and Rai can proceed with the plan and hopefully we will have an impact. People have to take notice. If we want to save our country the time is now."

Vana gazed at her husband, and relaxed, nodding in approval. A mix of wonder and admiration took over her as she now smiled, consented, and prepared to leave to the station. Thinking it better not to disturb the playful children, she and Baba then exited Rai mansion and rode their bicycle to the station.

Ten minutes later the couple were parking outside of Police station Sixty-two, Himayatnagar colony. They journeyed in through the old door, proceeding carefully so as not to startle anyone at this early hour. They were surprised to see Officer Reddy in attendance rather than a junior ranked official. Reddy, however, was even more surprised. "What brings you two here?"

"Actually, we have come to talk to you, perhaps admit fear has defeated us, and possibly turn ourselves in," Baba replied calmly.

"Alright then, sure. Take a seat. I will just get a pen and paper to take both of your statements. Can I bring you some coffee or chai?" Reddy asked sprightly.

"Er, yes, well, we would both love coffee," Baba answered, rather surprised at this sudden display of hospitality. The courageous couple enjoyed their refreshments before, once again, walking into the prison cell and seeing the gate lock.

Chapter Twenty-One: Netaji and Baba, 1941

It was an unusual situation; a telegram had arrived earlier that day, addressed to the Honorable Tirumakudlu Ramaswamy, alumnus, Oxford University.

"Dear Mr. Ramaswamy, we humbly request your presence at the reunion of "Brothers United" Association. Please join us in Calcutta for a reuniting of Indian Oxbridge alumni, on 18/1/41 at Calcutta's Law Quad garden.

Sincerely,
Rajesh Rai Yadav,
Class of 1929

Baba stared at the almond white parchment paper, up and down, rather surprised at the invitation. He pondered over each word, analytic as he was, and decided that it was probably a privilege that he had been invited. He didn't recognize the host. The time frame of his Oxbridge studies was accurate, but he did not recall this particular name. He took off his rimmed small-frame glasses and wiped them with his handkerchief. As he wore his glasses again, he lifted the letter up to the window in his bedroom. He studied it front and back, but was unable to gather any more clues about its origin. It was typed, in black ink, font traditional, classic format.

"What is that about?" Vanamali asked, entering the bedroom after putting Murali down for his nap.

"Well, it appears to be an invite to the Honorable Ramaswamy," Baba replied, now grinning and turning to address his wife, winking at her from the corner of his eye.

"Oh, how lovely!" Vana replied, ecstatic, as she usually was when her husband was being honored. "When is the event?"

"Mm, well, it is on January eighteenth, so just a few weeks away. I don't know, it may not be an ideal time to go, with your pregnancy and all. I don't think we should be traveling". Baba folded the letter along its creases, and set it on his bedside table. He sat on his bed, alongside his wife, and folded his legs, facing her and talking. "What do you make of all of this, wifey? I have been so busy over the last decade with the Freedom Movement, that it must have upset you in some ways. Murali has been without us when we were imprisoned. I have been consumed with leading the movement post war, yet we are in another war now. I don't know whether we will achieve freedom. The Britons are a proud group of entitled men, who lack compassion for other nations.

Now, this letter has arrived. I have suspicions, and I wonder if my involvement in the movement is driving you mad yet."

Vanamali giggled, just like the young girl who Baba had met in the forest years ago.

"Why do you think so much?" she said, holding her saree's free edging to her mouth, covering her teeth as she laughed. "You are a born leader. People respect and revere you. This is not the time to have doubts. Do what you need to do."

Baba stared at his wife, in awe of her supportive, kind words. He didn't really understand the sacrifices that she had made, until now, when, pregnant and a busy mother raising a young family, she still sang her husband's praises. Baba recognized that he had been gone a lot in the last few years, attending rallies, political meetings and offering support around the country. He was a part of a large movement, an undercurrent of social consciousness that was bubbling at its surface. Baba had the innate ability to listen and advise, without offending any fraction of the somewhat divided India, be it the reactive groups or passive resistance types. Yet, into World War Two now, he questioned himself and what was currently happening. Perhaps the time was now, to strike back and fight the British and kick them out of his homeland. Gandhiji was correct; we need to win over the Brits without violence. But, were we being ridiculed? Baba took Vanamali's hands in his, and gently began to speak.

"Vanamali, if I involve myself even more in the freedom struggle, you will have several days alone, while I may be traveling from city to city." He leaned in, as if being spied upon, "I even doubt the purpose of this invitation. I suspect there is more to the Oxford-Cambridge Indian alumni reunion than this letter reveals. I wish to attend, out of curiosity. But, if my suspicions are correct, I might have a higher purpose. Are you sure that you are fine with this plan? You will have to manage Murali on your own, till I return."

Vana leaned in towards Baba, smiling.

"What, you think that I did not know your talents when we were married?" she coyly responded. "This is what you are meant to do. The movement needs your guidance. So go ahead and do your duty. Murali is young and not affected by your travels. Plus, all of your sisters are here to help me. There is nothing for you to worry about.

The following morning, Baba's suitcase was packed and ready to be loaded from the platform to the station. Vanamali placed Baba's Kashmiri shawl over his left shoulder, lest he become cold on the train. "Take care of yourself," Vanamali said to her husband softly, as he embarked on his somewhat mysterious journey.

"Don't worry, I will be absolutely fine."

A day later, Baba had arrived in Calcutta, to a rather average day in the bustling city. Baba quickly found the Law Quad, and approached a bench that was flanking the North corner of the Quad lawns. After about five minutes of patient waiting, a well-dressed man, considerably younger than Ramaswamy, approached him. "Good sir, are you Mr. Ramaswamy?"

"Yes", Baba replied, with a smile.

"Please come this way, we are expecting you."

Baba followed Mr. Choksi eagerly, curiosity pounding on his chest as he walked the black and white tiled checkerboard hallway briskly. Choksi guided Ramaswamy into a small library in which a handful of distinguished men were already gathered.

"Please greet T.K. Ramaswamy, who has just arrived all the way from Hyderabad."

The men, all approximately Baba's age, greeted him kindly. Baba shook the hands of several invitees, introducing himself to unfamiliar faces. After circumventing the room, he turned to address Choksi.

"Mr. Choksi, kindly explain why I was asked here, for if this is an Oxbridge Reunion, I know but three of the attendees thus far?"

"Why, Mr. Ramaswamy, I am glad that you spoke up!" another man exclaimed, "I also wanted to ask this question. Were you a member of "Brothers United?" When I attended Oxford, there was no such organization, unless it was a secret society. I am somewhat confused and I would appreciate some clarification," he added. The young man stood up and walked towards the center of the small library, smiling gently as he addressed the group of anxious men.

"Welcome my friends. If you are questioning the circumstances of the Oxbridge reunion, then you are absolutely correct. I was not certain that any of you scholars would attend, given the inaccuracy of the content of the invite and your combined intellect. However, it is not I, but my brother who called this meeting. Let me introduce him now."

Choksi walked towards the bookshelf, on the right of which was a small door, which opened into a coatroom. A bright young man with a square face and firm, plastic rimmed spectacles, walked out. On seeing the man, the group of attendees simultaneously rose from their seats, in awe.

"Netaji, Netaji, you are here with us today? What an honor!" a portly man named Chandrasekhar exclaimed. Yadav, a Cambridge Alumnus who had sent the invites, hugged his friend Kekre, closely.

"Come and sit down with us. Let's have some chai!" he said. Baba approached Netaji, and shook his hand.

"So you must be Ramaswamy, I believe?" Netaji remarked.

"Why yes, that's right!" Baba replied. "How did you come to know? I don't think we have met before." Netaji nodded. He peered around the room, acknowledging the group of peers whom he and his brother had assembled. Smiling at each one, he spoke.

"Brothers, friends, it is I who requested Amitabh and Rajesh to call this meeting. I know that you know who I am. I have created attention all over the world for my approach to India's freedom struggle. However, I am a keen observer, and I do wish for peace. I have noticed the work that you have all done. And I do believe we are equipped, mentally, to start a global dialogue for change. Independence will happen and I am confident that within the walls of this room are the minds that will achieve this goal. We have different ideas of a free India, but I hope that we are truly "Brothers United" in this struggle. Just like Gandhiji and I have differences yet are able to talk about our goals, so shall we. So, without any further delay, let's construct a plan to conquer the British colonialists and their occupancy".

Kekre sat down next to his brother. There were whispers from the group of men, and a lot of fidgeting. Chandrasekhar, already thrilled to be in the presence of Netaji Kekre, approached Amitabh.

"Hi Amitabh. So, you are actually Netaji's brother? I had no idea he had a younger brother. How is it you introduced yourself as Choksi?"

Amitabh promptly responded, well aware that this question would arise.

"It's quite simple really. My brother has been in the news and political arenas a lot of late, and the attention has not often been pleasant. We fear British attack, so my brother advised me to change my name. I was anyhow moving from my college town to a different city, so I applied for a name change. I never speak of my connection. Indeed, it is a complete secret that Netaji is here. We need to keep absolutely quiet about Netaji's presence in Calcutta. He has received many death threats over the last few years; we cannot afford to take any risks. My brother and I have been communicating through secret names and societies, traveling to different locations and providing various mailing addresses. So far, this method has worked. However, this is the first time in a year that we have attempted to surface by way of new friends, such as Oxford and Cambridge alumni. We are not intending for you to now be targeted along with Kekre, but rather hope that you can construct a sort of method of communicating, then pass it on through your individual state freedom movements, if you so choose. I hope that you are with us."

Baba arose again, always charismatic, smiling as the young men stared at him, waiting for his next move. It was like a game of chess; each man calculating strategy, but patiently awaiting the other's move. Rajesh, who acting as an overseer having invited these brilliant minds together, introduced Baba again.

"Good men, Mr. T. Ramaswamy is a formidable force in the southern states of Andhra Pradesh and Karnataka. Over the last several years, I am sure you must have heard of the Osmania Rally shootings, the imprisonment of many nonviolent protesters, and the unlawful killings of many. Baba was involved in the freedom struggle for each and every one of these uprisings, and has proven his dedication to the mission. He also marched with Gandhi during the Dharasalam Salt March and survived the subsequent massacres and incarcerations. We salute you, dear Ramaswamy. We are hopeful that you will join forces with us and end India's incarceration."

" I am deeply honored by your kind words," Baba replied, "Yet I cannot take credit for the fight of many. Whatever little measures have been taken, whatever small victories we have had, whatever lives we have lost, have occurred thanks to a mass of passionate people, who deeply wish for unity. These are not the men of wealth and entitlement. These are the masses that don't even think of dreaming about universities and education. Each simply wish to earn his keep; raise his family and own his own home. Putting food on the table is what each wants; clothes that are clean and bear India's name is what each desires; this is what I believe in, also. Fighting nonviolently for India; for her strength;

for her industry; for her financial independence; this is what I strive for.

I can only speak for myself. Netaji, I am truly humbled to be in your presence. Indeed, it is true that I was suspicious of this sudden invitation. I had not been involved with "Brothers United" association, nor had I sought out alumni on my return. Gandhiji and I, of course, have crossed paths, but others were spread out in distant states and I was busy with settling back into my life. I was not certain that I would be involved in India's freedom movement, but my inner voice drew me to it. It was my calling, as I am fairly certain you each would say about yourselves.

My concern now, is how are we similar besides wanting freedom? There are several methods and several paths taken. I am in awe of Netaji, yet I believe I am very different in philosophy to you, sir. I will not bear arms against my enemy. So, let us each discuss if we even wish to be here, for those who are opposed should leave immediately. How do I know that we are each trustworthy? What do we each truly know about each other's darkest secrets? This is no trivial matter. Please think about this briefly and after a few moments of reflection, let's talk."

Baba was about to sit down, but he first turned to acknowledge Netaji once more. It was surreal; Baba felt inspired by the man who was a mere ten feet away from him, yet he was in disbelief. Almost like a dream, he smiled at Kekre, Baba's countenance kind and respectful, even with a few worry lines creasing his forehead. The group of attendees were mulling over their options. Brief, divided conversations now created a modest hum in the small library room. He felt a tap on his right shoulder, and turned to see that Kekre was trying to catch his attention, discretely.

"Yes Netaji, what can I do for you?" Ramaswamy asked, politely.

"Please, Ramaswamyji, come this way." Kekre led Baba into the very same closet door through which he had emerged earlier. This coatroom had a second entry, through which the two men exited. They were now in a classroom, perhaps a chemistry lab, with a large blackboard and several tiered arc-shaped tables. The men sat at the teacher's front desk, facing each other directly.

"Are you comfortable, Ramaswamy?" Kekre inquired.

"Er, yes, of course. It's been a while since I've been in a science lab-it's a little odd but brings back some fond memories!" he chuckled.

"I wanted to pull you aside and discuss some things on my mind, that I believe you would be interested in hearing," Kekre confessed. "Have you heard of the Islamabad's historic region of Saidpur? It has also been called Rawalpindi Market Street." Kekre paused, giving time for Baba to acknowledge this region.

"Well, if you remember from history, Saidpur was taken from the Sikh community by the British colonialists, who then built the largest barracks in the region".

"Yes," Baba replied, "I am familiar with this region. I had visited this area prior to entering university. It was very beautiful and I hope it still is."
Kekre pressed on.

"About three weeks ago, one of my junior supporters, Surinder Dhaliwal Singh and other INA members attempted to bomb the city cantonment. It was a failed attempt, and he is now being held captive by the British Army."

"Oh, that is very unfortunate", Baba reacted, empathetic always to any young life wasted. "Is he all right?" he added. "Why haven't we heard anything about this in the newspaper or on the radio?"

"Well, this is my exact concern. Why haven't we heard about this major incident? I suspect the British are employing some strange tactics to win their way over India. Can you believe, the barracks' head administrator is declining to comment on this incident, and is not even acknowledging that he has enslaved Dhaliwal. The young boy's family is terribly distraught and wrote to me, hoping I could help. I used my resources to inquire about the boy, but even my leads did not prove true. I fear that the British captives have either kept him hostage to be a ploy for me, or have killed him off to scare other INA members away. I believe I have been goaded, as Dhaliwal is used like bait.

I then set out on a mission to bring Dhaliwal back home to his loving family. I know you might think I am against passive resistance, but I am not. I simply think that it is not an effective strategy. I have been unsuccessful, but I am trying to use different approaches now. So I ask you now, can you help find him?"

Ramaswamy was now seated at the front of his wooden chair, attentive and shocked by this news.

"What can I do?" he responded, quickly. "We have opposing viewpoints, which is not the primary problem. But, if I, as well as other people here, show involvement, surely the British will come to know you are involved? After all, the INA is your inception, so why wouldn't they?" He stood up now, slowly pacing the room, stopping every so often as if finding answers in his head, to his very own questions. "Kekre, you could have us all assassinated, if you are not careful!" Baba returned to his seat, facing Kekre while wiping his brow with his handkerchief. His mind was already connecting dots as he frowned, ruminating on daydream about imprisonment and being caught in a conspiracy to release a British captive.

"You really should stop worrying so much!" Kekre remarked, seeing what the rapid change in Baba's countenance. "You won't be tried and hanged, trust me! You are the golden boy, always a peacekeeper, never a threat. All that you will do, hopefully, is to search for the young man. Can't you say that you know the family? The British would trust you over myself, and this can only count as a distinct advantage in gaining access to the barracks. You have not, and never will be linked to the INA, so this plan might actually work. Just tell the British army administration that you are searching for Dhaliwal, that he is a friend known to you by way of your brother, who is a friend of his father. Is it not right, that T.V .is a college professor? Dhaliwal's father is also in the education field. Perhaps you can claim that you were sent since T.V. has classes in session this term."

Baba listened, easing up his posture, and leaning in. "Why are you asking this of me? Aren't the other men more capable or qualified?" he asked.

"Yes, the room is a smorgasbord of brainy nerds who are free-thinkers, and I will ask them too. Out of respect for your input, I decided to approach you alone first. However, I think that a team approach would be much more successful. What do you think? Will you help me find Dhaliwal?"

"I'm not promising anything," Ramaswamy replied, "for I am a man of my word, and I do not wish to break my promises. But, I can tell you that I will do my level best to find out what has happened to Dhaliwal. Kekre, I request that you discuss this mission with our friends next door. Perhaps you can weed out the few who seem disinterested. It may amount to nothing, but at least we can set our standards that we believe in honesty and integrity with our Indian Independence Movement."

Netaji nodded, and shook Baba's hand firmly with both of his. Baba kept a firm grip on Kekre's hand for a long moment.

"Ramaswamy, is there something more on your mind?" Netaji asked.

"Only that I wish to say that I have lived my entire life based on the values of hope, honor and integrity. I am a peacekeeper through choice, and I wish no single man any harm. So, I am asking for your word that you will protect my values. Can you do that? Can you allow people to believe, if questioned, that we are friends with a passion for freedom, not conspirators who are plotting British India's downfall?"

Kekre had been waiting for this question. Why wouldn't he be criticized, or even disliked by his peers? Kekre had fought fear throughout his young adult life, extemporaneously engaging throngs of students in his zest for a free India. This, no doubt, had sparked criticism and anger from many who were either timid or strictly party-carrying political members. Kekre responded.

"I have a heart, you know. I've been pictured as an antagonist, a reactor, a violent self-righteous villain. But only a few good friends and my dear family know who I really am. I assure you, Ramaswamy, that I am on the side of freedom. We are together in this battle. I will not push you down and burn you; that is, after all, what the Brits do. They divide and conquer. I will fight with you for the common cause. Let's help each other achieve a common goal. I will not let you down."

Baba smiled and retorted, "Well, then, let us get a move on!"

The two men entered the library again, from the coatroom door. The alumni were mostly bunched around each other, having small conversations. Most of the men arose, when Netaji entered. "I want to know what is the plan? Why call this meeting unless there is a purpose. Please, Netaji, tell us what you know." The voice was of Chandrasekhar again. "I'm sure you realize that we have all journeyed from far across the country. Help us understand this."

Kekre approached the center of the room and faced the group of men.

"Whatever we discuss now, must stay within the walls of this room. Let me begin…"

Chapter Twenty-Two: Saidpur /Firozpur, July1941

Platform one, in Delhi's railway station, was a throng of activity, even on a Sunday morning. From there, Mr. and Mrs. Ramaswamy took a private car, given by Netaji's Delhi connections, mostly members of society with a keen eye to help the cause. They traveled from Punjab to Islamabad. Baba was happy to have the company of his wife for this trip. Vanamali, who was excited to be a part of her husband's adventurous life, was becoming nervous the further time spent away from her beloved son.

"Moggu must be missing us badly," she said gently, twisting the dress fabric into tiny coils as she spoke.

"Don't worry so much. Murali is such a good boy, I'm sure he is playing with Parth and Preethi as we speak. Just think of all the people you may be helping today, just by entering the cantonment. I am so pleased that you are here with me. I was shocked that the British Army refused my letter, but somehow they must have a heart for you; within such a short span of time they agreed to your visit. We must use this opportunity well and find out everything we can about the boy."

"But my spoken English is a bit out of practice, and I don't even speak Urdu like you do; what am I to do about that?" she fretted.

"Your English is excellent. Plus, I am right beside you, so I don't think there will be any issues. You just need to tell the guards that you have a scheduled appointment with the office, and show them your letter of confirmation. Once we are inside, all you have to do is remember what we discussed was the plan.

Think about what you are planning to say, just as we practiced it. Any clues from the wardens might help save the life of Dhaliwal, if he is still alive. Remember to say that you are a friend of his mother, who has asked you to help find her son. There is no need to add extra words, and try not to provide extra details", Baba instructed his wife. "Also, remember what Mrs. Singh told us about her son. These small details will make a difference if the British guards are interrogating you."

She was nervous. She had not been this involved in Baba's quest for freedom since they were imprisoned two years prior, and she was weary. Vanamali closed her eyes and listened to the heavy downpour of torrential rain that engulfed her senses.

"How much longer till we reach?" Baba asked the driver.

"Aur aas-paas beece kilometers Saab," the driver responded, explaining that they still had about twenty kilometers till Firozpur. "Baarish bahut hai aaj kal", he said, reasoning with how the rains were very heavy of late. Baba had spent almost six months determining the whereabouts of Dhaliwal. He was no longer in the Saidpur cantonment, but had been moved further North.

"At least someone had acknowledged his presence," Baba thought.

One hour later, Vanamali was peering out of the window enjoying the fresh scenery. There were green mountains on one side of the curvy road, while on the other side there was a small historic fort. Further along Vana saw people walking towards a mosque. It was quite beautiful, with white stone details that looked painted on, contrasting with the dark walls. It had a small dome on top, as well as a sidewall that had tiny diamond cut outs, also in a pattern. "Maybe there's a wedding, or something," Vana exclaimed, still admiring the scenery. Shortly after, the couple had arrived at the gates of the Firozpur Cantonment. It was massive; intimidating in size and was sectioned off by rather large gates. The journey was long, and the couple took time getting out of the car, taking a moment to enjoy the crisp zephyr of Punjab air.

"It's so much cooler here, no wonder Punjabis are so fair!" Vana remarked, to a grin from her husband. "So, he was moved to this cantonment?" she inquired.
Baba moved away from his driver's earshot, and whispered to Vanamali.

"Yes, Dhaliwal was moved, we think. At least, this is what Netaji and his connections have informed me. Yadav and Chandresekhar have already arrived here and are waiting to see if we can enter the cantonment successfully. If so, then we might actually have some success in our plea to let this young student free."

Baba approached the guard, who let the couple enter. A few moments later, a British Army official met the Ramaswamys and led them inside, to the administrator's office. A pale, skinny uniformed man sat at the office desk. He could not have been more than twenty-five.

"Perhaps his family have influence to give him such a title," Baba thought to himself. Vanamali, as previously instructed, began to talk.

"Hello, sir. I have an appointment to see a young man named Dhaliwal. You see, his mother is a friend of mine, and is distraught, worrying about her son. We are here to see him, and take word back. Can you help us please?" The skinny man leaned back in his chair. His badge was now more visible, the sun from the window shining on the letters of his name. Vanamali squinted at his badge. 'Watson' was this young officer's name. He pulled open his desk draw, and took out a document. It appeared to be some sort of ledger, with listings of various events of the week.

"Ah, yes, the Ramaswamys. You are down here-see?" He showed the couple, at which point Vanamali appeared to relax, smiling a little and sitting more at ease. "I have been advised to take you to meet Dhaliwal, but I will be staying for the five minute visit. You can understand I'm sure, that he is a prisoner for us, and we cannot take any risks." Watson looked at Baba as he was talking, and seemed to be studying him. He paused for a moment then began to speak again.

"Mr. Ramaswamy, I need to ask you and your wife a few questions before I can take you back to the cells. What is the nature of your visit?"

Baba, who had been preparing for this question for weeks, responded carefully.

"My wife is a friend of Dhaliwal's mother. I am sure she has made several attempts to have her son released, but this was to no avail. Now, she has asked my wife and I to try to assist her. I hope you know that we come peacefully, but with hope that we can start a conversation about Dhaliwal. He is just a young man who made a mistake. We just want to talk to him." It was at least, reasonable. Any investigations into Baba's history would serve only to reinforce his peaceful, nonviolent nature. Surely Watson would not suspect him of foul play? Watson peered at the request slip that Vanamali had originally sent to the cantonment.

"How did you and Dhaliwal family meet?" Watson probed. Vanamali looked at her husband, and then back at the officer.

"I had visited Punjab as a teenager, with my parents. We were attending a marriage of one of my father's colleagues and I met the young Mrs. Dhaliwal there. There were only a few teenage girls present for the music night, so being new to the town she kept me company. Ever since then we stayed in touch, although not as frequent as we would have liked. Nevertheless, we were able to stay pen pals throughout life. Recently, she sent me a letter explaining her distress over Dhaliwal's capture. He is her only son. She needs help. So, here we are."

"Do you still have those letters," Watson asked.

"Well, when I was married off, my father, in a frenzy to organize and build a new place, threw a lot of my belongings. He didn't realize that some of those possessions were dear to me. Anyway, they were discarded. There was a huge pile you know. After that, I didn't see the point in keeping any, once I had read them."

Watson appeared skeptical, but was interrupted by another officer's entrance.

"Sir", he saluted.

"At ease, Garrett. You may speak."

"Sir, there's a message for you." Watson read the letter while Baba and Vanamali patiently waited.

"Garrett, please inform the staff that we will be having visitors tomorrow morning, a tour of the barracks by other army officials. It is important that everything is proper", Watson responded.

"Very good Sir, yes Sir," the junior officer replied, and saluting, he left.

"Well, time is of essence. I think we should proceed". Watson led the way down several long hallways and down a few sets of stairs. Finally, Watson beckoned to a prison warden to open a door. This opened into a very small, dark room. Sitting with head down in the corner, was the young man, Dhaliwal. He looked even younger than how Netaji had described him, and he was emaciated. Baba and Vanamali looked at each other. They hoped the boy wouldn't expose them as people whom he had not even heard of. Baba decided to break the awkward silence.

"Son, I am Ramaswamy and this is my wife Vanamali. Your mother is a friend of Vanamali, and we have traveled from far to meet you and offer our help. We have a few minutes together. I hope this is alright with you." Dhaliwal cracked a slight smile, and squinted up, to get a better view of these strangers. Watson glared at the boy, eyeing every motion. Ramaswamy now decided it was time to use suggestion. Kekre had asked Baba to use a secret word that only Dhaliwal would understand. "Perhaps a code word from INA days," he had mentioned. It could backfire, but the hope was that the British people did not have a clue regarding the code words.

"Beta, aapki mataji aapke liye rosogola banayi thi. Lekin, rosogola raste mein kharaab ho gaye. Don't mind. I'm sure she will make it for you again. She just wants you home." "Rosogola," the favorite sweet of Dhaliwal, was a code word only he used in the presence of Netaji.

Baba was calm, inspite of Watson's constant vigil and Vanamali playing with her bangles, nervously. Dhaliwal similarly kept his cool, and gave the only response he knew to use in response. "I'll take rosogola at any given opportunity."

Watson was watching the clock, and tapped his wristwatch while informing the Indians that only two more minutes were left for the meeting. Vanamali now spoke. "Son, is there anything that you would like me to tell your mother?" Dhaliwal stood up, out of respect. He was weary, and held the wall as he arose, for balance. "You need some food," she added.

"Tell Ma, that I miss her. And tell her I want to get out of this place soon, and to do something! I didn't deserve to be stuck here," he lamented in fast Hindi, eager to communicate with some natives before being in solitary confinement again. He began to tear, but withered like a plant without water. "I was a kid. I did not know what I was doing. Just some fun, I thought. Why am I still incarcerated? Please help me," he pleaded. Baba held his hand, wanting to communicate so much more, but unable to.

Watson was already instructing the Ramaswamys to leave, and Dhaliwal shrank back down into the corner of the cell, defeated.

"Don't worry, there will be more rosogolas soon," Baba revealed, under his breathe.

The couple exited quickly, and were denied any further meeting opportunities. As they approached the main gate, Watson requested a signature, which Vanamali provided. Baba and Vanamali met their driver on the other side of the gate, and quickly left the block.

"That boy's in a lot of trouble," Baba summarized. "I don't see any signs of him being released. I just don't feel this is a good sign."

"What was all that about rosogolas?" Vanamali asked.

"Well, I can't be one hundred percent sure. Netaji told me to say 'rosogolas' which was their code word for someone in his inner mission. So saying, I believe Dhaliwal would have known that we are trustworthy and have spoken to Netaji. But, it was suggested to me that rosogolas also meant there would be reinforcements or others from Netaji's pack that would help in the release of the boy. We are now mixed up in this issue. I have played my part, but I do not think it safe for us to stay in town. Chandrasekhar is here, but he did not inform me of his role. It could be unsafe. It is late now. I think we should just go to our hotel, eat and sleep, then plan on leaving early tomorrow back home".

Baba appeared rather disappointed with himself. A sense of failure was glooming over him. In all his years with the freedom movement, never had he been in a position of not knowing what was the next step in the plan. It was weighing heavily on his mind. Would Chandrasekhar come through? Was

Yadav involved at the political end? Would there be riots opposing Dhaliwal's release plea?

The following morning, the couple left early on their long journey back home. The driver made good time. The Ramaswamys were at the Punjab train station by ten o'clock in the morning, early enough for chai and snacks before departing the platform.

Ten minutes into their train journey, the door of their train car connector opened and two men walked through. The faces were familiar. It was Yadav and Chandrasekhar.

"Oh, come and sit," Baba exclaimed, happy to see some of his friends. "What happened? I thought that I would see both of you yesterday? I was quite disappointed with the meeting yesterday. Do you have any updates?" Baba inquired.

"I actually do", Yadav stated, setting down his briefcase. He and Chandrasekhar glanced around the cabin. A young family was ahead of them, and some single young men, perhaps students, sat further along. Otherwise, the cabin was fairly empty. The men finally sat down and leaned in towards Baba.

"All is not what it seems," Yadav whispered.

"Meaning?" Baba responded quickly.

"Well, did you ever question the ease with which you walked into the barracks yesterday? Wasn't it a bit too easy?" The men studied Ramaswamy's expressions. He was pensive, but calm.

"I do not assume the worst. I mean, it took Vanamali and I approximately six months to be finally told the whereabouts of the boy, and then it was only a brief meeting, guarded. So, I am not convinced that was out of the ordinary, or too easy."

"Right, that is true. Well, after your visit, we were planning on meeting you both at the hotel. Netaji had asked us to stay in town, since he wanted to make sure you were both fine. Also, if any information needed to be communicated, he thought it would be easier if it were first hand. Although we could not enter the barracks ourselves, we had an informer who let us know when you left the facility. When that individual had left his post for the day, he came into the village and found the two of us. He claimed that there was an uprising in the prison camp shortly after your departure. Apparently, Dhaliwal was involved, and, in the brawl, he was pushed to the wall. This resulted in a loss of consciousness. He was supposed to be taken to the hospital. However, the guards were changing and the officer in charge waited for the shift workers to leave the premises.

At this moment, we do not know whether Dhaliwal is dead or alive. I sent word through Netaji's friend's office, via telegram, informing him that we are leaving the region. I don't know what to make of this - if it is the truth, or if it is a conspiracy to implicate us as troublemakers, or even, to provoke Netaji to visit? It is totally confusing. We decided to board the train without informing you, just so any eye witnesses would not assume we were all together."

Baba's face was now pale, in shock as to the sudden turn of events.

"I don't know what is the truth, but surely it is more suspicious to leave town? The cantonment officials would assume we are unaware of what transpired, so if they come to know that we have left, would we be targeted in some way?"

"No, Baba, I think that we are doing the right thing. If anything, I see it as the opposite. If we do not leave, these thugs will surely find cause to question us, hold us back, wonder why we are helping Dhaliwal, and bring unnecessary publicity or slander to our names. Let's get back to a safer region and then chalk out the next step," Chandrasekhar said. He turned and nodded at his friend, Yadav, who was clearly unsettled with the events of the last day. Vanamali, who had been quietly listening, spoke up now, frustrated.

"You mean to say that these British men will come after us, just for trying to inquire about the boy? Could it not just be deemed compassion, or concern for a young life? I do not understand this world. Any way, why would Dhaliwal have been attacked just at that moment? He has been held captive for almost six months, he seemed to be withered but unscathed when we saw him. Why is there fighting now? I'm confused! she said, shrinking back into her booth seat, defeated. Baba handed Vanamali their flask of water and box of snacks to munch on. He patted her hand gently, as if to remind her that she was not alone. Yadav spoke again.

"It's impossible to know, but I think something is unfolding, and this is why I feel the safest solution is this one. If my suspicions are correct, we will be hearing something about this in the news soon. There will be a chain of events unfolding. If we are able to keep our distance, perhaps we can still be effective.

"And what about our names, written in the prison ledger?" Baba reacted.

"It is simply what it is stated. You were registered to go for purpose of inquiring about the boy, sent by his mother. You did that and left. That's all there is to it." Yadav smiled at Baba, but spoke confidently.

"And what about the other steps in this plan? Are Choksi and the other members awaiting news, or are they hoping that we simply return to our homes and inform them of what went on," Baba asked.

"Well, I think they will react when we inform them, but there is a distinct possibility that they will come to know of the

boy's health even sooner. If I am correct, the British tactic may be to try to put fear in us, or weaken our resolve.
Let's simply move forward, and wait for more information."

Baba took a few deep breaths now, anxious and feeling weary. The journey had been long, and the sense of lack of control, massive. He pondered over his association with Kekre over the year, and wondered if the lack of control was actually stemming from differing viewpoints. When he had led the Freedom movement in Andhra, Baba had not really faced such confusion in planning. Difficult it had been, but not chaotic. His friends began to settle into their seats for the long journey ahead.

A week had passed since the Ramaswamys had returned to their hometown. Baba felt strange to be back into his daily routine, particularly since he had heard nothing from other "Brothers United" members on the Dhaliwal matter. Netaji had received the telegram, but there had been no response. "Give them time," Vanamali had commented, "communication is not that fast," she added. Of course, she was right. Another fortnight had passed when a letter was delivered, addressed to "Ramaswamyji." Baba closed the door behind the curious postman, who had been standing at the door waiting for the strange letter to be opened. The postage was different. Multiple colorful stamps adorned the envelope to the extent that the letter had probably been very expensive to mail.

"BY THE TIME YOU RECEIVE THIS LETTER, I WILL BE IN GERMANY. STOP. MISSION OF THE BOY INCOMPLETE. NO INFORMATION GIVEN ON HIS

STATUS. STOP. I.N.A WWII DUTIES AROSE. STOP. ALUMNI MEETING SEPT 13TH. STOP."

      Baba turned the letter over to see if other details were on it. Nothing. He held it up to the light, as was his habit, but nothing more was revealed.

He sighed to himself, muttering the word "Germany" over and over. Vanamali entered the foyer where Baba stood and set toddler Murali on the dining chair, ready to feed him breakfast. "Is it important?" she asked her husband.

      "Oh yes, it is I suppose. Take a look." Baba handed her the letter, which she read out loud.

      "Oh, so after all that, he has fled to Germany?" she remarked, sounding thoroughly disgusted with the whole matter. "Why would he do that?"

      "Well, he is a busy man, Vana. He is not only involved on the home front, but also with India's independence and representation globally. With the war happening, he is a man that is actually brave enough to participate freely and lead his men. I should guess that more important duties arose. But," he added, pausing for a moment, "who is to say that he did not flee the country due to threats? I mean, he has made several enemies too. There are a lot of possibilities. I would like to believe that he was hoping for a united, free India and, like Gandhi, tried to use a common connection to involve us with our homeland, before his departure. But, something must have gone wrong for this to have occurred so suddenly."

A few moments later, as though planned, there was another knock on the door. Baba reached for the doorknob. This time it was his brother-in-law, Dr. Rai.

"Come in, come in," Baba said, embracing Rai and sending Vanamali to get some refreshments. "Tell me, to what to I owe this pleasant surprise?"

Rai was tense, and agitated. Before even sitting down, he began to explain the events of his morning, rapidly. "Slow down good doctor, I am not following you!" Baba exclaimed.

"Did you listen to the news? It is all over the radio - put yours on!" he commanded.

"My radio is broken. We have had a quiet morning. I don't really know what is going on. The morning papers didn't say anything unusual," Baba replied.

"Well, it has only just happened. There's been a massacre of hundreds of Punjabi families, very close to where you and Vanamali had just visited. The news reports state that the massacre was the Briton's response to Kekre's bombings of the British Army cantonment in Firozpur that occurred late last night. Do you two know anything about this?" Dr. Rai asked.

"No. Nothing. If I had known that anything violent would be occurring, then I would not have been involved. You know that. The only matter that we were trying to tend to was in regards to a boy named Dhaliwal. He was imprisoned in the cantonment over precarious pretenses, and we went to try to talk to him, hoping we could assist in peaceful discussions that could eventually result in his release. Then we were informed that Dhaliwal had been injured in a skirmish, but friends and family could not contact him or even come to know of his whereabouts."

"Well, that's just it. Apparently, sources say he expired in the army's nursing wing. This information was eventually leaked out, and angry antiestablishment folk, led by some of Netaji's junior supporters, threw a bomb onto the premises. Now Netaji is in trouble, but he has fled. So, the Brits took it out on the villagers and their families. It's another bloody massacre. It is a tragedy.

We need to band together and have a protest march or do something. This is simply not right. Why are the lives of innocent families treated with no dignity? You have to do something, Rama. Get your movement people in order and do something."

"Hmm," Baba responded, clearly despondent. "Violence begets violence," he sighed, and raising his hands helplessly up to his face, he then grabbed the letter in his hand, tore it up neatly and took it out to his yard, throwing it in his compost pile.

A few hours later, Baba greeted his younger sister, Geetha Sastry, who paced quickly towards him, approaching the front entrance to his home.

"What is it Geetha? You seem distressed. Is everything fine?" he asked.

"Well, not really" Geetha replied. She approached her brother, entering the home and sitting down at the table, beckoning for Baba to join her. "I have important information and I need you to help me understand this, and fix this." Baba chuckled, accustomed to joking around with his younger sister. "No, Baba, no. You must take me seriously. Something happened this morning, and I need to discuss it. Let me explain." Geetha unfolded the newspaper that she was carrying under her arm, showing her brother the front page, with full page article on the upcoming unity talks between England and India's leaders.

"This is what happened just before I came here this morning. I was tending to my morning work in the house when there was an unexpected visitor, by the name of Noor. She said she was in need of my help, to stop an upcoming attack at the peace talks. She claimed to be from British Army intelligence, but could not give me exact details of her job. Noor stated that the main reason she rushed to India was based on a message that she had intercepted, while operating the radio systems in Europe. She mentioned something about a repetitive message mentioning the word "CHUTNEY BG"." Baba frowned, puzzled and surprised at his sister's story. He leaned in close to Geetha, listening intently.

"Noor explained that CHUTNEY is a code for Churchill, possibly, Nehru, Gandhi and possibly Bose".

"What is the UT and Y for then?" Baba asked.

"I don't know. But, Noor's the expert on finding and decoding messages. If she's suspicious, don't you think we should be? Anyway, then she said that my husband Vinayaka is probably the politician who is involved with the wrong side of justice. She believes he is permitting various fanatic groups to attend the talks (when they were not invited to do so). This will likely cause Hindu-Muslim riots that will distract the attention from the true terrorists who will attempt to assassinate Churchill and our nation's leaders. You need to do something Baba. Stop Vinay. Stop this attack".

Baba raised his hands to his head then slowly brought his hands together, tapping his index fingers together in the familiar habit of his, which he did while in deep thought. His elbows now leaned on the table and the gentle tapping of his fingers was the only vibration that could be felt.

"What else did this Noor lady say?" Baba inquired.

"Well, quite a bit really. She probably realized I was hesitant. But, to summarize, she is apparently of noble birth, with roots in Moghul India. She works for the British and French intelligence and only came here to prevent destruction to her motherland. She also explained that she had set things in motion already, but could not bank on the British alone, to save the lives of Indians. She made a plea to the heart, and stated that women play an important role in the backbone of the world, and if we did not act, we would regret this."

"Alright then. I will look into this matter further. Give me the instructions she had given, and let me investigate this right away. She may be right. You, however, should be mindful of your husband, and inconspicuous. Do not draw attention to yourself. Let my team do that. You need to take care of yourself." Baba took the newspaper from his sister's hand, and escorted her out of the door, as he left to research this mission.

Chapter Twenty-Three: Murali goes to school.1943

"This is how tomorrow will go. I will travel with you and the children, to Bangalore and drop you off at my cousin Reshma's house. The following morning, I will leave to Mumbai, where I am scheduled to meet with various members of the Freedom Movement. Don't worry so much; Murali will be absolutely fine. He loves Bishop Cotton's school. Remember when we toured it this summer? He will be very happy there." Baba advised Vanamali, the night before their journey. She was reluctant to go, since that would mean that she was in agreement with her beloved son to attend boarding school. She had taken such good care of her preschooler; now, she would barely be around for his precious moments of after school joy and stories of friendships.

"I still think Murali would be perfectly safe at a school in Himayatnagar. Why do you fight me so much on this issue? I do not wish to be away from him. What greater support can he have than his parents' love?" she cried, clearly distraught and restless.

"Vanamali, listen to me carefully. In ordinary circumstances, I would never ask this of you, or even myself for that matter. But, in this unstable world of War and differences, I am convinced that we would be putting Murali in harms way by allowing him to attend local schools, where I am very renowned. With the violence that occurred up North and Netaji now leading the INA's second division to battle, I just am leery about what secret intelligence knows about us. True we have done no wrong, but if someone wants to be disruptive, they could destabilize our Freedom Movement, and then our family could be hurt. Also,

Bishop Cotton's is a wonderful school. You said so yourself! It's honorable, and well guarded. He will have protection more so in Bangalore, than Himayatnagar. Once things settle down, which I believe will happen within the year, we will bring Murali back home."

Twenty-four hours later the Ramaswamy family was settling in to a hearty meal made by Baba's doting aunt, Shanti. Murali, who loved his aunt, was making a castle out of pots and pans in her kitchen, while Vanamali discussed with Baba the details of Murali's school schedule.

"Baba, come see my castle!" Ramaswamy peered into the kitchen to see his son's creation.

"Wow, that's very well made, Murali! Good. I like it, Moggu." Murali smiled broadly then ran into his mother's arms. Vanamali was smiling too.

"Such an amazing castle you have made! You should send your designs to Nehru! Maybe if he likes it, he will build it for India!" Vanamali told her son, happily. She was proud of her little boy, who was so happy with little pleasures, and never seemed to cry when his father took off on missions. She hugged her son, and gently teased him away from his creation, as she prepared him for bedtime. As she lay down next to Murali, reading him a Panchatantara fable, he began to ask more about his adventure to a new school far away.

"Amma, why is school away from you and Baba?"

"Well, because you are a smart boy, and this is the best school for brilliant boys," she lied gently, not wanting to disclose the truth of the matter.

"There is no good boy school next to our house?" he continued.

"Well, not yet. Perhaps you can build one when you get older!" Murali laughed out loud and then, humming softly, fell asleep while dreaming of all the castles he could build.

The following morning, Baba and Vanamali labeled Murali's empty notebook and showed him how to carry it nicely in one hand. Vanamali and Shanti prepared his tiffin lunch box and after a warm early breakfast, the Ramaswamys set off for the first day of school. The air was fresh, and the sounds of Bangalore's street vendors were already echoing over the school bell's chimes. "Oh yell neeru, yell neeru!" cried the coconut milk vendor, eager to capture the thirsty families on their way to school. Murali was enthralled by the vibrant colors and sounds of the city and stopped by the green coconut stand to watch it's owner. Baba, a disciplined man, tugged on his son's arm, signaling it was time to go.

"Your school will start in a couple of minutes. Surely you don't want to be late?" Vanamali reiterated this concern.

"Come on, son, or else you'll be late!" Murali entered eagerly and was received by one of the nuns, who quickly waved off the parents and took Murali inside. Baba smiled and stood erect, proud of his little boy. Vanamali was not so composed, however. She wiped away a few tears that were already streaming from her eyes. "Good heavens, Vana, you're acting as if we are sending him off to fight in the War! Pull yourself together!" Baba exclaimed.

"But I can't," she cried, "I just keep thinking that you will be gone, and eventually I will need to head back to Hyderabad, and how sad that will be for our son. We won't be around when he needs us. What is a mother to do?" Baba looked at his wife straight on.

"Everything will be just fine. This is the safest solution; please understand that. Whatever we do now, will shape the nation, yet one wrong move can hurt our family. These measures are temporary, but I believe, necessary. Let's keep focused on the cause, and what lies ahead."

As they walked along the street, it was now time for the couple to part ways, Vanamali to head back to Shanti's house and Baba, whose journey was now onwards to Mumbai. She handed her husband a wicker weaved bag containing several savory and sweet snacks that could be enjoyed on the train ride ahead.

"You will inform me of your arrival?" Vanamali asked Baba. He nodded, and began to walk toward the train.

"Remember what I said. Don't spend more than a week in Bangalore. There is a lot of work at home." Vanamali nodded slowly then, seeing the train departing, she turned and proceeded on her short journey back to Shanti's.

Chapter Twenty-Four: Baba's refusal

"This is not the time to divide amongst ourselves!"
Amitabh yelled, anguish clearly evident on his face. "The events
of Saidpur and Firozpur are done. Nobody can change that. Now
is the time to reach in to your inner voices and speak up together,
unified!" The room was rumbling with a mixture of disagreement
and fatigue. Yadav, again the coordinator, called for silence as
approximately thirty members seemed to now be arguing amongst
themselves.

" I think we should each take turns to speak, whoever
wishes to. Although we truly appreciate your presence and your
input, this type of verbal chaos only slows us all down and is
exhausting. Mr. Ramaswamyji, would you be able to say a few
words?" Baba arose and made his way to the front of the room
carefully.

"I can only speak for myself. Unfortunately, I am at a loss
with regards to our Brothers' United mission. What exactly
happened? I felt uneasy, undermined, and highly strange that
none of you communicated with the three members who made the
journey to Firozpur. Why? I put my wife in harms way as she
accompanied me on the trip. For what? Six months of planning to
free Dhaliwal dissolved into nothing in just twenty-four hours.
Then, it was none of you, but my brother-in-law who informed me
that Netaji was now in Germany. I have a lot of confusion now as
to who leads this part of the movement. Remember, just as many
of you, I also run the Hyderabad Freedom Movement. We have
plenty of work there. I cannot afford for a secret, separate mission
to undermine my group's efforts in the South! And it has taken a

full year to pass by before anyone called a meeting. That is just not acceptable. So, please, tell me what happened, for I am eager to listen." Baba sat down, to the side of where he had been speaking, making way for Amitabh to respond.

" I know you all must be feeling badly for my brother's absence today. He has been busy. I am sure you can understand what it means to be a political leader, on the international level. He was very much in tune with the beat of the Firozpur happenings, but he had just been called away. You know that when he met us all in Calcutta, it was secretly. He was under house arrest. He journeyed to Germany out of a passion to seek help from European nations. Surely you can understand the vital importance of that? We have been getting nowhere within India, fighting for freedom. It's time to call in other reinforcements. I can assure you that he will be back, and he will lead this nation to freedom."

Chandrasekhar now spoke, clearly upset, discussing the lack of strategy and concern with surprises. "Imagine how we felt, hearing that Dhaliwal was dead. And then, the British massacre? Don't you think that it was preventable? I have blood on my hands. You know, guilty by association. What nonsense is this? To try to free one boy but contribute to the massacre of hundreds, in the process. It is not right at all. Whatever we do needs to be peaceful. No lives lost."

"He's an important man, Chandrasekharji, he cannot guarantee his presence in one place, if other matters arise. That's the nature of the political climate right now," Choksi explained.

The men went back and forth discussing what they each felt was important in the mission, and how they would proceed henceforth. Yadav then requested Baba to direct them in strategy and guidance for their freedom movement activities. Baba took off his spectacles and cleaned them carefully with his handkerchief. He stayed seated this time, with the other closer members in earshot distance.

"Friends, I am again, truly humbled by your invitation to lead the mission. It has been my sincere wish to help others in their quest for India's freedom. It is my purpose and passion. I lead the Quit India movement in Hyderabad and have enjoyed working with similar people with a singular focus. However, I have pondered the Dhaliwal, Netaji issue over and over for the last year. I feel that I must pass that baton over to someone in this city, Delhi or Calcutta. I have some work in Hyderabad that is important as well as my own work. Please understand that my goal is to continue to work for freedom. In the light of the past year's events, I feel my skills are better used in Hyderabad, where I have a network of family and connections, as well as an infrastructure of mission members who I have known for quite a while. Forgive me for not accepting. I hope you will understand, and continue to keep me informed at least, so that I can participate within my region with confidence." The men began to mumble again and the whispers became louder.

"Netaji needs you, Ramaswamy!" another man yelled.

"Perhaps. But, if he is truly meeting political leaders in Germany, I fear that his political interests are far different than mine. I do not believe Germany holds the answers to our problems. Allegiance with the Germans would be a mistake. You see I have a very peaceful, national interest- not a global one."

Baba thanked the members again, then poised and calm, turned and left the meeting.

Chapter Twenty-Five: The Member of Parliament 1945

" "In this day of aggression, I differentiate between passive resistance and Satyagraha. Satyagraha is truth and freedom. I think these are important differences that one needs to recognize to understand my belief and passion for freedom." Mohandas K Gandhi was passionate about the truth, beginning back in his post-Oxford days in South Africa." " The reporter continued on, radio blasting in Baba's modest home, to gentle smiles from Murali, Vana and little Uma. Baba lifted Uma, now three, and swung her up in his arms as she giggled. Vana, who was more relaxed now that Baba was home and dinner was done, cuddled up against Murali and reviewed his elementary schoolwork.

"Is your math work done Moggu?" she asked him.

"Yes, Amma", Murali replied.

"Check your work, then I and Baba will. Make sure to read and re-read your extra work papers every night. That's how you get ahead in life," Vana continued, lecturing her child to smiles from Murali, who looked as if he could imitate his mother at that very moment word for word. Vana added, "You want to be the head of your class when you return to Bishop Cottons, don't you?"

"Yes, Amma, I do. I have already reviewed my work. You can ask me questions if you wish," he challenged. Vana, who appeared satisfied with her obedient son, proceeded to pick up Uma from her father's lap and carry her to the bathroom to get ready for bed. Uma seemed to squeal when taken from Baba's grasp, flailing her legs and looking at her mother with sullen expression.

"What is the matter with you child, don't you know it is time for bed?" Vana then turned to address her son, " Moggu, the laundry boy brought your school uniform neatly pressed and ready for you to take to Bangalore for the start of the semester next week. I have laid it out next to your bed. Be sure to check everything before you sleep." Murali obeyed his mother and went to bed quickly, while Baba picked up his pen and paper and began to write.

Vana returned, after tucking the children in bed. "What are you doing?" she asked.

" I am making a list of the items on the agenda for the upcoming meeting. We have a lot of things to discuss, including the political agenda of Nehru and how that affects Gandhi and his principles. Prasanna and Colonel Singh are going to be there. There is some talk of going to Delhi and Mumbai to meet with the government official and get the wheels in motion."

"Are T.V. and Rai going to be there?" Vana questioned. " They could really help here. Haven't heard much from them lately. Why is that?"

"Er, well," Baba paused, " They will be present, but I'm not sure how much help they will be today. You see T.V. has accepted the Member of Parliament position that was actually offered to me."

"WHAT?" Vana screamed, in shock. "I do not understand! You do all the hard work, go to jail, relinquish your dream of a private law practice, sacrifice high paying jobs and business interests all for the good of the Country and Satyagraha, yet T.V. gets the M.P. position? Why is that? Am I missing something??"

Vana was clearly shaken up. Baba spoke gently.

"Let us not get affected by these titles and happenings. Our mission is strong and needs support and honesty. Satyagraha is all about truth and freedom. T.V. said he was all about truth and freedom, but I always felt he really was looking for titles and moving up the ladder rungs. At this moment, our motherland needs to be free of the British squatters, and needs to be a unified force. Britain continues to divide and conquer. Our impoverished masses flock to rallies driven by politicians who promise them wealth, but in truth, they are being duped. The politicians only look out for their own interests by demanding votes and villagers' support. We need to stay focused. Do not look for monetary gain. We don't need the money. We have the education. We just need a force of brainpower that is honest."

Vana tried to smile, but was clearly upset. She paced a little, and pondered. She wondered why her spouse was so righteous, so honest all the time. She was troubled. Having grown up in a broken home, with a filthy rich father who gave her nothing and mistreated her mother, she had a hard time trusting men. But, she secretly craved for money and status. She wanted things. She wanted to be filthy rich. She would rather have jewels and keep them in her Godrej bureau, than not have them and feel all the wiser. "I'm going to bed," she remarked, and, turning away from Baba, she left the room.

Chapter Twenty-Six: Satyagraha, 1945

He wrapped his head and neck in the muffler Vana had made for him. She had been knitting a lot, and had even requested her brother-in-law to bring British lambs wool with him on his return from Oxford, just so that she could make her husband a warm muffler and sweater for his upcoming travels.

"I'm not going to the Antarctic!" Baba joked, looking at his wife and smiling proudly in acknowledgement of her concern.

"Delhi and Jammu are very cold" Vana explained. "My sister told me that you could never be too prepared for the weather up North. She was telling me to pack you more cotton woven blankets so that the train ride won't be as chilling." Baba listened while playing with little Uma at his feet. He peered down at his watch while reaching to pick up Uma.

"Oh my, look's like it is time to go," he exclaimed. He pecked Uma on the cheek, and inquired about Murali.

"He's finishing his bath. I will fetch him," Vana said, hurrying to the bathroom in search of her beloved son. In a couple of minutes she returned with Murali who was wrapped in a towel, hair dripping yet looking fresh.

"Yes Mother, what is it?"

"Your father is leaving shortly for Delhi and the Satyagraha movement. Why don't you talk to him before he goes? Who knows, but it is likely that on his return you will be back at Bishop Cotton's boarding school so you won't see him."

"Oh, right!" Murali acknowledged. "Baba, where are you going? Can I come? Do you know when you will return? Are

T.V. Uncle and Rai Uncle going too? Why can't we all go with you and make a holiday of it?"

"Son, I think you know the answers to these questions. At this moment, India is in a state of turmoil. Although I do not wish to leave you, I think it would be wrong of me to take you and cause stress to your school routine and home life. Dr. Rai Uncle and T.V. Uncle are coming also, but we are all journeying up north separately to avoid arousing suspicion from the police. You know Officers Reddy and Rao are always on my tail, and if I take you along too, they will know for sure that we won't be back for some time. I am just going to leave quietly and hope they believe my explanation of my whereabouts. As far as they are concerned, I am leaving on urgent work matters, and need to discuss some insurance claims of a major client in Delhi."

Murali, who had been listening patiently for the first few seconds, clearly was off the topic by the time his father started talking about the officers and insurance. Giving a salute to his father in a military fashion (something he had been imitating a lot of late) he winked at his mother and then ran back to his bedroom, picking up the towel that had begun to slip down his back and was now wiping the floor. Vana, smiling at her little "Moggu," turned to face her husband.

"Keep safe. How will I know where you are and what you are doing?"

"Just as we have done before, I will contact you if and when the moment arises. Do not worry about me. Take care of Murali and Uma. And, don't let any strangers in the house."

Baba boarded the Deccan Express and embarked on his journey to meet Gandhi and other Civil rights activists. The journey to Bombay would be a long one, and, knowing this, he had brought some novels and writing materials with him. He looked around the cabin. There were not too many other people traveling from this station yet - at least not from his viewpoint. About a twelve-hour ride, his research showed, but perhaps more with the multiple stops this train would make. He thought about switching to Express in a couple hours, if the journey became monotonous. After a good thirty minutes of feeling restless, he turned toward the window, leant his head on the glass, and dozed off into a gentle slumber.

The wheels screeched as the train rolled into Delhi's Punjab station. Baba was a ready as ever, newspaper and briefcase in one hand, and umbrella in the other. As he disembarked the morning chill of New Delhi's crisp cold air confronted him. He swiftly hurried through the swarm of people moving on the platform, watching the signs to figure out where he needed to go. As he approached the high street, he stopped to remove his muffler from his briefcase, remembering Vana, who had snuck it in with Baba's belongings prior to his leaving home. It felt much better now. He was comfortable, and ready to take on his new mission. He just needed to figure out the next step in the plan. All he knew at that moment was that followers and leaders of the Satyagraha movement would somehow communicate through papers. He had read all of the Indian Opinion pamphlets and circulars from the decade prior. Now, he and his resistance movement members had created another paper, which the friends had struggled to name. Finally, they decided on Punya Cote, the childhood fable of the mother cow and calf, and self-sacrifice.

Baba knew that he would recognize other members of the movement through their khadi cloth, pamphlet distribution and perhaps various chosen locations and times. He didn't have many names or specifics, intentionally, in order to protect the integrity of the mission.

He was eager for his typical morning coffee, but, well aware of his Northern location, he was willing to consent to chai. He stumbled upon a coffee shop close to the university where he was heading. After checking into the hostel guest quarters on campus, he ordered his Madras-style coffee with samosa and pakora snacks. Baba, loving sweets, also enjoyed the local treat of fresh milk sweets. He was finally beginning to settle in and was reading the local college circular, when he was disturbed by a rather loud firework sound coming from just outside his window. Baba peered up from the paper. There were only a handful of people in the coffee shop, since it was mid-morning already and college classes had begun. Baba gazed straight ahead, at the counter, and saw nobody in sight. Strange, he thought. A moment later he was startled by yet another blow. Baba stood up and peered out of the window. The activity outside seemed to be business as usual. There were students strolling along the campus entry, a few buses and cycle rickshaws taking guests from place to place, and many locals on their bikes, riding to and from work or on errands. He turned around to look at the coffee shop once more. He studied the faces of the inhabitants. There was a young couple, possible post-graduate students, who sat together having chai and discussing their classes. Then, an older gentleman, rather professorial in appearance, was reading his newspaper from cover to cover and seemed to be taking notes on current affairs. A group of adults, perhaps in their young thirties, was ordering chai and sitting together as if to discuss a project or review a book. Perhaps they were teachers, Baba thought to himself. Nowhere around the room did Baba see any suspicious activity. Funnily, nobody else seemed to be affected by the banging, explosive sounds coming from outside.

It was at that moment that Baba decided to finish off his coffee quickly and go outside to inspect the scene. When he reached the spot where he had heard the noise, he was surprised to see absolutely no evidence of any scurry or construction or explosive activity. He was even more puzzled now. He lent on the brick wall and, grabbing his handkerchief while keeping his newspaper and pouch in his underarm, he wiped his brow. He was more tired than he realized, and was feeling a little weary. He still had not heard, or been given any sign from The Satyagraha Movement friends, on where to meet or what to do. He was beginning to doubt their efficacy. At least, in his small branch of the movement back home, the warehouse operated like a smooth factory, churning out pamphlets and easily communicating through papers what the plan was and what events would be taking place. He was out of his comfort zone now, and felt a little like a fish out of water. Moreover, leaving his family behind made him a bit angry at the thought of not being taken care of at this moment. Baba was known to always be patient and calm. This was a double-edged compliment. Ninety-five percent calm nature and predicament just made for rare, fiery encounters on the five percent chance he was not having a good day. So far, besides finding coffee in Delhi, today was not turning out to be a good day.

A few moments later, Baba wiped his brow and turned back towards the cafe window, trying to decide whether he would while away more time seated inside the joint. As he slowly moved back towards the cafe, he caught a shadow in his blind spot. He noticed a small grayish window shutter that was dilapidated, but cracked ajar slightly. From there, a light was flickering. Baba turned and stared directly into the light. He moved a few steps forward toward the light and attempted to peer into the window. At that moment a whisper echoed from the window.

"Baba, come in," came a voice. "It's us- Punya Cote mission. Hurry inside." Relieved at the comfort of familiarity, Baba discretely stepped inside the building via a small side door that was visible only from one point of view. A torchlight glared at his face and, initially not recognizing the shadow, he held his arms up to his brow in defense. Then, to handshakes and hugs from a few familiar faces, the tension lifted from the cool air. Prasanna was the most welcoming, hugging Baba and patting his back with joy.

"How have you been? We have missed you tremendously. Where are you staying? How was your journey here? How is Vana?" The flood of questions was joy to Baba's ears, since his sense of belonging and purpose had suddenly returned.

"Well, I am quite fine. I arrived this morning, and checked into the hostel. I was just enjoying a coffee and pondering what I was going to do if I could not find you. I am thrilled that you are here. For a moment, I wasn't sure what my next step would be. Now, we can discuss our plans together."

Janaki then responded. "Baba, we also were beginning to wonder if anybody received our brief coded messages. With you in prison for some time, we couldn't afford to contact you for fear of being tapped. However, we knew you would come through. Where is Dr. Rai? Is he coming separately?"

" All I know is that the other senior members from Himayatnagar will come up in separate trickles, all with different stories, reasoning and alibis. I think this is the best we could come up with in the light of the heavy British troops and police force close to our homes. Has anyone of you been interrogated?" Baba asked. Janaki was walking towards the little window where Baba stood, responded slowly.

"Well, after you were imprisoned, the police came to most of us here, questioning us, excessively. They tried to, but didn't crack our shells. Purely frustrated, the officers left, swearing to follow us or charge us formally if our stories backfired. So far though, they haven't bothered us." Baba greeted every familiar face with a kind smile and a pat on the back. He was re-energized and eager to resume the mission planning.

"What's the plan now?" he asked.

Just then, Prasanna walked in, with a wad of newspapers and pamphlets under his right arm, and a wide grin on seeing Baba in his presence for the first time in the last year.

"Hello dear friends, great to see all of you." He made a circle, glancing at each and everyone's facial expressions as he turned around. He seemed to gain strength by the sheer number of members that just one night before seemed to have dwindled. "Well, hate to breakup the soiree but it's time to get to work." Prasanna moved toward a bench that was leant up against the grey wall. Taking a blank sheet of paper from his stack of documents, he proceeded to draw a few things onto the sheet.

"If my coding and intelligence serves me well, I think that Dr. Rai and Colonel Singh will be heading up a freedom march scheduled to begin from New Market Square at ten o'clock tomorrow morning. From what Janaki has gathered, the British army will conduct a processional, for ceremonial purposes, in the square starting at nine thirty, in honor of King George and the

Commonwealth lives lost. A memorial will be held following the grand procession. We were planning to be at the square sharp at nine fifteen. We will position a few members in opposite directions, facing the stage and members of Parliament. The Freedom Marchers are going to march against the tide of Brits at approximately a quarter to ten. If things go according to plan, the British Gentry will be offended by the Peaceful Protesters and may move to strike our members. We must be strong. The Indian Army, including Colonel Singh, will be present to some extent and with any luck, will come to our defense. If they do, we should have a chance to speak in the large crowd and be heard. If this does not happen, we may be harmed or even separated. We should plan for all of the possibilities. I think we need to plan some speeches incase the politicians do allow us to be heard. I think we need to spend the next few hours determining what needs to be said, and what we would like to accomplish. Also, in the event that we are attacked, what is our back up plan? How do we pull the plug? Do we have an inconspicuous exit strategy? What does Colonel Singh say about the tide in government and the armed forces at this time? Is the movement favorable or heading for doom? These are tough questions that I fear there are no easy answers to, but I need your input."

Baba now approached the front of the tiny storage room, and began to speak.

"I have some insight into these poignant questions. I met with both T.V. and Rai a few weeks ago, when we knew this trip was about to take place but were not sure how each would leave to come up. We decided that staying quiet and making our own plans to travel would be wiser than communicating of late. The emergency code phrase would still be "Punya Cote." We decided to communicate this through telegram if any emergency situation arose. Otherwise, the plan was to depart up North and somehow send a signal when at least six to eight members had arrived. The signal would call the members to the central square on a chosen day. The presumption was that an auspicious day would arrive on which members of parliament would gather. On that day, our group would stand in union and protest the British, and hopefully voice our views on the freedom movement. With Gandhiji doing hunger strikes all over, and time truly running out, we need to exercise more aggressive options yet still keep true to our ideals." Baba turned to Janaki now, who was standing alongside Prasanna.

"So, as you may know, I just arrived here earlier today. My question to you all now is, what have you been told? Is this event confirmed? I hesitate to believe everything I am told a week or two ago, since things seem to changes easily nowadays."

Janaki then came forward, in a hurry to detail Baba on the events upcoming.

"Yes, Baba. Tomorrow morning a processional will occur. Tonight many dignitaries are coming to present Nehru with an award. We want to use that moment to march in front of our city offices and guarantee some attention. There are three colleges whose student group leaders are planning on marching with us. Word from Colonel Singh is that Nehru will be giving a speech about Gandhiji so a big crowd is expected. All we need to do now is finalize our marching plan, and who is going to say what and when or how."

"Alright then," Baba added, "Every person here needs to take a paper and pen and brainstorm for the next ten minutes. I think between us we can come up with a genuinely innovative itinerary."

The group went to work, brainstorming their plans for a better world and how they would achieve it. Would they accomplish what they set out to? Ten minutes passed by, they had discussions and many opinions, and then it was time get ready for tomorrow.

The following day, the members reconvened at the city offices. A throng of important people comprised of activists, locals and British officials were in attendance. After a few minutes of ushers settling the crowd, an older gentleman took the stage and began to speak.

" Brothers and Sisters, please join me in giving India's future leader a warm welcome! Nehruji thank you for all that you do. I invite you to the stage now."

Nehru began with introductions.

" In a world of differences, India has been a melting pot. We pride ourselves in our abilities. We know many languages, love facets of each individual culture, religion and festival, and pride ourselves in our Mother India, a democratic culture of loving people. The unity that we seek, and freedom we will, is indebted to one man without whom we would not be moving forward. I would like to honor and pay homage to Mohandas K. Gandhiji, my brother and friend, my fellow lawyer and socialist, a man of the people, a man of tremendous strength and principle. I am thrilled to invite Gandhiji to join me in an embrace. Please sir, come to the stage."

At that very moment, Baba and Prasanna, who were side by side, leading one of the college groups, and positioned towards the right side front of the small stage, were both taken aback. They stood, turned and glanced at each other in disbelief. The

Indian Army now made a small marching processional in front of the stage and their foremen barricaded the stage steps from entry. Then Baba caught a glimpse of a familiar face from the corner of his eye. A fair-faced, tall man walked Gandhiji onto the stage. The man then turned and tracked the audience slowly, as if searching. When their eyes met, acknowledgement, relief and respect summed up their mutual expressions. T.V. smiled and nodded at his brother. Next, the British Army marched forward in a beautiful display of processional synchronicity, and Gandhiji smiled, applauding loudly. Gandhiji then spoke....

"Bhaiyo aur Beheno, in this tide of change, we need to keep the current flowing smoothly, rather than risk a flood. I love my Motherland. I am passionate about her. I believe India possesses all the qualities necessary to be a leading nation, but also has unique features that make her stronger. For example, we have the ability to mingle in spite of hundreds of languages within this great nation. We are a beautiful democracy, allowing all religions freedom to preach, pray and respect openly. We enjoy culture, music and dance. We strive to work hard every day. We embrace our seasons, rather than run and hibernate from them. We are tolerant, peaceful and accepting.

Satyagraha - this is my mission. This is not simply a move towards passive resistance, but rather, a search for the TRUTH. It has been years since I started this movement, with the belief that our glorious nation could unite as one in a movement for freedom. It is nineteen forty-five now and we are sitting on the brink of a tidal wave.
It is time to make a move, make a change, work on equality for all and equal rights. How much longer do we as a nation wait? Nehruji, what is our Indian government planning to do about the

rising tide of political unrest in the light discordance? Do you hear the heart beats of your people? What do your British counterparts have to compromise? Our Nation is bleeding with the cries of the people, urging for freedom from your British allies. Is there a consensus? Do the British occupants have an exit plan? My people have been patient, but now it is time to march as one, to demonstrate to you, our government, that we are not giving up. We will strive forward, with hope for a better India, one without British rule."

Baba felt a firm tug on his shirt, and followed Janaki who was in front of him. Janaki started to lead the members and college students toward the middle aisle, facing center stage. Then the college kids began to chant a familiar marching song, " An eye for an eye makes the whole world blind!" This phrase repeated many times, until the students were aligned neatly down the center aisle. Then the students, who were all dressed in cotton, began to dispense pamphlets to the crowd. "Remember the salt march", or "Home spun yarn," they said, referring to the salt taxes and Gandhiji's self-sufficient goal to use Indian salt and clothing only. The British army by now seemed to be a little restless, their schedule disregarded in favor of the public outcries for Satyagraha and Gandhiji's surprise attendance. One of the drill sergeants was seen approaching the podium and requesting a return to the scheduled events. Nehruji then took control of the situation, making a pleasant joke of the British peoples' stiff upper lip and gently cajoling them into staying calm. Nehru reminded the Brits that this was a momentous occasion and could possibly be a landmark event.

A half an hour passed by effortlessly, as the young student protesters were heard cheering on Gandhiji and chanting phrases as in times past. The Satyagraha movement seemed to be going well that morning in Delhi, and innocent attendees appeared to be taking heed.

Baba was overjoyed. Not only did he meet his hero and idol Gandhiji, but he also felt useful, energized and positive. The inspiring talk and surprise visit of Gandhiji gave Baba a sense that independence was near. He could almost touch freedom, he thought. He was also thrilled to be reunited with his brother T.V. in whom he had great pride and who, Baba had wrongly thought, was rather obtrusive of late. Now he understood that even T.V. was on a higher mission and had been called to Gandhiji's side, likely to accompany him to the Delhi march and assist him. Gandhiji did look frail now, with age and the withering after effects of multiple hunger strikes taking a toll on his body. But, oh, to be in the presence of such a great man was monumental.

Later that night, after the March and processions had ended without too many unruly outbursts Baba, Prasanna, Janaki, T.V. and other core members gathered around the local hotel lobby for chai and snacks. They were famished, the hunger of the last few days only now hitting, with the function being over.

"So, what now?" questioned Baba to the famished crowd.

"We wait for further word on the next move," replied Prasanna and Janaki, almost in unison. The members were content and inspired. They brainstormed various innovative ideas for the next freedom march. Where would they want to march? What would be the consequences of marching in another political rally? Could they attempt to directly approach the British government through newspapers, radio and college activists? Also, what if freedom and independence wasn't in their reach? What would happen to their careers at that time? Would they be at risk of losing their jobs or being imprisoned yet again? Indeed, each and every member had already pondered these risks prior to jumping onto the bandwagon and it really wasn't something that would prevent them from fighting the freedom battle. However, times were changing. India looked close to independence per some reports but looking at the Brits it was hard to tell. Perhaps it was the British stiff upper lip or poker face, but it really was difficult to tell. The new British Ambassador was more amicable, but that's where it ended.

The following morning, after an early hot breakfast and chai, the group was to convene one last time at the College Campus, to meet the young student leaders again and give some insight into how they could carry on the mission. The turn out was phenomenal. To Baba's surprise, the campus quadrangle was full of junior students, professors and some families of status. There were alumni who were invested in the college and the neighborhood combined. Some senior citizens were present too. Members of pro-Gandhi groups committed to seeing India free from colonization were out in full force. Then there were members of the farmers unions. Interesting, Baba thought. Why was this? Why such a large turnout today? Gandhi was gone. There were no processions today nor were there special notable speakers. The president of the college came rushing to the makeshift stage on the North side of the quad, rather startled by the large turnout.

"Bhaiyo aur Beheno, I am happy to see you all here today. I am rather shocked, but pleased. Today, we want to simply thank the college students who have been so active in the freedom fight and have achieved greatness in their efforts. Yesterday, those of you who were present on nearby grounds bore witness to Mahatma Gandhiji's surprise visit, the freedom March organized by members from all over our great nation, and the glorious processionals by the Indian and British Armies combined. It was spectacular. The senior members and youth came together in a peaceful march, a rally for freedom from oppression and independence from British rule. Today, our young students wanted to see off our honorable guests and respected members, alumni and neighbors with a goodbye farewell. Let me introduce Mandeep Singh, who will speak on behalf of the student body."

A young, burly sardaar came upfront to the stage, strong and athletic, beaming with energy and joy. He turned and looked at the front of the audience, smiling gently. As he started to talk, there was some rustling from the back of the audience. Mandeep paused, hearing some disturbance, but on not seeing any particular problem, he continued.

"Gandhij questioned what we can do for our country, stating yesterday that we are a fertile nation with a lot of resources, intellect and ability. We can make changes by using our own strengths, and unifying our goals to one free nation. Today, as we say farewell to our friends, let's make a pact to stay true to our goal of freedom from oppression. Let's pray for freedom from caste, creed, color and religion. Let's join hands and unite for change. In thanks to Gandhiji, T.V.Sir, Dr. Rai, Ramaswamy Baba, Colonel Singh Sir, Janaki and Prasanna Sir, I would like to invite them all to the stage for a small token of our appreciation. Please come forward."

Applause enveloped the quadrangle. The crescendo of claps and cheers began as Baba and friends came forward.

Fragrant flower bouquets were presented to the senior members, and hand shakes and smiles went all around. The cheers continued. But, there were some rustles again from the crowd. From the back, some shoving occurred. A little child started to cry but the crowd in the back was so thick that nobody quite knew what was happening. Mandeep Singh, who was still handshaking and garlanding the honorees, did not hear the shouts, from the back of audience, beckoning and gesturing him to get off the stage. No one had time to understand what the commotion was. Finally, Janaki, seeing Mandeep's young freshman friend frantically running toward the stage, began to tug on Mandeep's elbow.

" I think she's trying to tell you something." But before she could finish circumspection of the scene, several rounds of fire were heard. Mandeep, Janaki and the freshman student fell heavy to the ground. The color red oozed from tributaries all over the grounds. In the chaos, no one saw the disguised men leaving from different angles of the audience.

Chapter Twenty-Seven: Recouping. Tirumakudlu 1945

"Baba, why do you put yourself in harm's way?" his mother Susheila asked her youngest son. "I've already lost one son, I do not wish to lose another. I wouldn't be able to bear the pain. Now hurry up and get better, then we all need to talk." Baba's mother affectionately padded his brow with a warm washcloth and then gave him sips of lemon water from the silver glass. She saw he was drowsy and needed to rest. She left the room and approached her husband, who was in the living room with Vanamali.

"I do not understand why your children are fighting other people's battles. He could have died, you know," she scolded her husband, who was talking to Vanamali. He turned to face his wife, excusing himself from the conversation that he was having with Vana.

"He is a noble man, Sushi. He is not going to sit back and wait for freedom to happen. He sees himself as part of the movement for change and he is educated to help in this regard. Why not take a stand, I say? Why is this wrong?" Ananta was also troubled, seeing his son's wounds and fearing what could have been the outcome. But, he had raised his children to make a difference in the nation, and he was not going to shy away now. He turned back towards his daughter-in-law.

"Vana, what do you think of all of this? Is it wrong? Do you resent your husband for being an active part of the movement? What are your thoughts, my dear?" Vanamali paused, contemplating the swarm of thoughts in her head, particularly given Baba's predicament. She thought about her nights in prison, infant in arms, stressed and weary. She felt angry when her husband's priority was often his movement, not his wife. But she revered him, and she didn't feel that being negative at a time like present would be of any benefit.

"He is destined for greatness," she began. "When I listen to him speak to his movement members, he is on fire. He is so passionate about achieving freedom for India, that he can express his emotions with such love and joy and it becomes hard to not follow him. So I guess what I believe is that he is a born leader; this is his calling. I think he should continue with the Freedom Movement, but he should be better protected. Another thought is that he should delegate more work. He takes on too much, you know."

"But what about the children? Don't they miss him? How do you feel about Baba being gone so much? Does it affect you?" Ananta asked Vanamali.

"It does, but when I weigh this burden against the investment Baba gives in the nation, I cannot see any other path. This is the thing he was born to do, and I will stand by him through it all." Vana smiled, exhilarated at her freedom of speech, something rare for her within the walls of Himayatnagar where her voice was swallowed by her many sisters-in-law. She felt good right now. She couldn't believe that she was capable of such speech, but now that she had spoken her mind, she felt uplifted, spirited, like she was swimming again amongst the see of nature.

Ananta, equally thrilled at being Baba's champion, stood up and paced the room. After checking on his son and seeing he was fast asleep, he decided to go out for some fresh air. He took a cycle rickshaw across town by a couple kilometers, and approached the grand gated palace of the Mysore Raja (king), his friend and employer. The palace gates opened easily, since the staff of the palace knew Ananta very well, what with his title of being physician in service to the reigning monarch and his reverence in society. They let him in and straight to the drawing room, where high tea was being served. Looking at the Maharaja, Ananta smiled and walked towards him.

"Come, come my friend. To what do I owe this pleasure?" Maharaja asked.

"Oh, I hope you do not mind the intrusion, your highness, but I wanted to invite you to my home for a feast," Ananta spoke kindly. The Raja smiled, honored by the invitation.

"Come, sit down. Meet my cousin Motisa Baradsa, the Maharaja of Madhya Pradesh. He is visiting me today, on the way back from some lengthy travels. You know, he just returned from Delhi? He was updating me on the movement and progress there." Maharaja stood to introduce his cousin Motisa, to Dr. Ananta. Ananta, somewhat embarrassed realizing there was a visitor, did not immediately sit down. Instead, he chose to take two steps back, bowing as he did so.

"Oh, please, good doctor, please, do not bow to me. It is you who saves lives daily, I'm merely on vacation!" Motisa joked.

"Oh no, nothing like that. I just love to help those in need, medically. It's not so glamorous, but I do love it," Ananta responded. He sat down now, willingly receiving some hot Darjeeling tea in a fine china white and gold-leafed floral teacup.

"Tell me more about the dinner, good doctor. What is the occasion?" Maharaja asked.

"Well, my son Ramaswamy is visiting from Andhra. He actually was wounded at the Freedom Protest during Quit India presentations in Delhi last week. He was cleared by their staff surgeons but is still very weak. I brought him here. He will mend within days, under his mother's tender loving care. And now, I wish to celebrate him for his dedication to our nation. Please do come, I request you, your highness."

"Why it would be my honor, Ananta," Motisa replied instantly. "Why would I choose anything else over this? Your son is to be honored for his bravery. We are under trying times, and Britain continues to test our nation, greedily taking our possessions and goods, resources and produce. They have stolen our jewels, taken our tea and spices, and even used our homespun yarn and silks to adorn their ball gowns. Yet, it is our young men who suffer at the hands of the greedy occupants. We need to push on, but only a few brave warriors remain who can handle the conniving minds of the British. Your son represents the future, and we should support him in his efforts."

Ananta was speechless, not expecting such praise from the Maharajas. What struck him most was the tremendous support being given. In the past, he had wanted to question the kings, whom he felt were responsible for some of the problems in the country. He believed in his countrymen, but doubted that the kings' families had any clue as to the heartbeat of the nation.

"How could they possibly understand?" he wondered to himself, "they have never needed to work for money, nor fend for themselves." He knew that the Mysore Maharaja was, in fact, known for his empathetic nature towards his citizens. But, he knew of others that, rumor said, were compromising their values or undermining their citizens just to be in good favors of the British gentry and colonels and viceroy. He had the impression that the Rajas (kings) feared losing their status, which could happen with continued British rule. Ananta believed that the Maharajas would rather allow taxation of the farmers or poor citizens rather than fight against it and fear losing power or worse, even murder. But now, Motisa Maharaja's kind words of encouragement and praise rang loud in his mind. He also knew that his boss and revered Maharaja, was renowned for his kindness, and did truly represent all that was right with the Indian Imperialism.

"Thank you, your highnesses. You are honoring my family and myself by gracing this auspicious occasion, and I thank you from deep within my heart. Ramaswamy, my son, will be so thrilled. This is the medicine he needs to strengthen his resolve! He will be energized within no time!" So saying, Ananta graciously exited the palace, thanking the king's staff and other members on his way out.

Ananta hurried to the door to greet the royalty. He was still overcome with joy and wondered why Motisa raja would bother to come to his small, humble abode simply to honor Ananta's son. Yet there they were, wait staff bearing sweets and gifts, behind Motisa, who met his new friend with open arms. Baba was quick to join his father, bowing to Maharaja Motisa.

"Thank you, your highness, for gracing this occasion with your presence. I am truly honored," Baba said.

"Young man, it is I who must thank you for your courage and sacrifice, in moving India forward in her freedom battle. I present you this medal of honor and bravery, on behalf of my state and country." Motisa remained standing, in the foyer of the house, and turned to his wait staff. He raised a golden medal, strung onto a purple silk ribbon, and pinned it on Baba's lapel. Then, he again turned and, taking a golden necklace out of a red velvet box, he garlanded Baba with a golden bead necklace. It had five strands, a traditional "Mohan mala" necklace of the kings. Unlike the female version, this carried an emblem of Motisa's dynasty encrusted on the left side of the strings, effectively connecting them so they would not tangle up. Also, the emblem carried tiny ruby and emerald jewels that made an infinity sign underneath the crest. It was truly regal. Motisa garlanded Baba and then embraced him.

"But, your highness," Baba expressed, " I do not deserve all of these jewels. I'm not the only freedom fighter who sacrificed time, money, and even life, for the cause. It would be wrong of me to accept this." Baba looked at his father, hoping for clues of approval or concern. Instead, Ananta simply watched his son, admiring his humility and grace. Motisa now smiled again, this time agreeing to sit down with the family.

"Son, if I stratified all of the fighters out there, we would end up only acknowledging Gandhiji himself, and that would simply be untrue. All that has happened is the brainchild of Mohandas, but his army is you and all the other peaceful warriors like yourself. It is my pleasure and intent to praise, where praise is due. You are highly deserving of this medal and you should accept as a friend and as one of India's peace activists. Now please, let us embrace and enjoy the feast!"

Baba was thrilled and for the first time, speechless. Later that night, family and friends continued to gather in his childhood home, to honor Baba and celebrate his accomplishments. Vanamali, who was also thrilled to be celebrating Baba, took care of her royal guests and family friends. When the night was over,

Vana gazed around the room, remembering in her mind every little detail of that night, not wanting it to end.

"Amma, how come Maharaja Motisa presented me, and not our Mysore Maharaja?" Baba asked his mother.

"Well, technically, Motisa raja is higher in status than our state maharaja. It doesn't really matter, but since you were given a Medal of Honor, if a higher-ranking king presents you, it could prove more profitable in your life some day. Your father already knew that Mysore Maharaja pledged to honor you. However, due to Motisa's presence, the kings determined Motisa should present you. It's sort of a hidden protocol."

" I didn't realize you knew so much about the laws of the land!" Baba teased his doting mother.

"Well I certainly do!" Amma replied, making a face at her son. "Besides, if the British had their way, there will be no kings to honor us at all, so you and your kids will definitely not learn the royalty's ways. It's sad, really. Most of the Maharajas seem so nice. Except a few greedy ones I've heard about, they are a kind class of people. I think they too, want only what's best for our India."

Baba pondered this over and over. He did like his king, and Motisa maharaja, but could INDIA afford them?

Chapter Twenty-Eight: Flying Kites, Feb 1946

"Come on, hurry up!" Murali yelled to Patthabhi, his best friend. The boys rushed quickly down the stairs of their balcony and up the opposite staircase, reaching the neighbor's rooftop within minutes. "Get the kite, quickly!" he yelled energetically, "We need to cut Srini's kite down if we want a chance of winning!" Murali explained. The boys ran with the kite, attempting to make it soar into the skies quickly.

"Murali, our kite's not cutting the other string. We need to make the string stiff. I can't cut Srini's kite down," Patthabhi exclaimed.

"Here, hand the kite base slowly and carefully to me, but keep on feeding the string-don't lose sight of our kite," Murali explained. The boys skillfully released the feed of the string reel. Next, the other would pull the kite back in, observing the wind and the trend of kites above them. Initially about twenty kites in view, only four were contenders now. "I think I have one!" Murali exclaimed, attacking and then reeling his kite back in as the red diamond component became diminutive in the skyline before falling. The best friends cheered, then turned their attention back to the skies that were now beginning to cast a shadow.

"Murali, come on, let's do this! All we have to do now is cut down that flashy blue kite and we are through to the final round competition tomorrow! Let's finish this one off and then we can go eat. I'm famished!" Patthabi ran the length of the balcony rooftop looking closely at the kites remaining in the sky. "Pull it in, pull it in, the yellow kite is coming down on us!" he yelled. Murali quickly rolled the spool of his kite, nimbly rolling it in on his cupped palms.

"Watch out, Murali!" Patthabi screamed, but it was too late. The boys watched with necks craned upwards, as their kite fell to the ground. They plopped to the ground exhausted and defeated, at the end of an exhilarating, sweltering day.

"I'm sorry Putty, I messed up," Murali conceded, feeling guilty for not being swift enough with the kite.

"Oh, it was not your fault, that yellow one arose so quickly there was nothing we could do," Patthabi comforted his best friend. "Let's grab some food, I'm starving!"

"You're always starving!" Murali chuckled, teasing his friend.

As the boys descended the steps from the rooftop, Shiva, their classmate, came running towards them.

"Hey, Murali, hey Putty, you're still in! You are still in the competition!"

"What are you talking about?" Patthabi questioned.

"Your kite was one of the last four, didn't you notice? The finals are for the final four from Himayatnagar colony with the final four from the neighboring colony. You guys made it! Congrats!"

Murali was dazed, puzzled by the twist of fate and somewhat in disbelief.   "But, Shiva, I thought there were other kites in the field. Surely you're mistaken?"

"No, you are! Look, everyone's here to cheer you guys!" Shiva turned and pointed at the second grade class that was cheering and forming a circle around the two kite runners. "Three cheers for Murali and Putty. Hip Hip, Hooray! Hip Hip Hooray! Hip Hip Hooray!" Shiva and the young boys cheered.

"That's fantastic!" Putty and Murali acknowledged. "Come, let's go home and have some food!"

"Come to my Dad's snack house, it'll be more fun! We can talk about all the ways you can win tomorrow and eat lots of food too!" Sourya, one of the boys invited, and off the gang of children went.

The table was laid out with savory snacks and sweets, enough to fill the boys' stomachs for days. Sourya's Dad Mr. Gurusamy, forever an optimist, had prepared enough food to feed an army, as if the children had conquered the British Empire. "Boys, how are you going to win tomorrow?" he asked them.

"My brother says you can make a glue out of crushed glass pieces," Shiva exclaimed with glee.

"No, no, that won't work too well and is too difficult to do without hurting yourself. I have an idea for you, if you like," Mr. Gurusamy offered.

"What is it Uncle?" Murali and the boys asked.

"Eggs. Look, I'll show you." He went into the kitchen and fetched some eggs from the wicker basket. "Boys, all you need to do is break the egg into the white and the yolk. Discard the yolk. Then, dip the kite string into the egg white and watch how quickly it hardens. This is your winning trick!"

"Wow, Uncle, what a great idea! I love it!" Murali exclaimed.

"Sourya, your Dad's incredible. I think we are going to win tomorrow!"

As Mr. Gurusamy left the boys to their chatter, Murali whispered in Putty's ear. "There's only one problem."

"What?" Putty asked.

"Where am I going to get eggs from? My parents do not allow eggs or any animal things in the house. You know how they are," Murali sighed.

"Oh, yeah, I forgot about that. Well, let's ask if we can borrow some from Mr. Gurusamy then," Putty advised.

"But how are we going to practice?" Murali persisted.

"Well, we can use an egg from Mr. Gurusamy's kitchen as a trial, just to check how the thread rolls. If it works, then Sourya can bring some for us tomorrow before the match."

"Wow, Putty, sometimes you amaze me! That's fixed then."

Murali and Putty left the cafe, elated. Since it was already evening, the boys decided to rush home first, explain to their parents what had transpired, then go up on the rooftop to test the egg glaze method. Patthabi left Murali at the crossroads that connected their neighborhoods, waving his friend off quickly, so that they could reconvene shortly. Murali jogged down his street, grinning widely as he negotiated the box of sweet treats in one hand (given by Mr. Gurusamy for Ramaswamy and Vana) and two raw eggs in his other. But, the sweets kept on sliding in the box. He thought he would open it to check if the treats had mushed together, but he couldn't handle this attempt. Murali put the eggs in his pant side pocket and opened the take-out box. "Ahh, they are fine!" Murali said to himself, reassuringly. He resumed his journey, jogging a little faster as he approached his Himayatnagar house. As he entered through his front door, Vanamali called his name, hearing his footsteps and eager to inquire as to his whereabouts.

"Where have you been, son?" she asked, "The kite match ended hours ago."

"Amma, guess what? We made it through today's battle and will be in the final tomorrow. And guess what else?" Murali said, bending down to take off his sandals as he spoke, while still holding on to the goodie box. "Mr. Gurusamy sends you and

Baba his best wishes and gives you these sweets." As Murali again leaned forward to present his mother the sweets, he felt a crack and sudden wetness in his clothing.

"What is this Murali?" his mother asked, seeing the wet patch expand through his pocket. Murali peered down, realizing that the eggs had broken in his pocket.

"Amma, it is just an egg. I am going to use it to harden the kite strings."

Vanamali giggled, covering her mouth so as to not look like she was ridiculing her son.

"Moggu, this is not good for you! This is too fragile. Plus, where will you keep the eggs? Baba will be upset if he comes to know that you brought eggs into the house! You know how disciplined he is. It is not done in our home. Moggu, quickly go and take a bath, and I will wash your clothes."

Murali looked dejected, his small body even more tiny from his stance, shoulders now hunched as he felt the shell of the eggs in his pocket. A mere seven years old, he had always appeared older than stated, due to his quick and bright mind and maturity. Yet now, as he gazed at his mother, her expression changed from happiness to sadness as he winced to hold back tears. It was too late to hide the evidence. Baba walked in the front door, hung up his shawl and set his leather pouch down on the coffee table.

"Vanamali, I have news for you!" he called out, as he approached the kitchen.

"Yes, yes, just a moment, I'll be right there," Vana replied, shooing her son away as she moved swiftly by him. Baba was excited about his news, so rushed into the kitchen. He was too fast, and caught his son at the entryway to the kitchen.

"Murali, why are you dirty? Where have you been?" he inquired.

"Baba, I was flying kites in the competition the whole day, and Patthabi and I made it through to the finals tomorrow." Murali tried to ignore his sticky clothing, and made his best effort to stay confident and positive, like a good son.

"What happened to your attire?" Baba pressed on.

"Mr. Gurusamy said that we should use eggs to stiffen the kite strings. I wanted to give it a try before the finals tomorrow. I think it will work."

"So?"

"So, I was bringing some home to try it out, and I was leaning over to Amma to give her the box of sweet treats that Shiva's Dad sent for you, when the eggs that were in my pocket cracked. I did not mean to make a mess, it just happened." Baba searched the kitchen, and his wife's expressions, and then looked down at his son. He was at a loss for words. His mind had been full of his day's accomplishments, including a letter that he had received from the central office, requesting his presence at a meeting of delegates to discuss India's possible independence. He had come home joyous wanting to share this news with his young family. He pondered this over and over, but then began to dwell on things that could go horribly wrong if he did take the family with him to New Delhi. After a few still moments, Baba broke the silence.

"Murali, I am happy that you and Patthabi succeeded in your kite competition so far. But, my son, we do not bring eggs into our home. It is not accepted in our orthodox kitchen and I do not know how to help you now. You will have to be more careful with your things, and try not to get so filthy. Remember, cleanliness is next to Godliness."

So saying, he quietly dismissed his son, wishing him luck for the next day's finale. Baba smiled at Vanamali, accusing her of spoiling their son.

"No, Baba, he is not spoilt. He is a mere boy of seven, and was rejoicing after playing with his friends. So what if he cracked some eggs! It's sort of funny!" Vanamali expressed. Baba patiently listened, but then explained his events finally.

"So, I am going to take the next train out this Thursday, so that I can meet my colleagues beforehand, then attend and advise at this meeting. You will have to manage Murali alone till I am back." Vana smiled respectfully, setting Baba's coffee and savory snacks on the table along with the gift of sweets.

Vanamali studied her husband's face as he settled in to his routine of unwinding after work, and planning, on pen and paper, his strategy for the upcoming meeting. She loved his passion, his resolve, his focus, but as she stared at her husband, she couldn't help but feel sad for her Murali, who was missing the typical relationship of father and son. She wondered if Baba would ever truly play games with her son. Too often Murali was left to play with friends as Baba ran out on his freedom mission work. But, what could she say? He was fighting a bigger cause.

"Oh well", she sighed to herself, and then discretely left the room to check on her children.

Chapter Twenty-Nine: Bishop Cotton's, 1950

"Amma, do I really have to still stay away from you and father?" Murali asked, disappointed at again, being carted away by train to Bangalore, for secondary school. "The war is over and India is free. I just thought Baba would be done with his Quit India movement. What's the problem with me staying at home? Uma gets to attend the local grammar school. I don't understand. Have I done something to upset Daddy?"

"Oh my goodness no, son! Don't think this! Baba has been working hard with the Quit India members who are now members of parliament. There is still much work to be done, darling. Baba is so proud of how much you have accomplished and he believes you are best suited to Bishop Cotton's curriculum. Changing to the local school now would seem mediocre. You just have a few more years now. This school will lead you to the best colleges possible, and then you will be my pride! Your cousin Parth did it, and you are miles ahead of him! You must trust us, dear. Now hurry up and put your suitcase in the cycle rickshaw."

Murali was not convinced. He loved his mother, and believed that she honestly loved him more than anybody else in the world. But, the thought of his famous revered Baba began to corrode his mind. He had spent countless nights looking at the upper bunk bed while fighting insomnia and anxiety. Alone he was in the world, in a different state, far away from anyone who truly loved him. He remembered being in the bunk bed on his first night at Bishop Cotton's. The teacher had called for "lights out" but Baba had been tossing in his bed. When Priest Anthony, the residence hall teacher had come back to check on the young boys, Murali was out of bed.

"What happened, my son?" the priest inquired, kindly.

"I, umm, well, I needed to visit the toilet," young Murali had explained, truthfully.

"Is everything all right, my son?"

Murali nodded, but his gaze was on his pajama top, and he was tugging on it to pull it down. The priest smiled and walked Murali back to his bed. But Murali was walking rather funnily. After a few moments, priest Anthony crouched down beside Murali so that they were now face to face. Without words, he motioned for the child to stay put for a moment. The priest walked away, and within a minute, returned with a change of clothes for Murali.

"Here, put these clean clothes on, and leave your other set in the laundry basket. The laundry boy will take care of them in the morning." Murali obliged, and was relieved to not have to do any more talking. He took off his wet clothes and quickly changed. Nerves had taken over him, but luckily he did not have to sleep in his bed-wet clothes and linens. The first week of elementary school was the worst week in Murali's young life thus far. He had struggled with abandonment guilt anxiety and dysthymia, at the mere age of five while his Baba fought the world for India's freedom.

"Does India's independence equate to my independence, Amma?" he asked his mother, before climbing into the cycle rickshaw.

"I'm not sure that I understand you, Moggu," Vanamali replied, softly.

"Well, ever since Baba has been with the Quit India movement, and now the post-independence restructuring, he has left me alone in this world. Is that what Baba believes in?"

"Oh no, Murali! Don't think such bad things. Your father loves you so much that he wants you to have the best education. This involves sacrifice, separation and discipline sometimes. In the end, you will thank him," Vanamali explained, hugging her son one last time before climbing into the vehicle beside her son.

Murali turned his thoughts back to present time. He murmured under his breath, how thankful he was to at least have schoolteachers who seemed to care for his wellbeing above any other mission in life.

Two months had passed and Murali, a few inches taller than when he left home, was back on the train headed to Andhra, returning home for the Deepawali festivities. He was most looking forward to seeing his family and eating all of the delicacies they would have prepared. The train jerked a bit as it abruptly came to a halt at Himayatnagar's station. As he disembarked, Uma came running to hug her brother.

"Anna, happy Deepawali! How are you? How long are you staying? Did you receive the birthday card I sent you?" Her mother and two aunts, who quickly surrounded Murali, took out a jute bag and gave it to Uma.

"Feed your brother, Uma!" Brunda advised, eagerly telling her nephew of the special sweets that she had prepared only in his honor. "These are your favorite! I used to feed you milk sweets when you had only just learned to eat a proper meal!" she added.

"I have mango pickle rice for you, Moggu. Hurry up! Let me give you food!" Vanamali interjected, eager to take back her son's attention. Murali grinned happily. He had missed his family, but, growing up in a cantonment convent school, he felt it hard to express his feelings when it most mattered. "Never mind!" he muttered quietly, enjoying the love and affection with which he had been greeted.

Within the hour Murali had reached home. He placed his small suitcase in his room, washed his hands and face, and sat down comfortably on his living room sofa. Uma quickly joined him, watching her brother closely, perhaps to annoy him.

"Anna, aren't you wondering something?"

"No, not really", Murali chuckled.

"Oh gosh, Anna, you are impossible! Okay. Let me tell you. Did you hear about Pooja Aunty?"

"Yes, she is my paternal aunt number six"

"Anna, stop fooling around! I'm trying to tell you some gossip!" Uma explained.

"Go on," he added.

"Well, mother and father were having a talk recently, and Amma complained about how all of Baba's sisters molly-cuddle him. When he, and even I had a laugh about it, she said that Pooja Aunty was the worst of the lot. She accused her of teasing Amma to the point of an inferiority complex! Amma said that Pooja was unkind in her words and was making her angry. She said that because of Pooja Aunty she has to fight for her say in the household! Oh dear Amma! I just was bursting to tell you that! Of all the people, she's upset at Pooja Aunty the most!! What do you think of all of this?"

"Tell me how Baba responded," Murali requested, thoughtfully.

"Baba was triumphant!" Uma replied. "He giggled and explained that, in his mind, his little sister had had only sweet words to say about her kind sister-in-law, and that any type of accusation would be gravely wrong. Then he advised her to take up some hobbies to keep her mind calm".

Murali paused for a few moments, trying to imagine what life was like for his beloved Amma, particularly since he had left for school. He reflected on his mother's interactions that very morning. She picked him up from the station, but it was Brunda who did most of the talking. When Murali had left for Bishop Cotton's earlier that year, Vanamali had tears in her eyes. Murali remembered his own tears of separation, when his parents left him at the school for the very first time. How sad he felt. There were so many emotions in his head, as he mulled over the memories. She was imprisoned with Baba several times, but that did not seem to allay her fears or boost her confidence, Murali concluded.

"You know what, Uma?" he said. "Amma has done everything she was asked to, and more. She is working hard to support Baba, the freedom fighter. She was in jail when I was a baby, did you know? It was Amma who took me to my first day of school in Bishop Cotton's. Amma sent me letters and snacks. She's pretty cool. I think she just feels overshadowed sometimes, because others are quick-witted in response. I suppose things get to her, you know? I mean it must be fairly normal to feel upset at times. You need to be more understanding and less judgmental! Try that on for size!" Murali and Uma chuckled together seamlessly.

"Where is Baba?" Murali finally asked. It was the elephant in the room. Murali had been home an entire two hours, catching up with Uma, and had not laid eyes on his father still.

"He's on official business," Uma responded, importantly.

"To where?"

"I don't remember. Some really important place."

"That is so helpful," he teased Uma, sarcastically. "Amma, we need to talk, come here!" Murali yelled. Vanamali, who had just said her bye-byes to her sisters-in-law, came rushing to her children, eagerly.

"Yes, Moggu, what is it?"

"Where is Baba? I thought he would receive me at the station, too."

"Yes, my love, yes. Well, Baba had to leave on urgent business just yesterday night. As usual, he will provide more information when he arrives in Delhi. But, he was quite shaken up when he was told, by one of his old Oxford chums, that Netaji Kekre could be still alive, in Russia! We only knew he was killed in a plane crash, but this phone call came from a reputed source in the city. So, Baba had to go. I'm sorry that Baba is not here with you. The house feels incomplete."

Murali covered his face with his hands and sighed, deeply. Uma and her mother tried to cajole Murali into revealing his face, but he wouldn't. At least twenty minutes elapsed before Vanamali was able to shoo Uma away and gently pull Murali's hands away. He had shed some tears, and then fallen into a quiet sleep.

PART TWO

Chapter Thirty: Bangalore, September 1945

"Congratulations Prakash Sir, it's a beautiful baby girl. Wife and baby are both doing well. You may see them now." The doctor was pleased with the smooth delivery. Ratna was splendid in her postpartum glow. She was already thinking of baby names. The young Mrs. Murthy held her baby close to her heart and smiled widely, uncharacteristically revealing her larger front teeth, something she rarely showed. The spontaneous joy consumed the couple, as they gazed at their new bundle. Ratna knew, at that very instant, that she would do everything possible to make her girl the most educated girl she knew. " Seetha, that's what her name will be," she stated, handing baby Seetha to her husband.

Ratna was thrilled to have her own little baby to spoil and play with. She had always loved children and knew that she would enjoy every moment. While her young brother, a doctor, was more concerned with making sure Seetha had ten digits and a healthy heart, Ratna was up and about in her room, making sure everything in her home was running smoothly in spite of her recent confinement in the maternity hospital. She was tireless, always tending to others and never herself. The young mother was joyous, happily swaddling her newborn in one hand and scurrying to the kitchen to supervise the meals and daily preparations.

Seetha grew up quickly. A mere four years old now, Seetha could be heard reciting complex multiplication tables to her aunts and uncles and singing prayer songs to neighbors that requested them. She was known also as the little chatterbox, with plenty to say about everything, even things she didn't understand. Prakash was beginning to worry over why his wife was unable to keep another pregnancy. She had already had one miscarriage and the fear of not having a son consumed him. Prakash himself had suffered as the oldest son. One would think he wouldn't want a male heir, for fear of placing the son in the same destiny as his own. As a teenager, Prakash had been forced to choose work over college, since his father died young, leaving him, the eldest boy, with the household financial responsibilities. He had worked tirelessly, putting his younger brother through college and raising him into a fine young gentleman. He, on the other hand, was running the family mill and trying to keep up the small snack shop they owned. If it wasn't for his knowledge and love of family, he might not have been able to keep going. Life was tough. But still, he was pious, he was a good Brahmin, he performed his religious duties properly, so why was he still suffering? He longed for a son!

Chapter Thirty-One: A brother for Seetha

Some months, then years went by. Seetha still was an only child. Prakash's sisters had both conceived baby boys, but not Ratna. Prakash had taken his wife to the doctor for a complete medical checkup and she was given a clean bill of health. They were happy as a couple.

Soon, Ratna came to know that she was indeed expecting, but out of fear of an early miscarriage, she had hidden the news from her eager husband, until she felt confident things would proceed as normal. That weekend, amongst the hustle and bustle of Deepavali (festival of lights) celebrations, Ratna and Prakash seemed happier than ever. She had just given Prakash the exciting news.

"Seetha, my princess, you are going to be a sister soon!" Prakash smiled and exclaimed, lifting his preschooler in his arms and swaying her gently.

"Appa," Seetha addressed him, " am I going to have a sister or a brother?" she asked.

"Well," Prakash paused, "No one really knows the answer to that question. Only the Gods above know that answer. But, I feel it is going to be a boy. That's my guess."

"What shall we name him?" she pressed on, eagerly.

"You and Amma can think of names, but the priest will ultimately decide the choices depending on the stars alignment when he is born," Prakash explained.

It was only two months later that Ratna gave birth to a buxom baby boy, eight pounds per reports, which seemed massive compared to the mother's petite four feet seven inch frame. The parents were thrilled, and celebrated in the maternity ward as if he were their firstborn. After spending the day with his glowing wife, Mr. Murthy returned home to tend to Seetha. He prepared the cot within their bedroom, ready for the baby while Seetha arranged her dolls in a "welcoming committee" fashion at the entrance to her room.

The following day Prakash dressed Seetha, and they travelled by cycle rickshaw to the hospital. They rushed up the hospital steps and scurried quickly down the aisle towards Ratna's room. He was a bit disturbed when he didn't see his wife inside. Instead, an empty bed lay neatly made, void of people or decoration. Seetha and her father turned back towards the nursing station where they found some staff and inquired about their family's whereabouts. The portly nurse gave an expression of pity and, glancing back at Prakash and little Seetha, and then pointed in the direction of the other wing of the women's hospital. She also sent for the doctor, who came promptly to greet them.

"Mr. Murthy, I am so sorry to bear such sad news, but your baby son expired early this morning from respiratory distress. We did everything we could to resuscitate him but we failed. I am deeply sorry. Your wife is in room twenty-three. Please try to not let her see your grief, since she has carried her son for nine months but cradled him in her arms for barely one night. It is too much to bear."

" Doctor, please explain to me what went wrong. I do not understand. He was such a healthy-appearing boy at birth yesterday. What happened? Is it something we did? Could he be allergic to breast milk? Please explain."

Prakash was tilting his head down in disbelief, water dripping from his eyes in spite of every attempt on his part to hold them in. Seetha, unable to understand the gravity of the moment, turned her head up to her father. "Appa, don't worry, baby is in heaven. He will be safe there."

Prakash walked towards Ratna's room, smiles gone, saddened by unexpected news. He could not prevent the onslaught of negative thoughts within his mind. A usually happy, pious man momentarily fought the demons within poisoning his mind with hate. He could not understand why he was being made to suffer in this way. As he entered the room, Ratna was braiding her hair, which was full of knots and strands falling on the floor from a rough labor and now postpartum hormonal shifts combined with the depression that was trying to take hold of her. Seetha climbed onto the bed and hugged her mother, trying to kiss her on the cheeks.

"Seetha, my princess, stop that now, you know that kissing can make you sick", Ratna scolded, much to the astonishment of Seetha, who was used to cuddling with her mother. "

"That's okay", she replied to her Mom, adding, "everything will be okay Amma, baby's in heaven now. Don't worry."

The welts of tears mounted in her eyes, and dropped onto Seetha's head, under her. "Amma, can you come home with us?" she asked. Ratna didn't say anything, instead gazed up towards her husband with a fearful expression, as if she had disappointed him. Murthy, on the other hand, was a practical man. He understood that situations like this were out of human control. He just wanted to move on. He wanted to run from the hospital. He felt like escaping the area.

"Did the doctor say if you are well enough yet to come home today?" he asked.

"He wants to keep me for five days, since seven is regular confinement but five would suffice in my situation. However, I don't want to stay. I'm all right. Can you take me home?" she asked. The plan had been for Seetha to go to her mother's house in Mysore, where she would be pampered while recouping from delivery with the comforts of her mother's love. Now, everything had changed. Prakash wanted to ask whether Ratna still wanted to go but refrained from this, fearing it was too soon.

Dr. Bhatt now knocked and entered the room. 'How are you feeling today?" he asked Ratna.

"Well, I am fine. I have slight cramping, but I do not need anything for it. I think if I move around it would be good." "Well, let me check you first," he replied. A few minutes later, the exam was complete and Dr. Bhatt walked back into the hallway to talk to Mr. Murthy. He explained that Ratna would heal well physically, but mentally it would be trying. If Prakash was to take her home today, he needed to be considerate to her emotional needs.

"Try to limit visitors, keep Ratna busy with activities, and stay away from irresponsible public opinions into why and how the baby was lost. It does no good for this type of discussion to occur, at this critical time. The best I can say is that the baby was not physically able to survive in this world. If he had lived, then perhaps within a year something more drastic might have happened. We just never really know, but I would stay away from gossip. Keep Ratna surrounded by loved ones and keep her busy."

It was good advice Prakash thought, and he appreciated the kind yet honest words of the doctor.

Two hours later, the Murthys were packed and ready to go home. They squeezed into the back of the next cycle rickshaw and journeyed home.

Chapter Thirty-Two: The Exorcism

No sooner had they arrived home there was a knock at their front door. Ratna was in her bedroom resting, on strict orders from her doting spouse to not get up or busy herself with the household activities for a while. Prakash answered the door.

"Hello, brother, where have you been? We figured you were probably at the hospital since no one was home when we called on you earlier today, but we thought to try again after our breakfast. What's going on?"

Prakash invited his sister Lali and brother-in-law in and sat them down at the breakfast table. He explained, with a heavy heart, the turmoil and pendulum of emotions of his last twenty-four hours, from seeing his beautiful baby boy, to returning this morning to the hospital and discovering that his son was no more. Lali, Prakash's sister, held his hand and shed a tear.

"Why didn't you tell us? I could have come to the hospital yesterday, and stayed with Ratna," she expressed, frustrated and angry at her brother's loss. They sat together, trying to make sense of the tide of events. After a few minutes, Prakash collected his thoughts and inquired about Lali's visit. "What brings you and Rajanna here?" he asked. Lali and Raj shared looks of apprehension. Finally, she continued.

"We are having our baby Ravi's 'namakarna' naming ceremony next weekend and I wanted you to conduct it. I hope this is not too strange. You don't have to do it, we can call the priest."

"No, no, we should proceed. Little Ravi needs to be officially named and I would be happy to do this." Rajanna, at that moment, shook Prakash's hand while Lali stood up and proceeded towards Ratna's room. The women greeted each other and embraced. It was a different embrace, not their usual sprightly hugs but a soothing, gentle embrace as if to say, "I'm sorry you went through this." Though sister's-in-law, they were very close, probably the closest of all, and Ratna genuinely trusted Lali's compassion and intention. Lali sat for a while, then broached the subject of her son's upcoming naming ceremony.

"Would it be okay?" Lali asked. Ratna, very much on the same page as Prakash, took no time in responding. "Yes, of course!" the show would go on. Plus too, why should little baby Ravi suffer just because his aunt had not been so fortunate?

Prakash was up early the next Saturday morning and was taking his bath while saying prayers prior to sitting in service. Ratna, who normally would have been preparing sweets and snacks for the festivities, was busy cleaning her room. Her doctor and family forbade her from heavy activities. Instead, Lali's sister Shanti, who had travelled from Madras for the occasion, was helping in the kitchen, with the assistance of her maidservant.

"Hurry, Jaya, finish the cooking fast, the inauspicious time of 'rahu kala' starts in twenty minutes!" Shanti yelled at her. Far from the true meaning of her name, 'Shanti', or peace, she was a loud force, loving yet bossy and very rambunctious. But this was a welcome change for Ratna who was beginning to enjoy the comic relief. Plus too, Shanti was a loving aunt to Seetha and cuddled her endearingly like a doll.

"Oh, my, what's all the fuss for boys, I'd take a little girl to dress up any day!" she was often heard saying. Indeed, she had already spoiled her niece with a new party dress, lots of Tamilian sweets and even a doll of an intricate Bharatanatyam dancer, "straight out of Kalakshetra Dance Academy," Shanti had said. Seetha loved her aunt, and enjoyed being pampered in this way.

Twenty minutes later, Prakash dressed in his crisp white cloth lungi and scarf, sat down at the prayer area and began to chant. The rest of the family had arrived and now the small foyer was covered inch to inch with colorful people, seated on the floor cross-legged. Ratna was eager to join the throng but had been forbidden, being told that now was not yet the time for her to be celebrating, since she was still in mourning. She peered out from her bedroom door, cracking it ajar so that she could hear the beautiful rendition of mantras sung by her husband. His commanding voice resonated and was healing. Indeed, she felt lifted in spirits and happy that her husband was so gifted and kind. She could have created a fuss for him not to perform such duties, due to the recent demise of their baby, but she actually admired his kindred spirit and willingness to provide happiness to others even though he was suffering. That was a gift; being able to give even when you are spent. After an hour, baby Ravi was circled under and over his cradle several times by his other aunts, and blessings were conferred from well-wishers and godparents. The ceremony was now over, and the guests shared sweets and savories and then began their feast.

Later that day, as the crowd was dispersing, there was another unexpected knock at the door. Prakash answered, expecting some late attendees to take 'prasadam', or the religious offering and give blessings. He was about to explain that baby Ravi had fallen asleep and his parents were napping too, when he was taken aback by the presence of two more priests at his doorway.

"Hello, good sirs, what brings you here today?"

"We were asked to come by your community members and family. Where is baby Seetha?" they asked, rather sternly. Prakash questioned them but stayed calm, knowing that as priests they were to be respected at all times.

"I do not understand, please explain," he politely requested.

"You do not know? Your mother asked us to visit, to take off the evil eye that has afflicted your family of late." Murthy, puzzled, looked at his mother for answers and then responded.

"Please, I still do not understand the reason for your visit".

"Very well then, let us sit down and explain again, but we must get started quickly since time is running out. Your mother informed us that you and your wife have lost two full-term baby boys within the last two years. When things like this occur, we believe that an evil eye has been cast on you, causing your offspring to die. We are here to remove this evil eye. Please let us get started, unless you have any objection."

The two priests, dressed in black dhoti's and adorned with only grey ashes on their foreheads requested Prakash to bring his wife and young daughter to the prayer fire. Ratna and Prakash, still in relative shock, allowed the proceedings. Seetha sat cross legged in front of the fire, "just like a good student," she smiled, turning back towards her parents. A few long chants ensued and then the priests sat Seetha in front of them, with her back turned. Taking a long chain out from their loins, they proceeded to beat the child several times. Ratna began to scream.

"Stop this, Prakash, I cannot bear this. What are they doing to my child?" she cried. Tears ran down Seetha's pink cheeks as the pain of the metal chain hit her and scarred her skin. "Stop, Stop!" Ratna yelled, her cries dulled out by the louder chants of the priests, who appeared to be ignoring her. It was as if they were used to this scene, with other unassuming parents yelling at this atrocity. Prakash was confused as to what to do. He was a pious man and didn't want trouble. But now, his only child was being beaten. Ratna rushed towards her child and placed her body as a barrier in-between the chain and her child's back. The one older priest pulled her off, and beckoned Prakash to hold her back. Just when he was about to intervene, he recognized the mantras that signified the end of the prayer service.

"I think they are done now," he consoled his distraught wife, stroking her shoulder from behind.

"They'd better be," Ratna fired back, " or else they will be the cause of my only child's death. We have suffered so much, why are they killing my living child?" she sobbed.

The priests, now ending their rituals, took some ashes and the chain, and walking the entire perimeter of the house from inside and out, dropping Holy water as they went.
Prakash closed the door behind the men as they finished. Prakash turned his gaze towards his mother, staring her down with his angry eye.

"So, I guess what I can make of that is they believe that Seetha has caste the evil eye so no future baby is surviving. Thus, they beat her back to exorcise the evil within her."

"That's nonsense!" Ratna yelled, something so rare for her that her voice was cracking. "I will not forgive you for this!" she added, turning back to look at her mother-in-law and then taking little Seetha in her arms to the bedroom where the two wept in unison.

Chapter Thirty-Three: Mysore 1952

" Upala Amma, look, look!" Seetha shouted loudly, rushing in the door from school. " Come and see what I won today!" She was holding a chocolate ice cream on a lollypop stick and waving it in her left hand, right shoulder lifted as she steadied the heavy school backpack over her shoulder. As she enjoyed her moment, aunt Upala came rushing towards her. "Well, well, what do we have here?" she questioned, her voice thick and crackly from a congenital cleft lip.

"My teacher gifted me this ice cream since I scored top marks on my sixth grade math test!" She was thrilled. Upala, her aunt, was proud of her. But, most astonishing was that Seetha was a mere seven years old yet had mastered elementary schoolwork already and was jumping ahead of her peers in leaps and bounds.

"Congratulations little one!" she said endearingly. However, her attention was on the melting ice cream and her recently washed floors. "Hurry up and finish it off or else I shall have to throw it away," she commanded. Seetha tried to eat her ice cream quickly, but she was easily distracted by the footsteps she heard on the path outside her aunt's bungalow. Turning to look at the doorway, she quickly swung. The backpack slipped off of her shoulder. Now, the weight of her book-filled bag toppled the oozing ice-cream cone onto the tile floor. Upala, impatient as ever, started on one of her rants. It seemed to go on for hours.

"Haven't you learned anything from me?" she asked. "One thing at a time. Be mindful. Haste makes waste. Now we have a lot more cleaning to do thanks to your irresponsible behavior. You need to listen more and talk less. You need to eat tidily. You have a lot to learn, young Seetha. Wait till I speak to your mother!" When Upala upbraided Seetha, or anyone for that matter, her speech was unintelligible. Indeed, many neighbors without medical knowledge often mistook her for mentally impaired. Upala didn't let this bother her anymore. She had become used to her freedom now, no longer expecting a prince in shining armor to come into her life. She was an independent woman and enjoyed managing her own home, with the blessings of a caring younger brother and loving sisters. They would send their children over to spend time with Upala, so that she had company most of the year. She was also a talented cook, a passion that she would readily share with her friends and family, rather than eat alone.

The footsteps quieted down for a moment. Seetha and Upala were down on their hands and knees, wiping the floors together. But, a surprise visitor entered, causing Upala to fall back lightly onto the floor from the squatted position she was in.

"Hi Akka, surprise!" he yelled, gleaming from ear to ear and offering his elder sister a hand to pull herself up with. "Eh, Giri honey, how come? What brings you here? No telegram? What a marvelous surprise! Indeed, my legs are wobbly! Let's sit down and have some Mysore Coffee. What can I give you to eat? You must be famished after the long journey. I want to hear every single detail. Don't leave anything out," Upala demanded, hugging her brother and stroking his arm. Seetha, who had finished cleaning her ice-cream puddle, was now tugging on her uncle's suit blazer and found his hand dangling, which she promptly held.

"Giri Uncle, did you bring anything from Scotland back for me?" she inquired, curiously.

"Wow Seetha, what an amazing memory you have!" he exclaimed. "How did you remember that I was in Scotland?" He leant down and picked Seetha up in his arms, cuddling her before swinging her gently onto her seat at the dining table. Upala, a phenomenal cook and host laid the table with snacks, coffee and sweets, all homemade. It was a feast for Giri who, living abroad for his medical studies some years, had craved home food but not found anything to his liking there. A strict vegetarian, he had to concede and start eating egg, just to expand his diet with protein or risk malnutrition. His parcel of Mysore pickles, chutneys and cod-belles, had finished within two months, so for the remaining ten months he survived off of vegetarian soup cans, and the odd dried peas or beans and rice packet that he could find when he journeyed to London for conference work.

"Akka, how come little Seetha is with you?" he inquired.

"Oh well, you know Ratna is due for her next child and, thinking Seetha was taboo they asked for her to come and stay with me for the school year. So far it has faired well. She's a bright, helpful child; no trouble really. Plus, too, it's fun having some company around the house. She's a fast learner and is eager to do work in the kitchen. How about you, Giri? Are you here for good, or just for vacation?"

Giri grabbed another cod-belle, popped it in his mouth and then began reciting his itinerary for his summer in India. Upala tried to keep up, but seemed only to remember the words "surgical extern," and "hands-on experience," mentioned many times. He was a precocious student and was on his way to becoming a fine surgeon. Upala was simply thrilled to be surrounded by her loving brother; the house was full of life. She would prepare a feast for dinner and then plan the week.

A few days passed by; Upala and Seetha were in the kitchen working on some Indian sweet pies for the upcoming festival. Seetha would roll out the dough and cut it with a mold, while Upala stuffed the dough pocket, and then crimped the sides until a beautiful crescent moon shape was formed. The filling was a sweet blend of raisins, coconut and cardamom with sugar. Seetha loved the process and how pretty the final product looked. As the first batch of delicacies spluttered and shone a brilliant golden brown, Seetha danced in her spot, standing on tiptoe to see the sweets.

"Upala Amma, can I have one? Are they done? Do you need a taster?" she asked. Upala, growing impatient at her niece, tilted her body so that Seetha's view of the stove was blocked. She retorted, unkindly,

"Good girls do not taste the food while in the midst of cooking preparations. We taste only at the end of the process." Seetha continued her work, rolling out the pastry dough and cutting it into circles. Her aunt stuffed the dough with the sweetmeats and then closed and crimped the crescents again. When the oil was ready Upala carefully placed the sweets into the oil and watched them crackle again. Seetha, growing restless and hungry, sneakily took a 'cadgadbu' from the ready pile, and sank her teeth into it. It was scrumptious! The beautiful blend of sweet and savory played nicely in her mouth, and she savored every moment.

"They're yummy, Upala Amma, you are the best chef!" the child exclaimed, wiping her mouth with her scarf edge. Upala however, was not so thrilled by the praise. Instead, she grabbed her frying ladle and proceeded to wave it at young Seetha such that only a couple of inches separated the ladle from Seetha's nose.

"No means no! Doesn't your mother teach you anything?" she hollered, unaffected by the tears that were now rolling down Seetha's young face.

" I just wanted to try one," she confessed, sobbing terribly. "I'm hungry too. We've been working for hours," she added. Upala proceeded to upbraid the child, leaving no stone unturned. Finally, when all of her own anger had been thrown onto this child in a fit of rage, Seetha ran out of the kitchen and hid in her bedroom, crying herself into a deep sleep.

A few hours later Giri returned home from the teaching hospital close by. He greeted his sister, and taking off his shoes he entered the bungalow. After washing his face and sitting down at the table, he inquired as to the whereabouts of Seetha. Upala explained what had transpired.

"Akka, you know you are too harsh. Why didn't you just let her eat? She's a mere child of eight years only. She cannot understand patience, particularly on a task like cooking."

"I don't know what came over me. All I do know is that I cannot stand it when things do not go according to schedule. Things need to go according to plan. It irritates me when kids make a mess, or pick at their food and clothes in the midst of important tasks. I just can't stand it," she explained.

"Akka, you have to realize that she has a lot of growing up yet to do. You cannot scare her like this. She will think all adults are bad people. Or even worse, she could become like you! Just try to relax!"

"How am I to do that? It is not as easy as it looks. It takes me longer to correct all the mistakes of others than to just do it myself, yet I think I am being patient in teaching her. I'm doing a favor for my sister, you know. It is not easy. Where did I go wrong?"

Giri paused, reflected, but then proceeded. "Akka, if I tell you something, you will be upset, but I believe it needs to be said."

"Go on," Upala said.

"You are rather obsessive-compulsive and you enforce some very rigid ways on those around you. Most people are not like you and do not need things to be exactly perfect. Although this works for you, it is damaging on others on whom you push it. Take Seetha, for example. She is a young child. Words of encouragement would go a long way at this age. Yet, you chose to scold her for something as mundane as eating in between tasks. I think you need to work on your nature. I think you also possess a lot of underlying anger at the world outside. Perhaps this is due to your inability to marry from your cleft palate affliction. If you recognized this, you would try to make the world a better place. But, instead, you get even angrier with others and their imperfections. You are not very accepting. I do not know why you choose this path, but it is not too late to change it. I know the goodness within you, and I want you to get better. Please try, or else I will take Seetha back to Bangalore with me when I travel there this week."

Upala, initially stunned by the accusations, softened. Listening intently, she nodded, and chose not to speak further. Instead, the siblings gazed at each other, in silence. For a few moments, the silence was awkward, but then little Seetha awoke and ran into her uncle's arms at the dinner table.

A few months later and the news arrived via telegram that Ratna and Prakash had given birth to a healthy baby boy whom they had already named Nilkanth. Upala was thrilled. The surprises continued when there was an unexpected knock on the door. It was an impromptu visit from her elder sister, Sunela along with Seetha's favorite cousin Kalyani, who ran in to Upala's home with a suitcase full of homemade sweets and savories to celebrate the new family member. The sisters chatted while the cousins played. Upala came to know that another baby, too, had been born in Bangalore. This time, it was Prakash's sister, Lali, who had delivered a son on the same day as Ratna. The households had celebrated grandly, with sweets all around. Seetha wondered when she would be able to visit her new brother, but consoled herself with the knowledge that she still had school to finish and many examinations, which, in her standard, were getting pretty challenging. Kalyani, who was also a voracious reader, understood. The cousins, identical in age, related to each other well. Kalyani gave Seetha all the details of how her baby brother looked and what preparations were being made for the newborn's 'Namakarna' naming ceremony. They chatted all night, until their aunt came in and turned out their light.

Chapter Thirty-Four: Nilkanth, Bangalore 1953

The naming ceremony had gone off without any obstacles and now the joyous parents celebrated their family, with elder sister Seetha at Nilkanth's side. The family was happy to be together again. Seetha had completed her school year in flying colors, and was back home for the summer now that the 'coast was clear'. The infant had done well that year too, without any health problems to scare the paranoid parents. In fact, Ratna was embarrassed yet thrilled to let Prakash know that, indeed, she was expecting their next child by the end of the year, according to the doctor. She had been too engaged in the welfare of her infant that she had completely ignored the common signs of pregnancy such as fatigue, nausea and breast tenderness, putting these symptoms off to postpartum fatigue, nursing pains or anxiety. But Dr. Bhatt had confirmed Ratna's pregnancy earlier that week, and reassured her that the pregnancy appeared to be going along quite normally.

Later that week, Ratna, thrilled with her news, took her children for a walk in the park where she was to meet her sister-in-law, Lali, along with her newborn. When she arrived at the park and walked Seetha to the small merry-go-round, she tracked the park. Lali was nowhere in sight.

"Oh well," she sighed, "Lali will be here soon with cousin Ravi whom you can play with. For now, carry on alone. I will be sitting on the bench with your brother, watching you."

About half an hour later, Lali finally arrived, arms tiring as she pushed the stroller in one hand and held Ravi's in the other. She apologized profusely for her late arrival.

"Let me explain. I had baby Shiva's doctor check up this morning. I didn't think it would take long. But, when I explained to the pediatrician that Shiva had been slow to roll over, not laughing or smiling and often appeared limp, he wanted to examine him in detail. He," she hesitated, a small tear dropping from her dewy eyes, "He thinks Shiva is not normal. Like he has a birth defect or mental problem. He just says we have to wait and watch him grow. Only time will tell."

"I am so sorry to hear this," consoled Ratna. "But, we cannot believe everything this young doctor says. You know he doesn't even have children, right? Perhaps he is rushing to judgment."

The women continued to chat, confide and offer support, while young Seetha played with her cousin Ravi in the park. It was a truly beautiful afternoon in Bangalore, with a most temperate climate and pleasant skies. The city, although popular, was not crowded and the neighborhood and locals enjoyed the beauty of the South, yet all of the amenities of a big city. They loved their town, and prided themselves in being from Bangalore. Indeed, the Bombay movie industry had long since picked up on Bangalore's vast beauty and film studios and movie shootings had already taken place.

Ratna and Lali sat gazing at their children, enjoying the moment.

Months past and seasons changed. Soon, Ratna was off to the hospital again, for the familiar confinement of labor and delivery. Lali, hearing from her brother that Ratna was soon to deliver, came rushing to Prakash's side, eagerly. As the siblings waited in the hallway, Ratna hummed a lullaby, soothing herself into a hypnotic trance for the tiring finale.

"Push hard along with each contraction," the nurse was heard telling Ratna. "A few strong pushes and your newborn will be here." And he arrived. Baby Shiva, dark black eyes and strong eyebrows and hair, came rushing into this world. Prakash was thrilled. All the priests' talk about the 'evil eye' cast by the older sibling, yet here he sat, boy infant in one arm and toddler Nilkanth in the other. His life was complete. He had done his duty- healthy children and a beautiful wife. What more was there to achieve in life, he thought to himself.

Chapter Thirty-Five: Haasana

"Come quickly, the train is leaving shortly and we do not want to miss it," Prakash yelled from the bottom of the staircase at the children, slow to rise upstairs.

"Coming, Appa!" Seetha replied, rushing down in her new silky cotton maxi-dress, fresh and trim with neat plaits and jasmine flowers adorning her oil-treated, tidy hair. She had grown effortlessly over the summer holidays, and now her once childish smile had blossomed into a rosy glow. She was looking forward to her summer holiday with cousins in Haasana, with whom she got along royally. Also, her favorite cousin Kalyani was going to join her for a few weeks, and Seetha imagined the time she would spend chatting with her about college plans and music shows, all things she looked forward to with glee. Ratna came rushing down the stairs, hands full with jute bags filled with snacks to eat on the way, and some last minute additions to their suitcases.

"Hurry up, Nilkanth, I need you to bring Shiva and Apoorva down with you," she commanded. Now a full house, Ratna had Seetha, Nilkanth, Shiva and little Apoorva, who was already six years old.

"I'm not lifting her belongings," Nilkanth replied grumpily, "Apoorva has stuffed her bags too full. I'm not bringing them. You can if you want to."

"Why the fuss, Nilkanth, can't you just help Amma when she asks?" Seetha retorted, as she promptly ran up to assist her mother pack Apoorva's holiday bag and bring both Apoorva and Shiva down stairs.

"You can, you are the perfect one," he replied sarcastically, while combing his hair in the mirror and watching all the time for Seetha's facial expressions in the mirror.

Seetha chose to ignore her younger brother's comments, instead gracefully packing the remaining bags in the taxi and lifting Apoorva into the car. "Come on, it's time to go," she exclaimed with excitement.

"Akka, when are we going to get there?" Apoorva asked.

"Tomorrow. We are going to go on the night train, so we will reach Haasana in the morning. It's going to be lots of fun!" Seetha explained.

Prakash, who was taking time talking to the neighbors, explaining his family were leaving on holiday, now approached the car and got in the front seat. "All right children, it's off we go. I need you all to be alert and mindful. Do not leave each other. We are taking the night train to Haasana, from the train station. The platform is seven. You should not be alone, but for some reason if you get lost, look for platform seven. We are in car seventy, with cabin seats. Do NOT leave anywhere on your own!" Mr. Murthy warned his children. The taxi pulled out from the Murthy driveway and slowly drove away.

The following morning, Ratna took out her snacks of savory peanut chips, rounds of crispy fried bites and lemon rice, and served the family a picnic breakfast. The train had stopped at a large station for some minutes, and during this break, the snack cart seller entered. "Coffee, coffee", "all fruit-mix" he yelled. Prakash called for coffee for he and his wife. After breakfast, they freshened up, taking turns to visit the washroom. Only Nilkanth lagged behind.

"Come on, sleepyhead," Shiva teased, but it was to no avail. Nilkanth lay on the bed, covered in a blanket and not eager to move.

"Go away," he replied. His voice was sullen, yet soft. The rest of the family, used to Nilkanth's moody demeanor, didn't flinch. But, when Ratna called the children to prepare to disembark, Nilkanth still lay motionless.

"Something's wrong," she whispered to her husband, "He's never so still. Can you check on him? Maybe he's not well." Murthy rushed towards his elder son, while Ratna got down onto the platform, with luggage and kids in tow.

"Son, can you tell me what is happening to you?" the father questioned.

"Appa, I cannot breathe," Nilkanth replied, barely pushing the words out of his chest. Prakash lifted his son and carried him off of the train. Luckily, Ratna's youngest brother had come to greet them. Seeing young Nilkanth in his father's arms, Arun called for one car to go straight to the local medical clinic, and the other's to go straight home. Ratna was anxious to accompany her son, but realizing that her brothers were present, one a physician, she determined it would be better she rushed home to settle the rest of the family.

In the one hour that transpired between getting off of the train and reaching the hospital emergency room, Nilkanth had turned more limp and now was in a cyanotic state in respiratory distress. His face was puffy from trying to breathe, but it looked as if his lungs were failing him. He had no strength to talk, let alone sit upright.

"Mr. Murthy, I'm happy you brought Nilkanth when you did," Doctor stated, as he came to the side of Nilkanth and shook hands with him. " You were lucky," he went on, " I believe your son has diphtheria and is struggling for air due to the infection's control on the lungs. He is lucky to be alive. We will need to watch him here for a few days. If he continues to do well, turning this grave corner, then we can send him home, knowing that he will be in your brother-in-law's watchful care. For now, I have given him some medicines and I am hoping that the chest therapy, saline intravenous, plus antibiotics, will help his lungs heal." Prakash thanked the doctor on call, but then sat down besides his son and dropped his head into his hands.

"What's happening to my boys?" he sighed to himself. It was a recurring thought, something that he couldn't help but ponder over. After a few shed tears and a few mind games, he buckled up, tucking his shirt and sitting tall. He studied his son, who was now asleep, lying fairly peacefully in bed, with intravenous infusion running and monitors in place. Prakash prayed for good health more than anything else.

"Let my children live long, and have good health. Let them not be riddled with pain and suffering. This is my prayer." Kissing his son's forehead he left, as the night nurse advised the child no longer be disturbed.

Prakash was greeted by hugs and kisses from his family as he entered the Haasana home of his brother-in-law.

"Appa, is he going to be all right?" questioned little Apoorva, tugging her father's shirt.

"Yes, rani, he will be fine. The doctor wants to monitor him closely since his breathing was very shallow earlier in the day. We just have to wait and be patient. Anyway he is very tired, so staying in the hospital is a good idea."

"He's a dumbo," smirked Shiva, while running around tossing a ball up and down in the air.

"Shiva, that is no way to talk about your brother," Ratna scolded gently.

"But Amma, he never listens to us. Seetha Akka told him just last week to cut his nails because they were dirty. He ignored us. I told him last month to play cricket with me, and come out and get some fresh air, yet he refused. Now he's the first one of us to get sick."

"One day you two will learn to stop fighting and to take care of each other. For now, be thankful that he is going to be all right."

There was a loud ring of the doorbell. The maidservant headed towards the door but Seetha made it there first.

"Yay, Kalyani's here!" she exclaimed. The cousins greeted each other with hugs and kisses. Dodamma, Seetha's maternal aunt, came in neatly and gave her bags to the maidservant to put away.

"How are you Seetha rani?" she inquired, adding, "You have blossomed. You are looking like you mother," she complimented. This was well taken, since Dodamma was not one to praise undeservedly. Seetha was happy to have her favorite cousin to play with, chat with and confide in. As the youngsters played carrom in the sunroom, Seetha and Kalyani sat on their grandmother's four-poster bed, under the mosquito net, and chatted as if they had years of gossip to share and advice to offer each other.

Later, at the dinner table, Ratna and her sister and brothers caught up on all the fun times, and the difficult ones. Indeed, there was a lot to share between them. They exchanged opinions on Giri's surgical residency completion in North America, and his marriage which, till now had been kept "hush hush" from them.

"It's an American you know," they whispered, waiting for each other's opinions before offering up their own.

"You know, if they really love each other and look after each other, what difference does it make? After all, he is settling in America anyway," Ratna said.

"No, no, that's not right," contradicted Sunela, who was much more conservative in nature and didn't mind speaking her mind on her political and societal views. "What will the community say? What about us? Do you think he will care to visit us if his wife doesn't want to visit India? And what of his responsibilities here? Mother is still alive, then there's Chickakka in Mysore, who needs her supportive brother. What about all of that? Do you think he should simply forget us all and stay in America? I don't think that is right. He has a duty towards family. That's what our Appa used to always say. Family first. Blood is thicker than water. We need to always take care of each other. Brothers take care of their sisters –that is just how it goes. I don't see how this situation is acceptable."

"You can't expect everyone to do everything correctly all of the time, Akka," Haasana brother, Arun responded. "Look at his life. He has worked very hard and is now successful in his career. He has made us proud. Now, perhaps, he likes a woman. Life is different there. But, we cannot assume that living there takes his values and beliefs away. We just do not know. Hopefully one day, we will meet his woman. Then, we will discuss this again," he added, with a twinkle in his eyes.

"Well, let's talk about something closer to home, Guru, Sunela's husband, joined in. "Look at our girls, they are growing up. It's time to plan their college life and then find their life partners. Have you started to look at prospects?" he inquired. The two sisters, rather shocked, gazed at each other and then looked back at their brothers.

"Seetha is so young. She has to go to college yet. I haven't thought about it much. Definitely after she finishes college, but now, she is barely fifteen. She's too young. Kalyani too, is just fifteen," Ratna added quickly.

"But Akka, Seetha has already completed twelfth standard. She's already perceived as an eighteen year old, so what is the harm of looking now?"

"Don't be silly!" Dodamma scorned her younger brothers. "My Kalyani will be studying a lot. She won't be in the marriage market till at least completing her Master's degree. What's the hurry?"

"Wow!" Arun exclaimed. "You surprise me, Akka. In this day and age when are girls left unwed for so long? How long do you want to wait anyway?"

"As long as it takes to find someone good enough for my girl!"

The siblings cackled and jested, enjoying each other's company in a manner quite similar to their children, who were still gossiping in the bedroom.

PART THREE

Chapter Thirty-Six: Head Boy. Hyderabad, 1955

"Moggu, you're off then? Do write to Amma everyday, I will miss you too much," cried Vanamali, tears beginning to roll down from her almond eyes. "And don't forget to study hard!" she commanded, smiling and stroking her son with the pride of a lioness with her cub.

"Anna, why do you have to go? Can't you study here in Hyderabad? We have the best universities!" Uma cried. She dreaded being alone in the large house, with aging parents who did not really identify with the ways of the changing world. Baba, who was still sitting at the dining table eating his breakfast and drinking coffee, turned toward his daughter.

"Uma, don't you start fretting over Murali too, he will miss the train at this rate!" She hugged her brother, eagerly waiting for the slightest facial expression to acknowledge how she loved her elder brother. They were close siblings, always looking out for each other no matter what happened. Murali returned the hug with a wink, replying with a whisper in his sister's ear, "guess you're left holding up the fort now…. Sorry! You can write to me and update me on Amma and Baba's antics, while I move on into the real world!"

"Anna, don't say that!" she responded, "they are not so bad you know!"

Murali chuckled.

"Yes, right. I'll remember your words when I'm partying at the Institute and you and Dad are distributing more pamphlets on Peace and Freedom. Good luck with that!" he added, sarcastically.

"You know, you have to give Dad a lot of credit. He struggled for our future and at least is brave enough to continue on with his principles. Who else has done that? In fact, many of early Gandhi followers took money and political positions, yet our Dad stayed strong with the goal of Satyagraha. Even after "Freedom" and Independence of India occurred, he continued to fight a peaceful battle when others fell to the wayside. He's a Hero, Anna."

"Blah, Blah, Blah, save it for the jury. As far as I'm concerned I'm getting the hell out of this small town and off to bigger, better pastures. Thanks to Dad and Mum's freedom battle do you realize that we had nothing? I was never gifted anything fancy. We had to grow up practicing what Baba preaches. How is that fair? When I'm a father I will at least allow my children to make their own minds up about their political views and religious views rather than force it down their throats. It's all right to own something that is not made out of khadi cotton, you know!"

He was bitter, having suffered many nights alone studying till late, while Baba was off putting out skirmishes and representing the freedom party, as the peacekeeper. Now, at seventeen, Murali had decided enough was enough. He had devoted his student life to being the best, and had accomplished just that. He had studied so hard that he was awarded Head boy status in his school, and had achieved top honors in academics. He was on his way. He had already received admission to Kharagpur's prestigious Indian Institute of Technology, College of Engineering, an elite 'ivy league of the East', where only seventy of the best future engineer's from around the country were allowed admission. Vanamali was so proud she couldn't help but boast from time to time at her sisters-in-law who had so often made her feel inferior. But now, as the time to say goodbye to her beloved Moggu was fast approaching, she felt queasy and tearful.

Murali hugged his mother tightly, a rare moment in the Ramaswamy household, where displays of affection, even between mother and child, were considered immature. As they looked at each other face to face, they knew that they would not see each other for some time. Murali stroked his mother's hair, gently.

"Don't forget to oil your hair. And, make sure Uma takes you to the pool to swim every week. And, don't worry about sending me food at the dorm. I don't need it. It will spoil anyway till the time it reaches Kharagpur. Tell Dad to focus on Uma's studies now, and not so much on other people's disputes. She needs him. She's not as good a student as I", he added, pinching Uma on the cheek and receiving a blow with her magazine in response.

Baba finally arose from the dining table. "It's time to leave, Murali. Are you fully packed?"

"Yes Dad", Murali replied. With a final circle of hugs to the family and a prayer to Venkateshwara at their household prayer altar, they left from the front door and were off.

"Boarding platform six Calcutta Express train. Five minutes till departure!" bellowed the conductor. Murali carefully hung his backpack from his right shoulder and placed his suitcases down on the floor. He felt for his ticket in the breast pocket. Pulling it out carefully, he studied it slowly.

"Platform Six. Off I go!" he said to himself. He did not turn back to look at his father, who was several feet away now, having let Murali run ahead to confirm the train. As he hopped on to the train, a coolie lifted his luggage on the carriage behind him, and hopped on too, assisting the young man to his cabin.

"Sir, is this seat good?" the coolie questioned, knowing full well that the cabin selection was already assigned, yet pressing on for hope of a bigger tip. Murali took out his shiny wallet, a gift from his family for his college admission, and tipped the coolie, who left gracefully, saying "Thank you, Saab." Murali was eager, full of anticipation for his upcoming interview. He had Kharagpur orientation already, but had chosen to apply for the Indian Air force Academy, and had been selected for an interview the same week. He had opted not to tell his parents, for fear of unnecessarily worrying them to no avail. He was confident. He had studied all year, and was familiar with not just academics, something he excelled in, but also airplane safety, mechanics, flight instructions, just incase the interviewer would question his knowledge at this age. This was all he had ever wanted to do - fly planes on missions. He fancied himself for a top fighter pilot. Often, he consulted his elder cousins who were already in the army or military, and were fast moving up the ladder. How he admired them. Now, he hoped to bring glory to his family through service to India. Cousin Mohan had been his greatest influence, sharing with Murali his own escapades and experiences in the force. It sounded so amazing, and what an honor. Baba, who was not one to fight, had not really done anything to encourage or discourage Murali. This had frustrated the adolescent, who had taken to hanging out with his friends and listening to the radio, reading newspaper articles, and playing with planes and kites, imaging that their expertise would save the day. Murali was, after all, a World War II child, having grown up during such turbulent times. He wanted to serve his country.

Murali was slowly lulling into a soft sleep, when he reminisced over a time, some years prior, when he and his best friend Putty were flying kites during the kite festival season. He was winning, and wanted to win again the following day. So, the young boys had gone to the market, brought eggs from his friend's restaurant, and cracked them, to separate the whites. Murali had used the egg whites to coat the kite strings, thus making them stiff. The boys had hoped this would lead them to a win. On the practice flight, they had been successful. Jumping for joy, the boys had returned to the market again, buying a couple more eggs for the following day. Murali had placed them in his pocket and run home in time for dinner. As Vanamali grabbed him to see where he was off to in such a hurry, he had bent down to hide the pocket, which was bulging from its burden. At that very moment, the eggs had cracked and were running down his legs! Oh, what a sticky mess! Chuckling at the scene that followed in his head, he nodded off to sleep.

The train came to a screeching stop at Calcutta's central depot. Murali grabbed his luggage and disembarked. He was a bit apprehensive, being alone in a big, crowded city and not sure of where exactly he needed to go. He pulled out his interview admission ticket from his wallet. It was stuck behind the train ticket so that the only words conspicuous were "11:00a.m." on the top right of the stub and then the word "simulation." Murali eagerly gleamed while studying the ticket, excited to finally be following his dream. As he scanned the platform for any signs of transportation to the military academy, he came across another befuddled boy, in a similar state of anxiety. The boys looked at each other, and smiled. With an immediate sense of relief, Murali approached the boy and shook his hand.

"Going to the Military Academy?" Murali asked.

"Yes, and I think I'm running late. What time's your interview?" Mandeep asked. "Eleven o'clock for the simulation, and the written test is before. They've just requested I reach the exam room thirty minutes prior to scheduled exam time. I think I'm doing okay on time, but I have no idea how to get there," Murali responded. He felt better already just from having company. The boys helped each other with their luggage. As they were chatting, Murali suddenly stopped mid sentence and froze, glaring at Mandeep.

"What's the matter?" Mandeep asked.

"I...I, I have left my academy uniform on the train. I forgot all about it since the coolie that helped me board kept it on the upper bunk that was vacant. I need to run and get it otherwise the academy will disqualify me!" Running towards the front of the train, where his cabin had been, he tumbled on a small sack that was laying in the platform. He lifted himself up, seeing the train in his sight, smoke flowing from the spout of the engine as it fired up.

"Oh my God!" Murali exclaimed, as he realized that he had no time to make it. Nonetheless, he jumped up with all his might and leapt towards the cabin entrance. He was not fast enough. The train was now moving slowly. He didn't give up. He continued to run forward, hoping he would catch the attention of someone who would see him and stop the train. He ran further, lunging forward to the front driver. As he did so, the engine workers saw a boy trying to board the train. Startled, and fearful of a runaway, they flipped around, shovel and coal in hand. As they swung, a handful of coal pieces flew from the shovelhead and landed directly onto Murali's red face. As he yelled in pain from the burning heat, he gently fell backwards, tears pooling in his eyes and cheeks searing in pain. The conductor, by now, had stopped the train abruptly. Mandeep made it to his friend's side, aiding him. A medic had been called and Murali, now the center of unwanted attention, lay surrounded by people in all directions. Finally, the train conductor, who had gone to the boy's original cabin, came with the suit carrier in hand, containing a beautifully pressed military cadet suit. "All's well that ends well", Mandeep exclaimed.

"Er, if you say so", he said. Silently, Murali wept an extra tear.

"What's the matter?" Mandeep inquired.

"I can't see anything. My eyes are so swollen and we have a simulation test to take in two hours. I'm not going to pass."

"Well, at least you have the outfit. And you have the written test. Just wait, maybe the medic will give you something to help."

The following morning Murali sat patiently outside of the exam room where he had taken two tests already. He was tired now from the busy schedule, and the eye strain from the previous day's escapades was beginning to weigh on his mind.

"Oh well", he thought, "it's better to have seen it through, than given up beforehand." About ten minutes passed by. It seemed like eons. He could hear the chimes of the large grandfather clock's pendulum, swinging back and forth. The corridors of the institute were surprisingly quiet, in spite of classes being in session. Murali turned to look to his left and then right, scanning the hallway for signs of life. Another ten minutes nodded by, and Murali was beginning to doubt his prospects. He took out his handkerchief from his breast pocket, and wiped his brow. He was tempted to get up and search for somebody to ask about his status, but just as he thought it, a senior looking gentleman was seen marching towards Murali.

"Master Ramaswamy?" the man addressed him. "Yes, sir," Murali replied, anxiously.   "Come with me." Murali obeyed, and walked swiftly behind the man, who was marching rather hurriedly. They entered an office and were greeted by another official-looking man. Murali recognized this man as the one who had proctored him during the simulation part of his entrance examination.

"Good morning, son, take a seat." The officer immediately began to address Murali, making him feel comfortable. "Son, let me just say that we were all very impressed by your academic ability and general knowledge. You will make a fine officer one day." He went on. "You scored top marks in your written test, which is essentially unheard of when the examinee is an adolescent like yourself. Well done son, well done." Officer Malhotra proceeded, pacing up and down the long room, carefully marching with firm foot on the hardwood floors. He turned and finally sat down at his long mahogany desk. "Murali, you did not, unfortunately, perform as well on your simulation test." He studied the boy's face, trying to be gentle in his remarks. " Son, your simulation test was unsatisfactory. You were unable to steer your plane through tricky courses, and even the more easy pathways were trying for you. I see that your eyes are swollen. Did something happen to you?"

Murali replied readily, eager for a second chance. "Yes, Sir, actually something did happen. You see, I had just disembarked from the train and was standing on the platform, when I realized I had left my uniform behind. The train had already started to depart so I ran swiftly towards the engine, but as I reached it some of the coal from the engine was accidentally flung into my face. My eyes were burned, Sir. Luckily, the doctor expected my eyes to make a full recovery, but thinks my skin burns will scar slightly. I guess it could have been worse."

The major studied Murali kindly. "Son, I'm afraid with our academy's caliber of applicants, your score ranked on the lower part of the curve. It will simply not be enough to admit you this year."

"But, Sir, I can take it again. My eyes will be as good as new in no time!", Murali interrupted.
"Well, I understand that you are highly capable. But, I also spoke to your father too. Aren't you already on your way to IIT Kharagpur? That's our nation's greatest engineering college. What a privilege. And, I hear you were first pick. Congratulations."

"Thank you, Sir," Murali replied, "But, Sir, if I may say, becoming an air force pilot from your academy is my dream. I want this more than anything."

"Son, I'm afraid to say, that it is not possible for you this year. Our classes start next week and the simulation part begins immediately." He saw Murali's countenance drop, as the excitement from adrenaline and hope dwindled into frustration. "Murali, young men like you should be very proud. You are our nation's future. I think you will fly high and gloriously. Finish your education. If flying means that much to you, then come back to the air force or army after completing your engineering studies. We could use your intelligence. But for now, I will have to ask you to leave. Move on to Kharagpur and have a great time. I believe your friend is waiting outside for you". He nodded, shook hands with Murali, and said goodbye.

As Murali left the academy, emotions that he had held back for years, came streaming through, just like they had when he was crying in pain the night before. He rubbed his face to wipe away the tears. As the white metal gate of the academy closed behind him, he saw Mandeep, his new friend, waiting for him.

"Hey, there, how are you?" Mandeep inquired.

"Terrible. My eyes ruined everything."

"Hey, that's okay, at least it's not permanent." Murali shrugged his shoulders, not sure whether to react with anger or to cool off. He took a deep breathe of air. Then, he turned to look at his friend. Mandeep was also looking glum, but had been kind enough to ask about Murali. Realizing he was being selfish, Murali switched the topic over to his friend. "How was everything for you? Did you make it?" Murali asked.

"No, not even close. I was average in both simulation and written test. The officers were actually pretty nice to me to actually sit me down and explain how I had done one on one. I don't know why I even bothered. I guess I've been reading too many war novels and I though I'd make a great fighter pilot. Oh well."

The boys paced the high street for a while. After snacking on some street foods and ice cream, and then roaming the streets, they finally decided to take a dinner break prior to going to the station and confirming their tickets.

"You know what stinks?" Murali confessed to Mandeep over the chickpea curry and fried bread platter. He returned to his Air force Academy disappointment. "He called my father. He actually called my father. I thought the office would let me know first. Instead he had already talked to Baba, who is probably mad as hell at me now for trying to enter the military flight academy. I can just imagine Baba talking the officer out of giving me a second chance, just because he's much more proud of having a son in I.I.T. than one who is involved with the military. I don't get it. Not everyone is going to end up being a freedom fighter. At least if you're a pilot you can rescue people and go on important missions. People don't always settle disputes over milk and cookies."

"Hey, there, calm down boy!" Mandeep exclaimed, patting his friend on the back. "From what you've told me about your father, he's truly a great man. You don't have to have the same principles and dreams to love each other and believe in each other. Plus, too, whatever it is, you are both brave for trying so hard at the things that mean a lot to you. But don't beat him up so much just because you are disappointed. Just choose to move onward, to better opportunities."
They ate and chuckled, staying up all night before finally deciding to get to the station again.

Twelve hours later, Murali was seated on the train to Kharagpur. He was bored, too buzzed by three cups of chai, to actually fall asleep, and his emotions still stirring from his disappointment the previous day. As the train approached a screeching stop at the next major station, a snack vendor got on.

"Chai garam, garam chai!" he bellowed. Later the boy, who looked a mere twelve years old, exclaimed, "All fruit mix! All fruit mix!" and " samosa, pakora!" The food aromas were enticing. The fresh fried fritters and spices overcame him and he quickly grabbed his wallet and beckoned the boy kindly with a grin. He paid two paise only, for one pakora, one samosa, and then a bit more for the Deccan Herald morning newspaper. He turned to the back page, as a usual habit, and started completing the crossword puzzle. Puzzles and logic problems were his thing, and he truly believed that if it were not for his uncanny ability to solve every logic problem known to students his age, he probably would have been passed up at I.I.T. However, he was a topper. Nothing or no one could stop him when it came to academics. It was so easy for him that the nights prior to finals he was usually found in the local movie theater, "taking it easy". He moved along the down and across clues for the puzzle, choosing to pick "9A" to start.

" Our nation's leader in the fight for freedom; a great man. Seven and Six." Murali paused for only a second before filling in " Mahatma Gandhi. "Hmmph," he sighed. He looked out of the window as if to find an image to calm his mind from the emotions that he was feeling. "Can't understand why we believe that Ghandiji is the only solution to India's problems. Come on India. What about us youth? Do you think of us? One man cannot fight the battle alone. Even his army couldn't fight. We are independent but divided now. I just do not understand this country," he thought to himself. He had been building up angst towards the movement that his memories revealed, took his father away from his childhood. He tried not to feel so upset, but when he was alone he witnessed young families traveling together, a father holding on to his child as they enjoyed each other, and Murali felt deprived. Alone in his thoughts, Murali lulled into a soft sleep as the train took off from the station.

Chapter Thirty-Seven: Darkness falls

Vanamali was back to ordering around the maidservant, who was often frightened of her madam's moody moments. Kanchan, the new maid, had finished cleaning the kitchen and was now helping to prepare the menu for lunch.

"Cut the vegetables finely and don't mess up my countertops!" Vana yelled, not even making eye contact when talking. Kanchan nodded silently, then proceeded to follow the instructions given. Vana had now finished making her traditional raw mango pickle and lentil rice, and gave a few more instructions to Kanchan to complete. She left the kitchen, and headed to her bedroom to lie down.

"I cannot understand why I'm so tired," she said to herself, and lay down on the platform bed, wiping her forehead with her sari edge. She was not as energetic as usual and felt heaviness in her heart, now two children gone. Murali was gone, and Uma busy with friends and medical school. Baba was constantly preoccupied with the New India movement, and the couple had joked together that Baba was indeed married to the mission. But recently, Vana had felt her previously light spirited self was heavy, to the point of boredom. She couldn't shake the feeling. Her giggles that had become synonymous with her name were rarely heard, replaced with snaps and snide remarks, or apologies followed by silence. Vana had contemplated talking to her doctor about her mood swings, but her inner conscious had advised her this would be a bad idea. She imagined her in-laws somehow nosing into her business and finding out that she was seeking medical help. She continued to ruminate on her lonely empty-nester life, or dwell over the few caustic remarks she had made to poor Kanchan, just because she happened to be there. It was hard being without Baba for such lengthy periods of time. The nervous energy she had once felt when Baba was away now seemed to be turning into a major depression. She laid her head on the pillow, and closed her eyes, trying to not ruminate on her boy living far away, or her poor mother, who had refused to leave the vicinity of her home for years now. "Poor Amma," she thought to herself, recognizing that her own life was glamorous and happy compared to anything her mother had experienced. Hypnogogia weighed heavily as she closed her eyes and fell to sleep.

There was a harsh rap on the door. Vanamali, startled by the unexpected interruption, was apprehensive. "Hello, who is there?" she inquired, timidly.

"It's the postman, Mrs. Ramaswamy. You have a letter."

Vanamali opened the heavy door, and received the letter, then smiled and gently waved the postman goodbye. It was a small white letter, which she hurriedly opened with Baba's opener, conveniently hidden under the table lamp, just incase they suspected an intruder.
She wandered into her bedroom and sat down.

"Vana, it's Akka. I'm sorry, dear, but I must inform you that Appa died; Massive heart attack. Didn't even get to say goodbye. By the time you get this letter I will be reaching Amma's, so hopefully I'll see you there. If you cannot make it, I understand. Love, Manasa."

Vanamali dropped the paper knife and held her hands to her head. "Appa was only fifty-five or so. I don't understand," she cried. She laid her head back on the pillow and tried to get some rest, but she could not. Her mind kept on reflecting on her father, with whom she had tried so very hard to impress. "It's my fault," she told herself, thinking that if she had been a more impressive child, her father would have taken her and Manasa in, and even spent more time with Amma. Why? What had she done to deserve only the worst from her father, when the entire town knew him as the infamous lawyer? But as she tossed those thoughts in one corner of her head, others would arise.

"He was pure evil. Father succumbed to all the deadly sins and threw away what was pure. He did not deserve us," she concluded. "In fact, I am not going to attend the funeral. I don't care if he's gone; he did nothing for Amma or me. He was a rogue, a bully and a drunk. Who else would have all the wealth in the world but deprive his wife and children from those simple pleasures and pampering? He was evil." She continued to struggle, her night of fitful sleep, tossing and turning from anger and sadness, culminated with the early morning awakening by Birla Temple's bell ringing ceremonies at seven o'clock in the morning. Vanamali arose, wearily, shook her sari pleats, and stretched.

Chapter Thirty-Eight: Kharagpur, 1959

" You're a topper again T.R." his friend Satya exclaimed, tugging Murali on the sleeve. "Congratulations!" he exclaimed genuinely, shaking Murali's hand and then pushing him to the side, as he rushed towards other classmates.

"We are voting that you share your joy with a round of beer for us all!" Sandeep exclaimed, studying his friend's face closely to ensure he wasn't upset. After a few bated breaths, Murali turned and addressed his peers.

"Okay then, let's go!"

It was a joyous night. The 'freshers' prided themselves in their successful completion of semester one, and celebrated. It was the first time in a long while that Murali felt elation. There was a sense of freedom from convention or formality. Although he missed his family that night, he did not think once of heading back home to his parents. The only thoughts in his head were how grand it felt to be on top of the world. For once in his life he believed that his dream of being a famous engineer, would come true. It was in his reach; all he had to do was press on a little longer to finish his degree.

Much of Murali's college life mimicked that freshman semester. His success seemed to come with ease, with daily review of classwork paying off the week of final examinations. When others were cramming the night before their tests, he was in the movie theater relaxing his mind.

He sat in the theater one night, a year later, waiting for the movie to start. The headliner playing was "Ben Hur", already a phenomenal success in America. He waited for the movie with eagerness. The theater was quiet. It was a Monday evening. The movie was in English without subtitles. " Six o'clock national news headlines will precede the movie." Murali stretched his long legs in front of him and shifted in his seat. He removed his spectacles and wiped them with his handkerchief in preparation for the upcoming show.

Approximately thirteen hundred kilometers away, Baba and Vanamali too sat, in their local theater, watching the political news. The speakers bellowed:

"In the news: A Russian reporter who claimed to have witnessed Netaji Kekre still alive, has been found dead in a bus depot close to where he lived. At this time, the cause of death is not being revealed. India News reporters approached Nehru at his official residence earlier today, but he refused to comment on this matter. Also, the Shahnawaz Committee was asked to review the data for the purpose of Indian National interest. Lieutenant Colonel Rahman Khan, the sole survivor of the fateful plane crash, did issue a statement essentially repeating his oath of secrecy to his most trusted confidant and leader."

The couple was stunned and captivated by the ongoing conspiracy theories over Netaji's existence. "Maybe you should return to Calcutta to see if Choksi has a theory," Vanamali whispered in Baba's ear.

"Yes, that's not a bad idea!" Baba replied. Vanamali smiled, but secretly grinned with the realization that her husband was stuck in an era that had long gone; India was now independent, yet Baba and many freedom fighters and activists continued to dwell on that time. She closed her eyes for a moment and imagined what her boy would have said to the current news.

Back in Kharagpur, Murali was now becoming impatient.

"Not again!" he sighed, as the newsreel repeated the same headline in summary of the headline news of the day. "Let's get on with the movie!" he exclaimed.

Chapter Thirty-Nine: Bangalore, 1964

"Amma, I need the pepper spiced lentil soup to be perfectly peppered with coconut overtones. And, can you make mixed vegetable stew? We need a special dinner to celebrate exams being over, my first place ranking, and my veena recital success. Please Amma?" Seetha demanded, sweetly and happily, thrilled to be finally back home after months away from her Mom. Going away to college in Mysore had been tough on Seetha. She was already feeling so far removed in maturity and personality from her three younger siblings, but had missed her family all the same. She wished for her parents' undivided attention now that she was back home. She had risen to the challenge of attending college in Mysore, priding herself in the special relationship she shared with her aunt. In truth, suppressing the memory of the woman's oppressive, controlling, obsessive-compulsive nature was necessary now.

In fact, Seetha had changed. She remembered her innocence of middle school days, laughing over a teacher who stuttered or friend with whom she had crushed glass into a powder, hoping to make a diamond! Now, at a mere nineteen years old, she felt the pressures of adolescence and being the eldest child. She longed for carefree days where the plans for the day involved music or play, and she could giggle with her friends or cousins. But Ratna had already sent word to her sister, that Seetha, having successfully graduated with her degrees, was now of age to be married.

The hunt began. Prakash inquired about eligible bachelors, and the Indian marriage network unfolded like nowhere else in the world. Somehow, it only took a month before a pile of "candidates" had accumulated. On a daily basis, the local priest would stop by to review the prospects with Prakash and Ratna. Their topic of conversation revolved around Seetha and her horoscope.

"This boy seems highly suitable. Their charts match on most points, Prakashji. This is not easy to find. I think we should proceed, if you have no objections."

Seetha was apprehensive. She knew nothing of the ways of boys or men and the thought of marriage made her sick to her stomach. She went to the kitchen to help her mother make dinner, trying to not think too much about the plans for her future.

The following day the house was busy with action. "Come on Akka, hurry up, we need to leave NOW!!" Apoorva yelled at her sister who was in the bathroom still singing merrily while taking a bath. "Don't use up all of the hot water!" she continued.

An hour later, Prakash and his entire family were on their way to a wedding.

"Why are you all dressed up, it's not your wedding!" Shiv and Apoorva giggled, teasing their elder sister.

"Amma, tell them to stop bothering me, it's annoying. At least I know how to dress," Seetha responded.

"Children, quiet down now and don't trouble your sister. She has enough on her mind right now."

They entered the wedding hall. It was a grand event, but Seetha's younger siblings were more concerned with when it would be time to eat because they were famished. As the wedded couple took the oath of Saptapadi (seven steps around the sacred fire), some of the ushers directed the guests toward lunch and snacks. Apoorva, Nilkanth and Shiva rushed to the front of the queue with Seetha not too far behind, along with her cousin Kalyani. At that very moment, Prakash approached his daughter and beckoned her to follow. She did so, obediently, not knowing what the issue was. She observed Ratna happily chatting to her friends, in a group that included talking to a few elders whom Seetha did not recognize at all.

"Appa, who are those ladies?" she asked.

"Well, I am actually going to introduce you right now," Prakash responded in a somewhat jolly tone. He approached his beautiful wife and signaled her that Seetha was present.

"Ah, come Seetha, my princess! Let me introduce you to these aunties," Ratna said. "This is Vanamali aunty. She and her husband, T.K. Ramaswamy, have come for Naidu's wedding. They are visiting all the way from Hyderabad. They wanted to see you."

"Oh!" Seetha replied, a little taken off guard. She blushed, a second later realizing that the introduction probably was matrimonial related. But she remained pleasant, answering questions and meeting and greeting friends and family that she did know with respect and joy. Indeed, she was glowing. Adorned in a beautiful copper sulfate blue half-saree with a long braid and jasmine flowers, she was a natural beauty. She did not apply make-up on her face, since beautiful features and humility gave her classic appeal. A few minutes later, Ramaswamy arrived, sweetly smiling at young Seetha with delight.

"How are you, dear?" he asked. Seetha felt touched by his genuine concern for her, as if he already knew her and that she had recently returned home from college. She chatted with the

Ramaswamys for a while before her parents "released" her back to her cousins, while the adults continued their discussions.

"May we kindly request that you give us some idea now, so that we are not tense in the next few weeks?" Prakash asked Baba.

"Yes!" Baba quickly reacted. " We love her. Let's have Murali meet her and then we can set a date for their engagement."

And so it passed that the two were to meet. Murali returned home from Kharagpur the next week, and the parents arranged to meet in Hyderabad, thinking that Seetha would have more privacy away from Bangalore.

"I like the idea of a trip to Hyderabad, if you agree," Ratna stated. So the Murthy's were off, on a train ride to Hyderabad, while the youngsters stayed behind with their aunt.

"He's a good catch, Seetha," Ratna lectured to her eldest, discussing the importance of married life and the future ahead. "Plus his father is a highly respected man. He was a freedom fighter, and was instrumental in India's independence. He's from a good family, and is from our community. If you do not take him, then somebody else will, and then you'll be sorry."

"But Amma", she replied, " I know nothing about him. Does he sing, like I do? Does he perform religious rituals like Appa? Does he even speak Kannada? From the picture you showed me he looks British. He's not the only boy. What's the hurry?"

"Seetha," Ratna replied affectionately, " I think you're just nervous. Nobody is forcing you to do anything, but I know you better than anyone else and I feel strongly about this match. Even your horoscopes match. He is an IIT graduate and will give you a good life. It is time for you to marry and move on with your life. What better than to do so with the support of a life partner?"

As Seetha, Prakash and Ratna entered the Hyderabad bungalow, Baba ran out to the patio quickly to greet them. "Come, come, we are expecting you!" The Murthys entered the home to a very warm reception. As Baba's hospitality continued, Seetha observed her parents becoming relaxed within these strangers' home. She wondered what would happen next. She glanced around the house eager to see any signs of her prospective husband, but she didn't see anyone her age yet. Baba finally broke her silence as he began asking her questions about her degree. "Congratulations on your ranking. What do you plan to do now?" Seetha paused for a moment to look at her parents' expression, but then obediently replied.

"I want to go on with perhaps a Ph.D. The Master's program was rather straightforward, and I would like to advance further. However, I am ready to settle down too. I love to cook, and sing, and play the veena."

"Oh, you will love my daughter, Uma. She should be home any minute. You two will get on royally. She is just returning from medical school about now."

"Baba, when will your son be arriving?" asked Prakash, finally. It was the question everyone wanted to know the answer to.

"Oh, he is coming. He went to deliver some papers for me, and is expected shortly. Knowing Murali, he might even be picking his sister up and returning together.
Baba was right. Five minutes later Uma and Murali walked in merrily.

"Come, come my children," Baba requested. Vanamali, who was in and out of the kitchen preparing snacks and dinner, entered the living room and beckoned her son over to her.

"Moggu, come quickly and freshen up. Then go and talk to the Murthys; they have been eagerly awaiting you. Murali greeted his guests and then quickly freshened up. Seetha couldn't help but let out a smile widely after hearing Vanamali address her son so endearingly as "Moggu."

"So you heard that did you?" Uma, who had just freshened up and come to meet Seetha, spoke freely. "Oh, don't worry, I don't bite. I just think this is all so fantastic!" Uma exclaimed. "Now I have a sister to tease Murali with. He is such a geek you know!!!" Seetha's face relaxed, and she started glowing with her radiant smile, and began chatting with her would-be sister -in-law.

As Murali approached the living room, grabbing a cod belle before sitting down, Seetha noticed that his dress pants pocket looked full. She pondered, wondering if it was due to a heavy wallet, or, the more likely explanation, a pack of cigarettes. She looked at his smile, as Murali offered Seetha the tray of cod belles. "No thank you," she replied, inwardly wishing she could truly be herself and gobble up her favorite snack. His teeth were white, and his face white like a foreigner. He was tall, and well dressed. His shirt was crisply ironed with starch, and he wore a belt with his pants. Uma broke the silence, asking her brother to talk about something.

"Like what?" he replied, jovially to his younger sister, whom he doted over.

"Oh, I don't know. Tell Seetha what you do up there in IIT world, and what your interests are. She has already told us of her multi-talented self. She sings, and cooks perfectly and plays the veena, and she's a topper in University. What can you tell her? Come on, talk!" Uma demanded. Murali consented, and began discussing motorcars, his love of engineering and automotive design, and how he enjoyed puzzles and logic problems. He spoke only in English. Vanamali, entering the room to sit down and chat, discussed how her beloved son only studied in the best "English medium schools" and was head boy in the infamous Bishop Cottons' High School. She was truly proud of her son, whom she had raised with love through everything. Prakash was interested in Murali's education and was thrilled by his impressive degree, just like his eldest daughter. As they headed towards the dining table, Seetha, Baba, Ratna and Vanamali continued to discuss things, huddling around the coffee table.

"I think they are a good match for each other," Baba stated. "So, let's share sweets after dinner, and perhaps tomorrow we can have a small engagement ceremony, unless you had something else in mind." Prakash was thrilled, and he quickly agreed. The mothers embraced, and happily began discussing wedding arrangements.

After dinner, sweets were exchanged. "A round of kalakand from my favorite sweet!" Baba announced, and they fed each other in tradition of uniting families. A little later, the Murthy family took their leave, returning to the hotel close by to retire for the night.

The following day came quickly. Seetha and Murali exchanged rings and then garlanded each other. The rest of the Murthy children had arrived by overnight train with Prakash's siblings, while a few of Ratna's siblings chose to fly in. After a royal lunch, it was time to depart. Murali had to return to Kharagpur, and Seetha had to return to Bangalore to complete some music studies that she was enjoying with her aunt. She was a bit scared, not knowing at this point how soon the wedding would be. According to her mother, Murali needed to finish a few more things in Kharagpur. He was a new engineer at Hindustan motors, where he was soon to be moved to the head office in Calcutta. Seetha worried about this, having never moved out of Karnataka.

"Amma, what's Calcutta like?" she asked her mother. Ratna, sensing Seetha's apprehension, took her hand.

"It's fun. Some of our most famous poets and writers are from Calcutta. Take Rabindranath Tagore, for example. There's so much culture in Calcutta. There is also a strange blend of Western influence among deep-rooted Eastern tradition, which is a paradox; but works beautifully there. I think you will love it. Also, getting out of Karnataka for a bit will be good for you."

"But what if I don't want to leave Karnataka?" Seetha responded.

"Nonsense, you will love it. There's nothing to be afraid of. You will be a greater and stronger person in life if you fear not, but set out to new adventures. Now, you have a fine man as your fiancée, and you should follow him as he starts out his career. Everything will be an exciting adventure." At that moment, Apoorva and Shiva rushed in and sat on the bed.

"Amma, when is the marriage going to be? When is our brother-in-law coming to see Bangalore? Does he speak Kannada? I didn't hear him say any Kannada words when we met him. Is he really Kannada? Maybe he's English!!" The children laughed as Seetha pouted, eager to slap them but too conservative to even try. They teased her and she blushed, but eventually Ratna quieted them down.

Prakash returned home from his warehouse, beaming from ear to ear. "Ratna, the date is set. The horoscope and calendars both suggest that January is a perfect time. I will contact Baba and fix it up."

A few weeks passed, yet Prakash had not heard back from Baba regarding fixing the date. The Murthy's became a little nervous. The word had spread already within the family relatives, and people wondered why the marriage date was not yet set. Someone in the family rumored that Murali had been to see a distant relative for possible marriage. This only angered Prakash further. He reminded his daughter and wife to not be afflicted by doubt or fear, since he had the word of a noble man, Baba, and had no reason to worry. Seetha only had one picture, a black and white passport-sized photograph of Murali from his IIT graduation formal, which she showed to her best friends and cousins with glee. Yet, time passed on.

It seemed like ages but Friday, May thirteenth was the final date that the two fathers had settled upon, and it eventually came. Prakash had announced within his family that this would be the most lavish wedding in town. He was so proud of this day, and of his beautiful daughter, who had succeeded in meeting all of his expectations. The wedding hall was adorned with intricate flowers, and the musicians had been summoned from surrounding states. Even noblemen and dignitaries attended and blessed the happy couple. Apoorva, Nilkanth and Shiva were happily enjoying ushering in the guests and watching them intently, trying to make guesses as to which relative they were or whose side they belonged to. They screamed and giggled when their "Bhava" finally entered the wedding hall on route to the altar. He was tall, fair, with a small mustache and good posture, making him stand out in a crowd. He smiled on occasion, and looked slightly nervous as he tried to recognize his friends in the audience but saw so many new faces. His father and mother were already seated on the mandap and smiled joyfully as they saw Murali.

Baba looked so young, dressed in crisp white cotton kurtha shirt and pajama, with skin as white as an "Angrayzee," the term the locals would use for an Englishman. He was so handsome that many guests mistook him for the groom! Seetha, who could not yet see her fiancée, appeared frightened. She couldn't bring herself to smile, since a flurry of emotions had just arisen within her. She was leaving her family behind for life on the other side of the country, and the realization of this permanence set in. She had a pit in her stomach and, after hours of mantras already, she felt quite lightheaded. Her beloved cousin, Kalyani came to her side often, bringing requested items to the priest all the while smiling at the bride. She held the 'antarpatt" fabric veil between the bride and groom now, and winked a few times at her cousin gleefully. A few minutes later, the priest asked them to drop the veil and Seetha and Murali faced each other. It had been almost six months since the couple had set eyes on each other, and they gazed in each other's eyes with both fear and desire. Next was the garlanding, which occurred very easily since Murali stood a good foot taller than his new bride. The crowd laughed in unison, as the priest reminded the couple, jovially, that whoever was first to garland the other, would be the boss of the house. Finally, Seetha smiled at Murali, laughing at the improbability of a win on that one.

The priest continued, with the most beautiful sounding mantras. Seetha's parents had now left the mandap since the tradition of Kanyaadaan, or giving away the daughter was over. The 'mangalsutra' marriage necklace was tied on the bride and the couple then took the seven sacred circles around the fire.

A few hours later, Seetha changed into another beautiful zhari sari. She stood on the stage with her new husband. The young Mr. & Mrs. T. R. Murali greeted people at the receiving line, which seemed endless. Prakash proudly introduced his new son and daughter to a famous recording artist that knew and respected him. Then, other esteemed guests and loving family greeted them. So far, it was royal being Mrs. Murali. She struggled a bit keeping track of all of her father-in-law's sisters. But Uma, who was an absolute joy to be in the company of, helped her remember with little details. She would add funny comments that would tease her elder brother, cheekily mocking how he himself was terrible at names and at languages. Baba also, seemed to be already very proud of Seetha introducing her as their new daughter, someone to take care of the family, but particularly their son. She smiled in recognition of Baba's sweetness. Her mother-in-law on the other hand, seemed very quiet, in a shy way. She was kind, but had not been able to direct Seetha at all during the engagement or wedding functions. "I suppose it's better than her being a witch," Seetha thought to herself. She had observed Vanamali being pushed aside, often bossily, by some of Baba's sisters, and this bothered Seetha. She felt her mother-in-law was too soft, somewhat like herself. Perhaps they would get along just fine.

The couple was able to eat, finally, when the receiving line was over. They fed each other sweets and enjoyed some of the best cuisine in the whole of Karnataka. Seetha felt truly royal that night. Prakash was heard gleefully telling his own siblings that this was the most lavish wedding he would ever conduct. Ratna, noticing that her husband was in eves shot of their younger children, nudged him to stop. Apoorva looked up at her father, frowning. "Why does he keep saying that Amma?" she asked.

"Oh, I don't know," Ratna replied quickly, "He's just excited about his daughter and how everything is going on so well. That's all." Secretly though, Ratna pondered the knowledge that was deep in the pit of her stomach. Prakash's horoscope, which he himself had redone recently, confirmed that Prakash would not live long enough to marry off his other children. It was for this reason that he spent his entire savings on Seetha's wedding. He believed this ancient astrology culture, and had no doubts that this prediction would prove true...

The following morning the couple attended more rituals and ceremonies recognizing them as a married couple. She mingled with the new family, and sneaked glances at them, observing each one's style, whenever it was inconspicuous. She was nervous. Baba was seated at a wicker rocking chair, next to his brother, and brother-in-law Rai. They appeared to be in a heated discussion, albeit pleasant. Murali and Uma, eavesdropping on the elders, came to realize soon the topic that was so engaging. Uma picked up the newspaper that her father had set down on the coffee table, and approached her new sister-in-law. She grabbed Seetha's hand and led her into the kitchen.

"Sit, let's look at this together," Uma ordered. The ladies gladly sat and read the article together. Seetha read the title page, "Partition, by WH Auden". It was a poem that documented the offending blunder of Sir Cyril Radcliffe, who was responsible for drawing the boundary between Independent India and the newly created Pakistan. Seetha recited the poem in a loud whisper, easy enough to understand but still avoiding unnecessary attention.

Unbiased at least he was when he arrived on his mission,
Having never set eyes on this land he was called to partition
Between two peoples fanatically at odds,
With their different diets and incompatible gods.
"Time,' they had briefed him in London, 'is short. It's too late
For mutual reconciliation or rational debate:
The only solution now lies in separation.
The viceroy thinks, as you will see from his letter,
That the less you are seen in his company the better,
So we've arranged to provide you with other accommodation.
We can give your four judges, two Moslem and two Hindu'
To consult with, but the final decision must rest with you.'

Shut up in a lonely mansion, with police at night and day
Patrolling the gardens to keep assassins away,
He got down to work, to the task of settling the fate
Of millions. The maps at his disposal were out of date
And the Census Returns almost certainly incorrect,
But there was no time to check them, no time to inspect,
Contested areas. The weather was frightfully hot,
And a bout of dysentery kept him on the trot,
But in seven weeks it was done, the frontiers decided,
A continent for better or worse divided.

The next day he sailed for England, where he quickly forgot
The case, as a good lawyer must. Return he would not,
Afraid, as he told his Club, that he might get shot."

The ladies giggled with full knowledge of their spite of the lawyer, who had done no good with dividing their homeland.

"No wonder Baba was red in the face! This must have conjured up a lot of emotions! Oh well, now you get to leave and I have to deal with the folks!" Uma joked.

It was now time to leave, and after tears and kisses from her parents, and lots of pickles, and sweets, stuffing of suitcases and words of advice from her in-laws, the newlyweds were off to Calcutta. Uma had the last word before the couple boarded the plane.

"Akka, Murali Anna is terrible with names and speaking Kannada, and in fact, anything related to Kannada. So, remember to keep track of all of that. And, for God's sake, please get him to quit smoking! It's bad for health!"

Vanamali felt emptier than she had ever in her life. Her son was gone, and she had very little in common with her daughter, who was anyway busy with medical school. Baba had left the next day, to attend a Freedom Fighters' reunion in Bangalore, leaving Vanamali alone. She had made plans to visit her sister, Manasa, who was settled in Bangalore.

"Come, Vana, come," Manasa welcomed her little sister. The two had still remained very close, in spite of the different paths and states that marriage had led them to.

"How are you, Vanamali?" she asked.

"   I am fine, Akka, just fine. The wedding went off very well, so I am very satisfied. And you? How are you?"

"Oh, quite well, you know. Raji is busy with her studies, and he is gone most of the time with his line of work, so, it's just me keeping the house cozy. But, you and I are accustomed to that, isn't that right?" she exclaimed. "Amma gave us excellent training." Manasa paused to look at her sister, who was distracted by a photograph of her father, judge Shrikantayya that was lying on top of the Bangalore newspaper. "I see that caught your attention too," Manasa blurted.

"What's this all about?" Vana asked, genuinely surprised. She lifted the newspaper to her face, and read slowly.

"Honorable Judge Shrikantayya, born 1900 deceased 1955, is to be honored by the state of Karnataka for his contributions to the legal profession and court. He not only wrote some of the state's most significant amendments and laws, but he was instrumental in the capture and sentencing for many pivotal cases, including the drug trade that hit the country at the turn of the century. We will be honoring him in many ways, but first in dedication, by naming Bangalore's court district street after him. The high street has been recently renovated and worthy of the honorable judge's name. We invite all family, friends, colleagues, and respectable members of the city council to attend this grand ribbon cutting event."

The sisters stared at each other, Vana bursting into chatter after just a couple of seconds.

"What do you make of all of this nonsense? Honorable? What an oxymoron! The word "honor" should be removed from all of the judges' names when addressing them. It's so untrue! The pig didn't even leave anything to Amma. This is so wrong!" she screamed, and marched to the sofa to sit down. Manasa was not so angry.

"Do you always have to be so dramatic?" she asked, rhetorically. She approached her younger sister, and stroked her hair. "Listen, I for sure know that we did not have life easy, growing up. But, I just am not so angry because he meant nothing to me. He wasn't involved, Vana, he did not make an impression and then abandon me. So, does it really affect us? No. He didn't make us who we are today, Amma did."

"Does Amma know about this?

"Yes, I informed her via telegram. She will not attend, of that I'm sure. But, I think we should go down and take a look at the street. Spit on it if you have to, but let's go!"

The sisters decided to go to the ceremony, since it was on the Friday of that very same week. As the politicians of the town gathered and pressed the flesh of other aristocrats and power-hungry leaches, Vana and Manasa took in the crowd. It was a much larger group than anticipated by the women, and some local reporters were in attendance. After a short presentation and speeches, the mayor announced the city street name. "Shri H.K Srikantayya Boulevard." Vanamali glared up at the street sign and smirked. She waited some time for the people to disperse, then grabbed a pebble from the sidewalk and threw it with all of her force at the sign. Manasa, who caught only the end of the act, shook her head in disagreement.

"Vana, just calm down! This type of vandalism is not going to win you any awards! Just relax. Look at things the bright way- at least we could end up being known as the daughters of the famous lawyer! I mean common folk don't know how horrible a father he was!"

"But I want them to know! He was a terrible man," Vana cried out in vain. "My children would be better off with the guidance of such an influential grandfather, but instead they struggled on their own. How is that fair?" she rambled on.

"It's not, but then again, it all worked out fine, didn't it? They are successful, and we should be proud that the children are successful based on their own talents. They cannot fall back on influence and nepotism. At the end of the day, I believe karma rules. Father is gone, but it really makes no difference now. You are fine, your children are amazing, and that's really all that matters." Manasa comforted her sister, as the two proceeded to leave the street. "And remember, you at least, have a principled man as your husband, one who will never give in to money or bribes. Life is not that bad, Vana."

Vanamali nodded, acknowledging her sister's comforting words.

"Thanks Akka", she said, putting her arms around her sister. "I think we should stop by Mysore Tiffin Room for coffee and dosa, don't you?" The sisters chuckled, finally loosening up and starting to enjoy their day together in the city.

Chapter Forty: Married life

"Bhabhiji, andar aaeeye", Sandeep politely addressed his best friend's wife. Seetha felt that all too familiar pit in her stomach, as surroundings of this very crowded city, and new faces, seemed just too much to take in. Sandeep showed Seetha the apartment while Murali rushed to the kitchen to look for the maid. "Jaldi chai bunaao" he requested politely, and the maidservant hurried to fulfill her master's request to make some tea. It was a high rise apartment complex, overlooking some gardens in central Calcutta's busy business district. In fact, the apartment faced Hindustan Motors, where both Murali and Sandeep worked as mechanical and automotive engineers. They pointed this fact out to Seetha, who was a bit too distracted by the maidservant, who kept lolly-gagging about, staring at Seetha as if she were a statue. "Saab, I thought your wife would be a white girl and fair, just like you," she exclaimed rather crudely in Bengali. She then remarked, "She's like wheat. Not so fair."

"I think I'm going to need to fire her, if she keeps that up!" Seetha exclaimed, rather embarrassed and frustrated at the maidservant's words.

Life was different in Calcutta. Seetha found herself the minority, where locals had no clue of where Bangalore was, and simply referred to her as the "Madrassi." After weeks of explaining that Madras was in a completely different state, she gave up, deciding instead to continue the charade. Seetha was beginning to enjoy her new surroundings, home in the daytime setting up house while her husband was busy in the office. However, she was missing out on her chat sessions with friends and cousins. She didn't enjoy speaking only in English or Hindi, and found herself being very different from Murali's friends' wives, all of whom typically had not pursued higher education, or were business class individuals. These women worried about whether their haircut was in vogue with the latest movie heroine, and compared sarees and punjabi suits with the latest trend from popular movies. Seetha was foreign to all of this, and worried about her place in life. Would she go to work or try for her Ph.D.? What should she do with her time besides cooking and tending to the household?

Murali and Seetha made a couple trips back to Hyderabad, to visit family, or to attend an important ceremony. Baba greeted them at the train station, as was his custom.

"Come my children, mother is waiting for you with food. She's been in the kitchen all morning", he said with a smile. "Seetha, how are you finding Calcutta?"

"I like it Baba," Seetha replied. "It's a bit too crowded, and people are very different, but they are friendly. We are settling in."

"Good. Tell me about Murali, is he behaving?" Baba inquired with a wink.

"Yes, except for the tobacco," she bravely added. "Nobody told me he was a smoker. I wish I would have known."

"Oh, it must have been something he picked up in college. He has never smoked in front of us. Hopefully he will listen to you and not smoke any longer." The happy couple entered their home and greeted Vanamali with joy.

"Moggu, you are home. Good. Come, come eat."
Vanamali, who was overcome with joy at seeing her son, held his
hand and led him to the dining table.

"Amma, we have some news," Murali confided in her.
"Seetha and I wanted to tell you that you are going to be a
grandmother." Tears of joy filled her eyes and trickled down her
face. Baba, hearing the commotion, sat beside her at the table, as
Seetha settled in. "Yes, Baba, you are going to be a grandfather".
Uma, who had been showering when her brother had arrived,
rushed down the hallway and, understanding what had just been
revealed, hugged her sister-in-law happily.

Months passed by quickly. Seetha was now in Bangalore
in her third trimester, awaiting delivery. She was thrilled to have
her mother around, to dote on her in this uncomfortable state.
When their baby finally arrived, Murali and Seetha were
enthusiastic new parents. They decided to wait on naming her,
until their elders had provided input. According to the stars, she
would be named with the sound "Ru." One month later, Rukmini
was presented to joyful friends and family.

Chapter Forty-One: Uma's time

"Anna, I'm getting married!" Uma screamed in excitement.

"Are you sure he was wearing glasses?" her brother retorted, cheekily.

"You are terrible! Let me talk to Seetha."

"Congratulations! We are thrilled. So, lots of doctors in the family, huh! Let's get all the details. What does he look like? Is he tall, like your brother? Is he serious, or funny?" Seetha went on, questioning her sister-in-law eagerly. They got along royally, and this news was the icing on the cake.

Weeks passed by quickly, and soon the family was together again, as Uma wed her betrothed, Dr. Nagpal Verchas. Tall, svelte and beautiful, Uma was the stunning bride, looking more like a movie star than an upcoming physician. "Does she do the catwalk, sort-of runway walk, on purpose?" Apoorva asked her sister.

"No, that's just how her body moves. It's sort of her individual style. She's so stunning, you know, like a model. We even needed to stitch extra fabric on to the top of her sarees just so that she could tuck them. Such a beautiful height she has!" Seetha explained.

The wedding festivities went off without a hitch. Murali had earned well, yet gave most of his earnings towards Uma's wedding expenses. Dr. Nagpal seemed kind and gentle, but his meddling sisters were eager to drain the young family of their savings. "Don't worry, we have many more years to work and save up," Murali was heard telling Seetha.

Baba, now retired, was busy making sure every attendee of the wedding was well taken care of. "Ayyo, Motisa Raj's address has changed? The invite came back. I hope I can locate him now. It would have been such an honor if he graced our family event, as he did for Murali," Baba said. Seetha, listening to her father-in-law, remembered her conversation with her own Upala Amma, earlier that week.

"Baba, my Upala Amma said that she heard the town folk discussing a transition plan in Mysore. They were told that Maharaja is retiring his duties by the end of the year. It was apparently a national governmental decision."

"I have not heard about this till now," Baba remarked, somewhat astonished. "I wonder why? Surely the Raj was successful in running his town? This makes me quite sad; it is as if our country's culture and traditions will be forgotten soon."

"Baba, don't feel too sad. This way, the citizens are not paying taxes for the kings' upkeep. I would think our Mysore Maharaja would still have a lot of political influence to do right? Maybe he will be given a state or national position. He is certainly well loved," Seetha added, trying her best to sound logical but comforting her father-in-law at the same time.

The family returned to packing snacks and suitcases for Uma and putting them together in preparation for Uma's big move.

As Uma left, the following morning, to enter her new home, she turned to look at her parents. 'Baba, will you be okay?" she asked, with a small tear beginning to trickle from the corner of her eye.

"Oh, baby, don't you go worrying about us. We have a lot of things to keep busy with. Also, it's not like you'll be too far away," Baba replied. Uma hugged her parents, saying goodbye, before proceeding to the car with her husband. The future seemed so unpredictable and new, but she faced it with her usual sense of optimism. Vanamali was more apprehensive, however. She worried about her husband, who was so deeply attached to his only daughter that she feared Uma's separation would spiral him into a depression. He was always so active and busy. Now, with neither of their children nearby, she feared what was next in their lives. "Come inside," she beckoned Baba. "I'm making coffee."

Chapter Forty-Two: London, 1968

As Murali and his young family began to thrive in the "old meets new" blend of Calcutta life, he found himself becoming restless. He enjoyed the work, but wanted more. Some IIT graduates were immigrating to America and Murali and Seetha thought they could both make a prosperous life for themselves there. However, as the decision-making drew near, things around them seemed to be more complicated.

"I got in to Indiana University for a Ph.D. program!" Seetha proudly exclaimed, as she opened up the large letter, covered in many stamps.

"That's great", Murali said. "Shall we leave to America then?" he asked. It was rare for Murali to ask his wife opinions to which he already knew the answer, but this situation was difficult. The radios were bellowing news of war in Vietnam, waged by Americans, and that young civilians were losing their lives. As he held his young infant, he began feeling uneasy about the plan to flee to the "land of the free." Sandeep, one of his closest friends, urged Murali to turn in his resignation, since he was planning the same, citing stories of friends less intelligent who had found golden engineering opportunities in USA. Murali eventually followed suit, turning in his resignation to a rather stunned company manager. He was honored with glowing recommendation letters from Hindustan Motors. But, he was leaving without a job aligned, and this made both he and Seetha nervous.

"I have an idea!" Sandeep had said, "Let's just move to England." Seetha was okay with this plan but still apprehensive of a new country. She was also not too keen on working in England right away. She was enjoying motherhood and being home. She was frightened. Uma cheered her sister-in-law up with words of encouragement.

"I'll join you there one day. You should just go! If it doesn't work out there is always a plan B!"

A few weeks later, Seetha stood with baby in arms, and her lifetime of belongings compressed into two suitcases. A telegram had arrived from Bangalore, which she read, with weepy eyes.

"Take care of your family, dear. Sorry we cannot come to Calcutta to see you off, but Nilkanth has fallen a bit sick again and with his exams fast approaching, I thought I should stay back. Be safe, and try to write to me every week! We will miss you, Seetha! I hope you enjoy the United Kingdom. You will become quite the English fair lady, I'm sure! Stay safe, and keep warm. First and foremost, take care of baby Rukmini. Visit us soon! Love, Amma."

Seetha wiped a tear from the corner of her left eye, and kept Rukmini down, grasping her child's hand and proceeding to walk with her instead. She took a deep breathe, thinking to herself how already tired she was, and with such a long flight ahead, she wondered how she would manage with a small child in tow and probably no edible Indian food on the flight. With formal handshakes from Baba to Murali, they were soon forced to part. The young family moved through the security gates and within minutes was no longer in Baba's sight.

It was a strange country, Seetha observed. She saw a lot of white faces wearing gray or black pants and white shirts, but no color. People were busy, not stopping to smile or chat. Yet, she felt strange, as a few passers by would glare at her long hair and ethnic dress, as if she were a witch. In reality, she wasn't properly dressed. Her feet were in Indian slippers, and she was feeling a bit cold. The couple boarded the red London double decker, heading towards Belmont Avenue, where Sandeep had recommended Murali to stay.

"There are some flats there, for rent. The landlord is Indian, and he usually has space. You can tell him I sent you if you like". The couple made it down the city street where the bus had dropped them off. It was chilly, and besides a muffler and cardigan that Uma had made for her sister-in-law, Seetha was now freezing. She was unaccustomed to the grey skies and wet weather, and was growing wearier by the minute. Finally, they reached their destination. "Five, Belmont Avenue, Highgate." Murali climbed up the steps to the first floor doorbell, and rang it. A fair, mustached man wearing a sky blue bush-shirt and grey slacks opened the door. "

Hello!" Murali addressed the man. "My name is T.R Murali and I have just arrived here from India. My friend Sandeep, advised me to contact you for possible accommodations." The man looked at Murali kindly, and invited him in.

" So, are you staying a while?" he asked. "My wife and I have a one bedroom flat upstairs that is available for rent. My previous tenant just left. You can see it if you like." Murali agreed, and the two men took the tall front stairs up, leaving Seetha and Rukmini on the first floor. A long five minutes passed, and baby Rukmini was getting restless and hungry. She crawled out of her mother's arms and waddled about the main floor, peering into the rooms ahead.

"Bedama, mari. Don't snoop darling. This is not our home, and we do not want to get into trouble," Seetha explained. The toddler, however, was too curious to listen. She grabbed ahold of the doorknob and turned it firmly. The door opened into a long hallway leading to a kitchen, where fish curry spice aroma filled the air. Seetha's stomach churned with a mixture of panic from Rukmini's curiosity and nausea from the strong emotions and smells that now overtook the foyer. Next Mopsy, a stout young woman with raucous voice was heard yelling to her husband above.

"Hurry up then, lunch is ready. What's taking you so long?" She came towards the foyer, realizing that an intruder had set path in her kitchen. "Oh, so you're the little terror who found my kitchen? Like fish curry do you?" she screamed, smiling as well while stooping to come to face level of the child. Rukmini, getting a little scared of the stranger, ran back towards her mother.

"I'm so sorry. She was just exploring. We just got off a very long flight and she's tired. I'm sorry, again. I'm sure you understand, little ones can't keep still for too long."

"Actually, we do not have children. But I suppose it's to be expected." Mopsy opened her mouth as if to say more, but then closed it the moment she saw her husband entering the foyer from upstairs.

" Oh, I'm glad you two ladies have already made acquaintance. Mr. Murali here will take the flat upstairs, starting right away. You must be famished. Care to join us for lunch?" His invite was genuine, but Mopsy glared at her husband, effectively taking the invite away in that brief moment.

"Oh, thank you," Murali responded, "but we are fine. I think we just would like to rest. Thank you, though." Arun, the landlord, kindly helped Murali lift the suitcase up the steep stairs. Seetha, weary and now becoming nauseous from the wafts of fishy scents passing again through the hallway pushed her hand luggage into the bedroom and plopped down onto the sofa. She was in a deep slumber within a few moments.

The next few months were trying for the young family, alone in culture in the western world. Seetha felt quite homesick, while Murali continued to put on a brave face as he went from job interview to library, looking for opportunities and surprisingly coming up short. They had made the decision to not settle down in America, but some dark thoughts began to creep into their minds, suggesting that they had made the wrong decision. Nonetheless, they pressed on, with that very British style that Murali had grown to love. He was happy here, in spite of being jobless yet. It had only been a couple of weeks but Murali, who was no stranger to loneliness, was loving his new nuclear family's independent state. He admired the British way of life, and was only thrilled to suggest to his wife that she, too, look for a job since they were still beginning to get established.

"This way, I can start to think of starting my own company and making big money, then you can quit later," he said. She was taken aback.

"But, who will care for Rukmini?" Seetha asked. "We can't leave her with strangers, it's just not right." Murali calmed her, slowly. "Don't think so hard, it's just until I get established. Plus, there's always Mopsy; I'm sure she could help us out." Seetha, hearing this, couldn't hold back her feelings any longer.

"You must be joking!" she exclaimed. "That lady has no common decency. She complains about our baby walking too heavily upstairs and making noise. Do you know, I don't even let

Rukmini play with musical toys just because of that woman? She's strange. She doesn't like me and she hates children. I had to give our baby a bath this afternoon and Mopsy complained that I was wasting good water. Even though I'm putting money in the meter, she still runs her mouth off. What am I to do? There is just no way. I need to be home with Rukmini or we come up with somebody else to help us. There is no other way of thinking about this." Murali grinned, understanding his wife's concerns.

"We will find a way, don't worry. I spoke to Sandeep this morning and he thinks there may be an opening at the company where he is working. I'm going in tomorrow. Hopefully, everything will fall into place."

Chapter Forty-Three: Petticoat Lane. Spring 1970

"I can't wait!" Seetha exclaimed as she packed full her jute shopping bag with snacks and water bottles, in preparation for her busy day ahead. "Meera said Petticoat Lane has everything you could possibly want at wonderful prices. I have made a list and if we can find what we are looking for that would be super. Plus, too, we do need to stock up prior to Manni Uncle coming," she added. Her uncle was scheduled to arrive the following week, but the aerogram announcing this had only just arrived. She knew she would be on her feet preparing homemade meals for the man who knew nothing different, yet would be the first to inform her family back home if things were not quite up to snuff. So, she carried on, with the energy of a new battery, excited for the future events. Murali grabbed the bags, and they walked a short distance to the Underground station. "I think Meera and Sandeep will meet us down there," Seetha informed Murali, while waiting for the tube to arrive. Murali, who had his hands full with two jute bags in one hand and little Rukmini in the other, mumbled under his breathe,

" I wouldn't count on it. She wanted to hire a babysitter for Rahul but they were unsuccessful. I doubt she will come with the baby."

"Well, that sure surprises me. She made it sound like she would die rather than miss this market!"

A half hour later the family arrived at the crowded, infamous, Petticoat lane. It was time now for Seetha to grab onto her child, for fear of her getting lost in the crowd.

"Excuse me sir, but where may we find fabrics?" Murali inquired of one of the vendors.

"Down the other corner, mate!" the portly man replied. The couple journeyed to the cloth counter, gently excusing their self in order to pass ahead of slower groups of people. Seetha took her time studying the cottons, polyester, and new imitation silk that had just hit the market.

"Oh its beautiful!" she exclaimed, holding up a large meter against her skin and imagining making a sari out of it. Murali, patient as always, nodded, but gently tried to move his wife along.

"Remember your list", he said, "Is that on it?"

"Okay, okay, let's get the list items first," Seetha agreed.

Time flew by. They drudged through crowds of people in the cool spring London air, grey with the occasional sprinkle, as if to remind them that they did, after all, live in London. "Daddy, chippi, Daddy, hungry!" Rukmini yelled.

"Honey, do you want something to eat?" her mother asked.

"I'll go round the street and get her something. You stay right here, you have already reached the counter you want" Murali advised. Daddy and daughter left while Seetha studied the vast array of grains, lentils and legumes. After a few moments, the attendant asked,

"Can I get you something ma'am?"

"Um, yes sir. I'll take the yellow lentils, the jasmine rice, and the chickpeas."

"How much ma'am? A kilo?"

"Um, maybe five kilo of the rice, and 2kilo of the lentils and peas please." The storekeeper handed Seetha the lentils and rice. He then placed the bag of rice on the counter in front of her. She had a heavy winter coat on, buttoned to the neck, to spare her from the slightest draft that could come her way. Colin didn't notice behind her thick layers, that she was with child. As Seetha steadied herself, trying to negotiate the bags in front and the crowds behind, she thanked Colin and then turned slightly to check for her husband. "No where in sight," she muttered to herself, as she pondered her next move. She felt a chill within her, and shook as if she could warm her body up.

"Are you alright Ma'am?" Colin inquired.

"Oh, well, I'm not sure," she blurted out, rather taken off guard. "I felt a bit of a chill. Oh well, I am sure it will pass. Good day."

As she turned, bags in each hand, she felt a gush of fluid between her legs, and a cramp in her abdomen. "Oh no, something's wrong," she cried, gently. She was embarrassed and in pain. Colin saw her grabbing her tummy. As he approached her to assess, there was another cramp and Seetha fell to the ground. The last thing she remembered was the sight of blood on her new shoes.

When she came to, she was on a gurney being wheeled quickly into the operating room. 'Mrs. Murali, we are going to have to let you rest now. You are losing a lot of blood. Please take a slow, deep breath into the mask." Within moments she was unconscious.

Seetha awoke to a sterile gray-white tiled operating room.

"Your husband will be in again in a moment. You will feel a bit groggy for a while, but I suspect you will feel better tomorrow."

"What happened?" Seetha asked. But it was too late; the nurse had already left the room.

Her throat was dry, and she felt dizzy when she tried to move. Something seemed frightfully wrong. She was not supposed to be admitted for at least two more months, not now. It was only March, and her due date was May fifteenth. Seetha attempted to turn, to see if her purse was next to her, but she couldn't muster the strength. The intravenous bore through her right arm and prevented it from bending fully. Even lifting her arm to run her fingers through her tangled hair was a struggle. She held her left hand to her forehead and slowly wept. Just at that moment, Murali walked in. He took her hand and stroked it.

"You did well, you were so brave!" he explained. She wept some more. "Why are you crying? Is it the medication? You're not acting like yourself."

"Why are you speaking like this?" Seetha sobbed. "I've just lost our baby, I'm in pain, and I cannot even recall anything. What did the babies look like? Did we have twins like Dr. Begum expected? Why are these ghastly rooms so grey?"

"Oh my, what nonsense you speak! Didn't the nurse tell you? We have a beautiful baby girl. She's downstairs in the baby intensive care unit. I had to go with them to the NICU, so I didn't stay with you at that moment. Sorry. I thought I'd perhaps get back before you awoke. There's nothing to worry about, everything's perfectly fine."

Seetha smiled the biggest smile Murali had ever seen. She had had no clue as to what had happened. The ammonia mask stench was the last thing that she could recall. She had associated that odor as well as the blood on her shoes, with the loss of her baby. Anyway, it was two months too soon. But, in her eyes, a miracle had occurred, and little baby girl had survived. She felt blessed.

"But what about what the doctor said about twins? Any truth to that?" she asked.

"No, not at all. It was just an educated guess, but she was wrong. Why, do you want three?" Murali chuckled.

" I want to see my baby. Take me there," Seetha demanded.

"Not just yet. You're not allowed. You are very anemic, and the nurse does not think it is safe for you do go down a floor yet. You'll have to wait."

The following day, Seetha finally persuaded her nurse to wheel her down a floor to the neonatal intensive care unit. There she was, her beautiful baby girl, with fair white skin and thick black hair. But she was so tiny, and tubes pervaded her body, one in her nose, and one in her tiny arm. "Will she be all right?" Seetha asked the nurse, holding back tears from her eyes.

"Oh, Mrs. Murali, you don't need to worry. She is going to be just fine. We have the best neonatal doctors here, and she already looks very comfortable." Seetha was relieved to hear this. She wanted to stay longer, hold her baby in her arms and nurse her. But she could not. The pediatrician and the gynecologist both felt Seetha was too weak to nurse. Her baby was too early to know how to suck, and taking her off of the unit to nurse could delay her progress. They opted to continue to feed the neonate through the nasal feeding tube and hydrate her with intravenous fluids.

"She's just not ready for breast or bottle feeding yet. Be patient, she will be full term in a couple of months. Then you can take her home and feed her all you want," the neonatal nurse consoled the young mother. And Seetha needed to recoup, with iron and blood transfusions already in progress for the treatment of her critical anemia. Thankfully, the physicians reassured Seetha that she would probably make it home in a couple of days. Seetha kissed her baby girl's fingers and, pressing her fingers to the incubator, she said good night. As she turned away, she gazed at the sterile white NICU, void of the feeling of fresh, young life, yet functional, practical.

"Come on then," the nurse said, turning Seetha's wheelchair away from the ward, "Let's get you back to your room. I wonder what's on your lunch menu today?" Seetha listened, but wasn't paying attention when the nurse on the ward brought in her food tray. "That's splendid!" the nurse added, smelling the aroma of hot mashed potatoes with gravy and meat "It's Beef Wellington today, you are so lucky!" She placed the tray on the bed table, after helping Seetha back to her bed. "Maybe I should ask for anemia diets for everyone, if the meals are that great," the nurse excitedly suggested. She turned and closed the door of the room giving Seetha her privacy. She was famished, and eager to get some tasty food into her tired body. Seetha raised the food lid and studied the strange concoction. A red piece of thick meat covered with gravy and to its right some mashed potatoes covered with brown gravy. There was a side of green beans too. The smell repulsed her. The sight of meat made her uncomfortable and she wondered if this Westernized nation even knew what a Hindu person was. The beef was out of the question. The mashed potatoes looked inviting but the gravy irritated her. And the beans were touching the beef. She covered the lid and looked over her tray one last time.

"Ah yes," she said to herself, "a bread roll and butter. That will do nicely". She ate the roll then pushed the table away from herself, and fell to sleep.

As the next day came and went, Seetha made frequent visits to her infant in the NICU. The staff had now become accustomed to the beautiful young mother with a long braid of black, silky hair. They smiled, both affectionately and curiously, as Seetha spoke her language to her child. It did not seem to matter what language she spoke, the baby babble seemed to be universally understood. Still, the staff enjoyed the differences in words that Seetha made.

"When can I hold her?" Seetha asked.

"Not for a bit, Mrs. Murali. You see she is just not quite ready to come out. She needs the medical support."

"Very well," Seetha replied dejectedly, "How many days do you think she will need to be in an incubator?" she asked.

"Oh, ma'am, it will be several weeks before she comes out of that machine. Probably five or six weeks."

Seetha returned to her room, this time feeling homesick. The nurse had already asked her several times where the father of the baby was, and what about family. Seetha longed for her mother, her sister, her family by her side through all of this difficulty. She didn't fear moving to England a few years prior, since she never placed herself in these situations. Now, she felt alone.

"Ma'am, when's Mr. Murali coming back?" nurse Mary asked again.

"He will come but not for a week. He caught the mumps. He has Rukmini too, and she is also not feeling well. I do not know if they will make it back prior to my discharge." Nurse Mary left the room, turning her head down to the floor as if to acknowledge she had pried too much. Seetha also began to feel the weight of reality. A new baby, yet no one to tend to her besides the NICU nurse. It didn't seem right. For the first time in a year, Seetha longed to be back in India. She missed her mother who, at that very moment, would have been fussing over her and the baby if she were in town.

"Oh Rama, please give me the strength to get up and walk around soon, so that I can tend to my baby girl," Seetha silently prayed, hoping for a speedy recovery. Her mouth was dry and her appetite soured by the smell of dinner being served in the ward. The stench of meats and gravy filled the hallway. Seetha closed her eyes and drifted off into a deep sleep.

The day finally arrived for Seetha to be discharged. She felt strange leaving the hospital without her newborn baby. Manni, her uncle, had met Seetha at the hospital, since Murali had still not been given permission to return until the mumps was fully resolved. Seetha returned home but rather than recouping as most postpartum women would, she found herself fussing over the men, cooking and cleaning in order to make a good impression.

"Seetha, you really should be resting. Let the men handle their dinners," Mopsy advised. "You are still anemic and you look it. Plus, when are you visiting the baby next?"

"This evening we will go. I think Murali has the all clear now, so we will have a early dinner and go." The young mother had returned home weak but eager, and promptly started fussing about the house and home. Two hours later, weary and weak, dinner done and plates washed, the family looked at their kitchen clock, hopeful that a hospital visit was on the horizon. Seetha glanced at the clock and then turned to look at Murali and uncle. "It's too late now, we will have to go there in the morning." Disappointed, Seetha said her goodnights and turned in for the night.

Chapter Forty-Four: Uma. London, September 1970

"Anna, let's take Seetha Akka shopping tomorrow; I have only one more free day before the internship starts."

"You women will never tire of shopping will you?" Murali chuckled.

"Well, we need to change with the times. We are British people now!" Uma replied, enthusiastically.

"Yes, I'm ready. If you can just wait a moment till I change Maya's diaper, then we can carry the pram and go," Seetha said. Uma grabbed the infant away from her mother, kissing her pink cheeks and gazing at her beautiful blue eyes. "So how do you make a baby with blue eyes? Amazing Seetha Akka, how do you do that?"

"I know! It is quite shocking. Our landlord told us the neighbor saw the baby and thought she was someone else's!" The little one wiggled out of her mother's arms and happily babbled, playing with her aunt's hair. Maya's blue eyes stunned her aunt still, who gazed at her niece, holding her up closer and giving her butterfly kisses.

"Ammaloo!" Uma called her affectionately, "Whom are you going to look like? I can't tell. You look different every time I see you. Hmm, I think you're like me. That's my opinion and I'm sticking with it!"

A few minutes later, the family was packed and ready to head out for shopping.

Chapter Forty-Five: Baba's India, 1971

He had aged yet was still a handsome man. He was dressed in a khadi cotton shirt, linen pants and a waistcoat, and carried a leather pouch under his right arm. He wore Gandhi-style spectacles and sandals. He approached his brother-in-law's house, and rang the doorbell. Brunda his sister rushed to the door. "Come Anna, come inside."

Dr. Rai was sitting in the living room, serving coffee that his wife had just placed on the mahogany coffee table. To Baba's surprise, Vanamali was also present, seated in the living room next to Brunda. He beckoned to Baba to join him, and poured him a cup.

"You look perturbed, Baba. What's troubling you?" Dr. Rai asked. Baba paused, taking in the surroundings and trying to make sense of the setting, with his wife present. He answered, thoughtfully.

"Nothing like that. I just keep on thinking about the movement and where we stand today. So many promises were made for the nation, yet nobody came through. I cannot help but worry about the future of our nation. Plus, all of the people we trusted to carry on the mission, seemed to have been bought off. What is to become of this country? I cannot get over this. What are your thoughts?"

"I think you are worrying too much. Whatever happened in decades past was not in vain. You have paved the way for countless others and there are still good people in this nation. Just because one mission failed, doesn't mean the message did not go through. In fact, several people in the government were disappointed that you did not accept a parliamentary position. You are a golden boy who could affect change. I can do some things, but I do not have your abilities. Now that your children are grown and settled, you should resume your activism work. Gandhi would have said the same. Just let's come up with a plan now."

Baba listened, his right pointer finger gently tapping on his left as he pondered over the conversation. He felt like the last two decades were weighing heavily on him, marking his beautiful face with frown lines and crows feet. How could he sum up his life, he thought. A life dedicated to the freedom movement and what had he been able to accomplish? Yes, Murali and Uma were educated and independent, but what of his own personal wealth? A mere insurance underwriter lawyer with his own small business, he neither felt prosperous nor important. Agreed, he was renowned within his community for his social service and representation, but he felt deep dissatisfaction with his status. Marriages had come and gone and he had nothing left to show for it. One son had graduated from IIT, but Baba felt only regret at not truly knowing his son.

"He's so distant," he remembered telling Vanamali. "Why is he like that?" At that time, Vanamali had tried to explain to her husband that he had spent a decade fighting a nonviolent war, leaving his son at home most of the time. Baba had not spent his weekends playing kites in the festival with Murali (a festival that Murali ultimately won.) He had given up his political share for freedom party representation, choosing an honest life rather than rise in the lines of the parliament. Yet, he felt great personal strife. Now, at the brink of another decision, he felt like retreating, just like a horse in front of a cliff edge.

"Baba, why the hesitation? What are your worries, do tell me?" Dr. Rai asked kindly.

I just fear for this country. And, most of all, I fear for Murali. He ran away to England, leaving us and not even moving on to USA, where he would be thriving currently. I do not see the joy of living in England, and it troubles me. Great Britain is a nation that has made a living out of ruining other nations, foraging and stealing their wealth and jewels, then putting up a flag and claiming it as theirs. Is that even humane? Yet, where does my son pick to set up home? England. It just makes no sense. At least I thought my baby girl would stay with me, but she goes running after her brother. What does our son want in life?"

Baba paused, rather emotional, as Vanamali frowned slightly at the suggestion that her "Moggu" was anything less than perfect. She retorted,

"He has worked very hard his entire young life to live up to your expectations, perfect grades and perfect schools. Don't misunderstand his intentions."

Vana and Baba left Dr. Rai's home, and continued their conversation on the ride back home.

Baba, frowned, his forehead creasing as he tried to nonverbally communicate with his usually quiet wife, to keep mute at this delicate time, with his beloved sister present. Vanamali conceded with a frown and her head tilted down, but Baba had already continued her rants in his head- sermons that he was all too familiar with. His mind echoed with her words.

"He has fought off criticism and cynicism from your siblings, leaving jealousy aside I just took their remarks. How they provoked me constantly. Only when Murali was off to IIT did they acknowledge that our son has accomplished more than each of their own children combined. And, Murali never asked for anybody's recommendation or influence. You don't think you could have requested your brother-in-law or brother, politicians both, to put in a good word to the Deans of the engineering colleges? But, they just praise you in face and laugh at us from behind since we haven't amassed the type of wealth that they are accustomed to. But our boy showed them all. In one entrance exam, he succeeded in acceptance to the college by direct admission. Now he chooses to make a life for himself and his young family in England, again never asking for your help, and all you can dwell on is the honor of the country? You really need to let it go."

Vanamali turned away, disgusted at her husband's rare negativity and that too, aimed towards her beloved son. She herself was uneasy ever since Murali left her and moved abroad. She yearned for her son, more so than her daughter. With Murali gone she felt aimless. She loved her husband, but decades of being muted by the sisters-in-law had made her slightly bitter, and very anxious. She craved wealth; she craved attention. To Vana, Baba was constantly preoccupied by his mission and entertained by his siblings. The happiness and independence she once felt had slowly been replaced by feelings of worthlessness. She had not gone for a swim in twenty years. She had steadily gained weight, and her once petite body had now molded into a plump, pear shaped woman, yet still with a beautiful face. Her hair had withered and she had resorted to braiding the fine strands and clipping the tail onto her head with a pin. She joked to her children that it was a "piljuttu" or a priest's hair tuft but, jokes aside, she was becoming dysthymic. Neither happy, nor totally sad, just down. She couldn't figure out how to rid herself of her mind's negative thoughts. Decades of others speaking behind her back and putting her down had finally taken its toll and she began to believe these remarks. "Fat," "lazy" and "no talents" were phrases that had stuck to her mind and she began to believe them. When Seetha would send her a beautiful sari from England, "Italian viscose" or something very special from Europe, Vanamali would appreciate it, but rather than wear it she would lock it in her infamous Godrej closet. There were several occasions where Baba would ask her to dress up, or adorn the beautiful jewelry or clothing she had, yet Vana couldn't do it. She had grown up without the love of her father, and after her own mother's passing the year prior and now Murali's emigration, Vana had been lost in her own negative thoughts. She began to believe that she was incapable of happiness and love, since those loved ones in her life had left her. Even though Baba loved her, their relationship had changed, and Vanamali felt outnumbered and outvoted in his henpecked family household. Even their baby girl Uma would lovingly tease her mother, proudly stating, on her medical school graduation, that her smarts she had inherited from her father's genes, and her looks too. Vanamali struggled with her emotions, often left to her own company while Baba went out to work or meet with his siblings. Who knew what would become of their relationship as time went on in this empty nest.

Baba came out from the bedroom where he had gone to get refreshed.

"Vanamali, I am leaving for work now. I was thinking of sending a telegram to Uma, is there something you wanted to say?"

"Tell Uma to come back quickly for a visit. It's Gowri-Ganesha festival and we would love to see her."

"All right, no problem. Anyway I was going to tell her the same thing. Any message for Murali?" Baba inquired.

"Tell Moggu to bring baby Maya and Rukmini back fast, with Seetha, of course. We can have fun times together. I'm going nuts in this house alone!" Baba and Vanamali exchanged smiles as things in the Ramaswamy household reverted back to normal. "How strange yet sweet life is," Vanamali realized, bearing witness to her own mood swings that had spiked like a violent fever taking control over her body and seizing yet now dramatically cured with the mere mention of her children. Baba had assumed long before now, that Vanamali's affliction was simply that she longed for the presence of her children. The moment at hand only served to prove this, in Baba's mind.

"I will be home early this evening," Baba said as he sipped his coffee. He finished his Mysore coffee, picked up his leather pouch and stack of newspapers and headed out the door.

He decided he would walk. The weather was perfect for a long walk, not too hot or too humid. As he passed by the paper recycling shop, he presented the pile of newspapers to the assistant. "Ten rupees," he stated. Baba nodded, took the money and moved on. His next stop was the telephone S.T.D. booth. He was about to send the telegram to England, and was pondering his choice of words. As he stood at the counter the booth attendant addressed Baba.

"Saab, you can send a telegram or you can make a phone call. The rates are good today. Ganapathi special!"

"How much?" Baba asked, not accustomed to holiday specials and rather taken aback by the suggestion.

"Fifty rupees, five minutes," the attendant replied. As Baba looked around, making sure he was not holding up the queue, he reflected on the immediate gratification of speaking to his son and daughter, as opposed to awaiting a response to a letter that could take up to three weeks to reach, or a telegram that could reach, but could also not.

"Yes, um, I would like to purchase the phone use for five minutes," Baba politely stated. The man took Baba's money before he could change his mind, and then continued,

"The number, Saab (sir)." Baba appeared a little bewildered, expecting to take the telephone himself and dial the number. He looked down at his address book, pointed his finger down to the name "Moggu," for his son, and then read the number.

"It is a UK number, I am showing it now." The attendant was prepared, and he proceeded to dial the phone number to place the call. He continued to hold the phone, waiting for Murali to pick up. After the fourth ring Baba was beckoning to the man to hang up, when Murali's voice was heard on the other end.

"Hello? Hello? Who is this please?"

The attendant explained that he was giving the phone to Baba for five minutes, and Baba took the phone with pleasure.

"Hello Murali, Baba here. How are you, son? How are the children? Amma and I want you all to come home soon. Are you able to do that?" He paused, realizing that the string of questions had resulted in Murali not getting an opportunity to speak.

"Yes, Baba, we are all very fine. Maya is growing, Rukmini is a mischievous little charmer, and Seetha is keeping well. How are you and Amma?" he asked.

"Very well, very well indeed. Amma has made enough mango pickle to last a year and it is sitting here in jars waiting for you and Uma. Have you spoken to Uma? How is she?" Baba asked. There was an unusually long pause. "Moggu, did you hear me? Is all well over there? Uma and Nagpal are fine?"

Murali, who was using the kitchen phone downstairs by Mopsy's living room, found himself gazing at Seetha's face, a tear welting up in the corner of his eyes. Seetha shook her head slowly, an instruction to not discuss this matter over the phone.

"All is well, Baba, all is well," Murali finally responded softly, dissatisfied with what he had just stated.

"Very well then, very well. Please tell Uma to come back next month. I want her here for Gowri-Ganesha festival. Please convey this message to her." Baba looked at his wristwatch. There was only one minute left till he would be forced to disconnect. "Murali, how is your work? Are you enjoying? Is there anything we can send you from here?" His son's response was quick and typical, knee-jerk reaction style.

"No, nothing at all. We are all fine. We have everything we need. We can always shop when we visit." Baba listened, hoping for a few more words out of his son's mouth. He missed him, yet they had never really told his son this in a conversation. Baba was uncertain why. Now, strangely, he longed for his children yet could not bring himself to pour out these thoughts in words.

"Okay then, it is time to end the call. Do come, all of you. We miss you."

The phone cut, and the receiver returned to the attendant. Baba acknowledged the man's guidance, and turned to take the steps down from the short storefront entrance.

As Baba made his typical walk down the main street, across the post office and onward to his office, he felt a chill running down his spine. Murali had been rather quiet, he reflected. Why did he not chat some more about the family's plan to visit? Were the grandchildren truly fine? A ray of sunlight bounced off of his youthful face, causing Baba to look up to the skies. He closed his eyes for a moment and took a deep breath. "Everything is fine," he said to himself soothingly, as he unlocked the door to his office.

The freedom fighter sat at his desk, completing the necessary tasks of paying bills and responding to inquiries. After a couple of hours he sat gazing at his antique watch that his father-in-law had gifted him on Baba's wedding day. It ran like a charm and was an old classic piece that never looked out of vogue. As Ramu the servant boy brought tea around to Baba, he quickly fell into a daydream, taking his china teacup and studying its intricate china pattern.

"It's so complicated," Baba said to himself. "Our nation loves the china teacups, the fine formality, the pomp and circumstance of what the British have left behind, yet we still have the Indian politicians bleeding our system, stealing from our folks and pocketing money that is not their own. Indian chai in a china teacup-that's the India we are. Confused." He struggled with his thoughts. Baba ruminated over which direction to take his passion for India; whether to be involved in India's movement again, take a back seat, or even, throw in the towel.

The cup was half empty as Baba glanced out of his office window. A small shadow fluctuated from the corner of his eye in the dim light of eve. Baba wondered what it was. He stood up quickly, suspicious of the shadow and what could follow. Still haunted by the post traumatic stress of his earlier movement days and the attacks in both Delhi and Firozpur, he proceeded to the door holding his office umbrella in his left hand, just in case. There were no unusual sounds outside and when he peered out of the front window, he failed to notice the tall woman with dark hair turning the corner to the front office door.

There was a rap on the door. Baba, seeing that this was rather normal behavior, decided not to panic. "Who is this?" he inquired without opening the door. There was another knock, but when Baba refused to reply this time, the voice answered.

"Baba, it is I, Lakshmi, Janaki's sister. Remember me? It's been a while. I need to talk to you."

Baba opened the door quickly, thoroughly surprised to hear of his old friend and partner in crime, Janaki. It had been over fifteen years since they had met in one place as part of the movement. The previous traumatic events had concluded with the fracture of the movement, and death of dear Janaki and Prasanna. Temporarily, so as to protect its members, the movement had dispersed, to intentionally prevent the police and others from tracking them. Now, Baba and Lakshmi stood together opposite each other as if no time had elapsed at all. Lakshmi shook Baba's hand, her younger age more obvious now. She looked the same. She possessed such bright eyes and an ever-eager attitude.

"Baba, we need you," she said firmly, looking her mentor in the eyes and gently looking down for a moment with respect.

"Why? And, why should I be involved now? Independence has already happened, what could be happening now that you need me?" Baba exclaimed. He beckoned Lakshmi towards some wicker chairs that faced his desk, and the two sat opposite each other, in thought.

"Baba, there is a lot you do not know. Many things are happening right now. Independence has indeed happened, but we are still not at peace. India is really not unified. Are you happy? Most people we know are troubled by the fragmented India and Pakistan chaos and want things back to the way they were prior to partition and prior to British rule. We can achieve this if you help us. Let's come together again to fight this nonsense."

Baba paused, reflectively, and sighed gently. Decades had passed and although he continued to carry the Indian pride that could engage any young audience, he felt dismissed by friends and family who held political power. He also longed for his children close by, and his wife at his side the way she used to be. Indeed, since Murali's birth, Vana and he had been imprisoned nine times, and had attended political rallies at least twenty four times. He enjoyed the movement, and loved having a sense of purpose. Yet now, as he contemplated Lakshmi's invite, he felt disappointed at where India had come, decades later. Had anything actually been achieved for the better of the nation? He doubted this, and an internal struggle brewed in his ponderous mind.

"Who is with us now, Lakshmi? Who is even joining the movement? Only new blood can keep the spirit alive. What is our mission? Previously it was freedom, now that has happened, where are we? I am as confused as anyone here. I don't know what to do or where to stand. All I know is India today is not what I had envisioned."

Lakshmi listened intently, but chose her words wisely, waiting until Baba had spoken his mind and thrown in the flag.

"Baba, our work was never completed. I never avenged my sister and brother-in-law's deaths. Forget me; we as a team never reunited to discuss and plan the future. That's not how we end things. What happened with India's independence was a compromise, and very few citizens are truly happy now, on either side of the border. There is always work to be done, and only you can motivate people to do it. They listen to you. You are untouched by the riches of political gains, and you command attention by living and breathing your patriotism. Moreover, unlike the Bhagat Singh's and Harmeet Singh's of the country, you have maintained the Mahatma's principles of nonviolence. This gives you leverage since the establishment cannot hurt you if you are not doing anything wrong. I think we have a platform. Let's climb it. Let's do something. You are the last person I would have pegged to sit still in the face of injustice."

Baba nodded. He felt uplifted by the words of his friend and student. With his everlasting smile he cupped his hands, then, folding them into "namaste" pose, he acknowledged Lakshmi's words. He stood up, grabbed his umbrella once more, and led his friend out the door. "Come, let's take a stroll. There is much to talk about."

Chapter Forty-Six: Gowri-Ganesha, August 1972

"Baba, here I am, finally! Did you miss me much?" Uma exclaimed, hugging her father and giving him a peck on the cheek.

"Arre, naughty girl! I enquired about you constantly. Didn't Murali tell you?"

Uma gazed in her father's eyes, kindly acknowledging this information.

"He did, Baba, but I could not contact you immediately. Phone conversations from U.K. to India are more difficult than I would ever have imagined." She paused, had the cabdriver bring in her suitcases and then headed to the kitchen to find her mother. "Hi, Amma!" she exclaimed, matching the enthusiasm she had shown her father and hugging her mother tightly.

"Ayyo, be careful or else you will get pickle stains on your beautiful sari," Vanamali reacted. The family was reunited again, excepting Murali's family who could not make the trip this soon. Uma felt pampered in her parents' home, enjoying her mother's mango pickle and spicy lentil soup specialties, while Baba took care of his baby girl with all the things she wanted.

The family asked for a minute- to- minute account of her daily activities while living in England. She had become a young internal medicine doctor and enjoyed her lifestyle there. Her parents probed her as to why she had not yet started a family, to which Uma replied,

"Do you want me to be an accomplished doctor, or a homemaker?" They quickly dropped the subject on this quick reply, which Uma had no trouble giving. She was known for her fiery style and intelligence, quick wit and affection. They had indeed missed her, and she filled the void that had been left when she emigrated.

A few days later the home became more hectic as all of her paternal aunts dropped in to see her. Oh how they fussed and commented. But Uma was gifted in gab, making everyone feel welcome and loved. It had been a long day. The fatigue was setting in. As the last of the aunts, Pooja, left Uma with a tight handshake and some words of advice, Uma literally dropped to the floor as she closed the door shut. Baba and Vanamali came running.

"What happened here?" he exclaimed, "is everything all right?"

"Um, yes, fine Baba, fine. I will just need some help lifting myself up since I'm thoroughly exhausted."

Vanamali tucked Uma in bed, as though she was a little girl again.

"Rani, it is Gowri festival tomorrow. You will need to take good rest tonight since tomorrow you will be fasting, then puja ceremony, then only a late dinner. It will be tiring. Then you leave us the following day. Not fair. Too short a trip," Vana vented. But then, directing her mind to the positive, she resumed her conversation. "Rani, tell me something."

"Yes, Amma."

"I have noticed that you are walking very differently. Is this a new style, or is something going on? You look different to me too," Vanamali added, "Perhaps marriage has changed you?"

"Movie-star walks, you know, full of style and glamour!" Uma smiled, giggling with her father and dismissing her mother's fears, just like in her childhood. "Oh well then, you just don't understand! You two are always ignoring my words. That's fine.

If you don't want to listen you don't have to. I just thought something had changed," Vanamali repeated.

Uma turned her head towards her mother, but Vana, in a moment of frustration, had already turned her back to walk out of the door. Baba gave his daughter a kiss on the forehead, and left her alone in her room. The parents did not see the tears rolling down her cheeks, nor did they notice Uma's shallow breathing, as she propped herself up with three pillows, just to try to ease her distress.

The following day Gowri-Ganesha festivities were in full swing in the Ramaswamy household. Freshly picked jasmine flowers adorned the household, and holy basil, or tulsi leaves decorated the entrance to the house. There was a beautiful drawing of 'rangoli' on the doorstep and the fragrant scent of sandalwood incense followed the prayer altar around the house. The pundit was done by about twelve o'clock, and next Vanamali began to serve Uma's plate, beside her father's. As Uma began to eat, Vanamali again noticed something strange about her daughter's expression. She looked exhausted. "Uma, are you okay?" her mother asked.

"Yes Amma, just tired. And starving. I tell you, who invented fasting anyway?" Uma always joked around, and this was something the parents had missed when Uma had left the home. As she finished her food, she slowly lifted herself up from the dining table and took out a plate of her dad's favorite sweets from the kitchen. "Kalakand, Daddy. Just for you!" She fed him, as was tradition for Gowri-Ganesha festival, as the daughter returned home to enjoy the love of her family. Baba easily obliged, as the sweetmeat pieces melted in his mouth. Uma gave him one last hug, then went into her bedroom to recline, the events of the day taking their toll on her body.

Two weeks had gone by too quickly, and Uma was yet again packed and dressed to travel home to her husband and brother, in London. She kissed her mother, and pressed her father's hand close to her cheek as she stared him directly in the eyes.

"Baba, I'm going to miss you", she said, tears welting up in her eyes. "Don't worry, you will come again," Baba replied, choking up as well.

"Come visit us in England now. You have no excuses. Both Murali and I are there. Plus the grandchildren need you. Come fast!"

"This is the last boarding call for passengers on British Airways Flight three-zero-two to London Heathrow. All passengers are kindly requested to come to gate twelve A for boarding." Uma left with a stylish wave, her long hair braided down her back, reaching her lower spine. Her hips swayed musically, which attracted attention from all who observed her. Her tall, voluptuous five foot ten inch frame and beautiful face were not inconspicuous. Her hand luggage was small, which surprised her mother, who knew Uma to be an avid shopper, only wearing the latest brands. But, this time she had traveled light and came and went with one check in baggage only. Before proceeding down the gangway to the plane, she gave a final turn, now tears rolling down her cheeks uncontrollably. She waved as she caught her parents' attention, and boarded the plane.

The flight was well in the air, having taken off rather turbulently in the harsh monsoon rains. Uma had closed her eyes to avoid the rush of emotions and shaking plane sensations. She slept, thinking of the home away from home that she would return to.

A few hours had passed, when a young male passenger pressed his assist light to request help from the airline hostess. "How can I help you sir?" she asked rather curtly, since he had pulled her away from her power nap before the first flight service.

"Please, ma'am, help. I am trying to get up to the washrooms but the lady next to me will not get up. I think something is wrong."

Rose the stewardess, politely tried to awaken the woman. When she did not respond, Rose nudged her. No response. The stewardess called for help. Two women came rushing to assist her, one the main cabin purser and the other the first class cabin hostess. They seemed to be more experienced. They nudged her, and prodded her. She did not wake up. Finally, Sally, the first class hostess ran to the pilot's cabin.

"We need to divert the plane and land immediately. We have an unresponsive passenger. It's not looking good."

Within half an hour the plane had made an emergency landing in Kabul, Afghanistan. The other passengers began to panic, or even show anger at the rerouting, still not knowing the events that had transpired. The med-alert team was fast on the scene. After a quick airways-breathing-circulation assessment the team lifted Uma onto a stretcher and attempted resuscitation. The other passengers were restless, some crying, some pushing their way out of their seats. Others on board attempted to move closer to the action. It was to no avail. A young doctor, by the name Al-Ejel, spoke. "Time of death four minutes past five o'clock a.m. Kabul, Afghanistan."

It was amazing how efficiently the events of the morning took place from that moment forth. An ambulance came to take Uma's body away while the airport managers and safety teams also arrived to discuss protocol. Indeed, deaths in the air were rare, something that the managers would be pulled out of bed for. Next came the phone calls. There was no easy method to notify the family. Luckily, Uma had been carrying a small address book in which page one was marked and highlighted. "Murali and Seetha. 01-681-4727. Belmont Ave, London, UK"

It was now ten o'clock in the morning, G.M.T, when the phone rang in London. Seetha and Murali both happened to be home, tending to the children who were scheduled to go in for wellness visits later that day.

"Urgent call for Mr. Murali, please. To whom am I speaking?" the operator asked.

"Yes, this is he," Murali replied.

"Sir, I am sorry to report to you some very sad news today." The lady continued. " A person known to you, by the name of Uma Nagpal, was pronounced dead on the airplane over the skies of Kabul, in transit from India to London this morning." Murali handed his wife the phone, unable to tolerate the injustice. He was in disbelief. The voice on the other end continued.

"Are you there, sir? Are you there? I need to confirm this is your relative." Seetha now took over, witnessing a pain in her husband's countenance that she had never witnessed before.

"Hello, ma'am, I am his wife and I will take over now. He is rather distressed. Please explain what is the nature of the phone call?"

The woman spoke again, more slowly and very clearly, reiterating what she had just told Murali.

"I'm sorry ma'am. Is there anyone else we can notify for you? I need you to take down the following number of how to contact me, so that we can make arrangements of how to get the body to you and your family. By the way, by law, we can only hold the body for three days, after which point we will take care of the body. I'm sure you can understand this."

Seetha took down the number and then put the phone down. This was possibly the worst day of her life. She loved her sister-in-law, and, even though she and Murali were aware of her terminal diagnosis, she and Murali had given consent for Uma to travel since she had taken an upswing.

Murali lay frozen, clinging to his wife's sari fabric, in shock. The woman's last words were that they had attempted to call a Baba Ramaswamy, but no one had answered. Indeed, the phone had only recently been installed and had given the parents some trouble. So now, Seetha looked at her husband in shock, and realized she would have to be the one to send a telegram. She got to work, hurrying before the children would trouble her for lunch or play.

Chapter Forty-Seven: The Funeral. 1972

"Uma expired above the seas of Afghanistan, August 25 1972 STOP. Body being flown back to you STOP. Seetha the children and I coming today. STOP. IA flight 347. Nagpal closing clinic and flying tonight. STOP"

Baba read the telegram over and over, his hands trembling with fear, a feeling he had never experienced in his life. He had so many questions, but no answers. Did she get a rare flu? Was there something already wrong? Nobody had bothered to tell him. He felt emotions now that he couldn't control. The once majestic, tall man fell to the ground of his foyer, clutching the letter in his right hand while holding his horror-struck face in his left. Vanamali came running from the kitchen when she heard the thud of a grown man hitting the floor.

"What happened?" she exclaimed, meeting his eyes with her own. "What happened?"

"She's gone, Vanamali. Our baby has gone. She has left us. How could this be? This is not supposed to happen. She had only just come for a short while. What if we had forced her to stay? Maybe this would not have been the outcome. Vanamali, what are we going to do?" He lay on the ground sobbing in his wife's arms.

"Hush, Baba, hush," Vana consoled him, rubbing his back and rocking him like an infant trying to fall asleep. She too was in shock. Dare she tell her husband that she had suspected all was not as it seemed? Only last week she had noticed Uma's walk, a

Trendelenberg gait, hips swinging to control the loss of muscle tone and function that was progressively weakening her young body. No, she decided, that would not bring Uma back now. She would need to just wait. See what God's plan was for them. But she wept. Her body too, was now trembling with a feeling she could not control. She had given up all of her own dreams to be a dutiful wife and supporter of the freedom movement, yet now she sat with her husband grief-struck, and desolate. What was it all for? She could not comprehend the grief that she felt. Nothing made sense anymore.

By suppertime, all of Baba's sisters and brothers had convened, and were tending to matters in Baba's house. Aradhana made hot packs and tinctures and balms to apply to Baba's forehead so that he could rest and ease tension in his muscles. Brunda had taken over the kitchen to prepare foods for the night. Geetha was helping with the police, hospital and airlines communications of how and when they would expect Uma's body back in her homeland. By midnight, the family had tackled most of the pending work and duties needed to arrange the funeral cremation ceremonies. Brunda's husband approached Baba quietly.

"Baba, I can go to the airport to pick up Murali and family. You needn't worry about that. Try to get some sleep."

"No, no," Baba exclaimed, rather firmly, "That is something I and Vana will do. If you can keep the house warm we will all be home within the hour. It shouldn't take long, since it's just the train ride-no customs at the station."

"Very well," Dr. Rai acknowledged. We will stay here and wait for you to return. But, if it is acceptable, I would like at least our boy Parth to accompany you. Just incase you don't have a driver at this hour."

Baba agreed, and the Ramaswamy's left with nephew at side, to go to the airport.

The train rhythmically entered the station at Hyderabad, coming to a screeching halt at the end of the platform. It was a covered station, which felt cozier at midnight compared to the following local stops that were over ground. Baba stepped out of the ambassador as Parth held the door open for his aunt and uncle. Baba grabbed the boy's hand unexpectedly. Parth, acknowledging the flood of emotions that Baba was experiencing, smiled kindly at his uncle and held his arm to support him from falling. Vanamali, on the other hand, was walking quite fast, ahead of her husband but still in view. She was anxious to see her son and grandchildren, and eager for some comfort. She was emotionally drained, yet felt a sense of deep-seated depression that her own family were consoling Baba, but not her, as much. Only Geetha, who had a daughter Uma's age, had commented that there is no such deeper pain as that of a mother mourning her child. As the family stopped at the platform and waited for their loved ones to dismount, Baba requested Parth to take a seat on the bench behind them.

"Are you sure, Baba?" young Parth asked.

"Yes, son, I just want you to take rest. You do not need to be afflicted with this sight."

Parth acknowledged and retreated to the bench. Just at that moment, Seetha climbed down the final step from the cabin above, holding Maya in her arms as Murali assisted her descent. She saw her father-in-law immediately and turned to hug him, handing Maya to Vana.

"Baba, I'm so sorry for your loss. She was like a sister to me. I cannot bear this pain."
Baba began to weep, looking Seetha in the eye and feeling overwhelming grief.

"This is too much for me to bear. I do not know what I have done to have this suffering." Baba turned and hugged his son, who was standing behind him with Rukmini's hand in one hand and his other on his mother's forehead. Just then, Murali also began to tear, noticing that the warm embrace from his father was the first hug that he could ever remember having from his austere father. Baba was trembling now, the flood of emotions coming to his head, and the uncontrollable urge to speak his mind, something he just had not done yet in his home, full of caregivers. "You would not believe what they said to me, Seetha. It was so hurtful. I do not understand people."

"What did they say?" Seetha asked, concerned for her father- in -law, who was a kind-hearted man, never known to upset a soul.

"They said that her marriage was wrong. They accused us and claimed we wronged Nagpal and insulted his family by arranging his marriage to our Uma. They said we must have known she was sick but arranged her marriage for pride and other silly reasons. Does it even make sense? How could they do this?" As Baba sobbed in the loving arms of his daughter-in-law, Seetha found herself speechless for the first time in her life. She paused, stroking Baba's back and getting a handkerchief from Murali to wipe away the tears.

"You know, Baba, you are a kind, sweet man whom everyone reveres. In fact, people flock to you for words of advice and wisdom. It is amazing in this time of pain, how a few people can show their true colors. Am I right in assuming it was Shakuntala, Nagpal's elder sister, who made these false claims?"

Vanamali, now listening in, nodded. "Well then" Seetha stated firmly, "Let's not waste our energy and thoughts on such evil-minded people. We just have to focus on healing and on our own nuclear family. That's all. Please don't take her words to heart."

The Ramaswamy family left the station swiftly, and sped away in the Ambassador, ready and waiting thanks to Parth,

The following morning the young family helped their parents get dressed and ready for the thirteenth day rites. A lengthy prayer service followed by lavish spread of the best home made foods, to signify the passing of a loved one, and help her spirit go to the heavens above. Seetha's family arrived from Bangalore the previous night and was thrilled to reunite with Seetha. But, it was bittersweet for Seetha. She had felt a loving, strong bond between herself and Uma and now, the void that existed within her felt irreplaceable. She explained to her parents what had happened, and what she herself had witnessed with respect to Uma's deteriorating health in England.

"But she looked so lovely at her wedding, just like a movie star!" young Apoorva had expressed, still not quite understanding how precious life could end with no significant warning. "I know. That is what we are all struggling with. She was fine. We didn't even realize she was sick until the very end." Murali, on the other hand, could only manage a few smiles of acknowledgement and grimaced at times. He was suffering. He was not a talker, never had been. Now, his familiar quiet demeanor was only more noticeable, like a typical Englishman, reserved and soft-spoken. He couldn't find words to chatter, and didn't wish to mince words on the rare occasion that he did speak. Moreover, he pondered over his parents' relationship with him and between each other now. Baba's love had and always would be his baby girl Uma, yet now, with Uma gone, Murali feared that Baba would become introvert and avoid connecting with his family. Vanamali was a doting mother to both children, but again, had favored her son most obviously, something that Uma would openly tease her about. He wondered whether his parents' love would be enough to see them through this catastrophe.

The family were just ending the function, beginning to speak with the priests and settle accounts, when Shakuntala and her parents walked in. Nagpal, who was already present and had been civil, looked surprised by his family's sudden entrance. Shakuntala approached her brother, grabbed his arm and dragged him towards Baba and Murali. Her parents were already with the grieving family but were quiet, awaiting their fiery daughter's arrival. Shakuntala glared at Vanamali and Baba and, flailing her brother's arm in the air, she spoke.

"What is my brother going to do now? He is a widower and so young. How are we able to marry him again so soon? You know what, I think? You married off your daughter with full knowledge that she was sick, just so you need not worry about her health. I think you set us up for failure and now we stand, empty. I think you all should be ashamed of yourselves."

Vanamali cried, always emotional but unable to hold back her tears in the presence of her loving family. She looked at Murali and wept.

"Moggu, you see how they are treating us? We do not deserve this. Baba is the most respected man in this community and everybody adores him. That lady is casting such an evil eye I'm not sure how Baba will recover from this. It's wrong, Moggu, it's wrong." Just at that moment, Brunda and her husband approached Baba and stood with him in support. Murali was able to leave his mother's clutch now, since Seetha took over and held her now. He looked around the room, feeling the grey mood of bereavement and frustration. He gazed, momentarily at Nagpal's parents, hoping for a sign of kindness. When no acknowledgement came, Murali glared at the rabid Shakuntala, and spoke firmly.

"I have just lost my sister, my one and only sibling and my best friend. My parents are suffering from an irreplaceable loss, that of their daughter. The pain of loss is unbearable, and we reunite today on sad terms as we say our goodbyes. Yet, it is only petty-minded people who prevent the healing by false accusations. Talk is cheap. If you had any love in your heart, and if you actually cared to know Uma, Baba and Vanamali, you would not even dare to make such accusations. But you are only human, a mere mortal who will live and keep living in the hellish existence that you have created for yourself since this is your Karma. You only know hell, not love. I simply ask you to leave the premises before I call the police. I owe you no explanation for my sister's demise. And your own brother, a doctor, was with us when she became ill. Even he knew that this was a sudden progressive disease, not something pre-existing. But if you still doubt, then go ahead. Just keep my unfortunate parents out of your hell. At least your sibling is alive. That's all I have to say. Now I am requesting you to leave."

Baba and Vanamali took a seat by the door, and silently watched the Verchas family leave the room, heads bowed and mute, finally. Vanamali felt proud of her son, whom she had taught to be always well behaved and non-confrontational. She wished she could express her feelings of love and appreciation. She knew something had to be said to the naysayers, but she didn't expect Murali to speak up. Seetha, too, was preoccupied with young children and didn't really respond well to confrontation. Murali had always walked away from such situations. And Baba, a nonviolence preacher, would rather sit and meditate than come across as angry. Indeed, he was always in control of such reactive emotions, and Vanamali had felt cheated from that advocate voice that she, at times, deserved. So now, with all the pain and tears within her, she could sigh a breath of relief that there was a voice advocating for truth, and it was her Moggu's.

Chapter Forty-Eight: Bangalore 1975

Where are you bringing me?" Seetha asked her brothers as they drove her and the family from the airport to Jayanagar.

"It's our new home" Shiva replied, smiling as he held his nieces in the cycle rickshaw and gave further directions to the driver.

"What happened to the big house? Were you planning on telling me?" Seetha accused, fearing the worst.

"I will Akka, let's just get home first," Shiva replied.

As the Murthy's and the Murali's reached their Bangalore home, Seetha disembarked, unable to comprehend the new surroundings. Seetha, realizing now was not the opportune moment to broach the subject took the children in each of her hands and set off up the dark stairwell to the door of her new India home. Her mother, already awaiting her, grabbed her hand and gave her a hug.

"You came, good. Was everything fine on the plane ride?" Ratna asked her daughter.

"Yes, Amma, everything was quite smooth. I am so happy to see you. How are you? How are you here? Tell me," Seetha asked her mother privately, wanting her parents' rendition of the tale before taking her younger siblings' explanations. Ratna, forever patient, sighed, putting her hand to her hips and leading her daughter into the bedroom.

"Sit", she said, beckoning her eldest to the corner rocking chair positioned next to the Godrej cupboard in her room. Ratna opened the cupboard with her key, attached to a small bunch hanging from a silver decorative keychain on her sari waist. She removed a thick black ledger book and a plastic folder that contained various important documents. Ratna then paged through the black ledger and, pointing to the last few pages marked in red, she sat down close to her daughter and showed her the accounts.

"Look, Seetha, our businesses were completely down. Appa did not realize how severe the situation was until it was too late. The mill was no longer profitable and the auto rickshaw business was hard due to no money to pay the employees."

"But why didn't you ask the drivers to manage on their tips for a few months until we took advice of an accountant? I cannot believe this!" Seetha expressed, concerned and upset at her family's living situation. Indeed, the home was poor, a far cry from the comfortable bungalow that Seetha had called home, years prior. Her worries had already taken her to thoughts of marriages for her siblings being unable to happen due to financial worries, and her brothers' education being at stake.

"It was not so simple, Seetha," Ratna explained. "We were desperate. Prakash is a man of great pride. He was not willing to ask for help from his younger siblings, even though they owe him their success for raising them. So, he kept the truth from all of us. Months went by and we had no idea that the mill was failing. We couldn't pay the bills. We were living paycheck to paycheck, and also had taken on loans and verbal agreements from friends who owe us money, but since nothing was in writing, when we attempted to get payback, those individuals turned their backs. We were helpless."

"So how did everything fall apart?"

"It was Apoorva's last year of college. Nilkanth and Shiva had already started factory jobs in order to help pay the bills. Apoorva had already tried to help in her own way by talking to friends in her college neighborhood. The boys had also tried their best.   Your Appa talked to a few friends, but his pride made him avoid the reality of the situation, for some time. We ended up with only one offer. It was not great, but we didn't feel we had a choice. It was at the time, our only offer. So, we took it. We moved out the following week. It was hard for me, since my Appa had given a lot of money to support our home and business, yet we had to leave or face living on the streets. But, we couldn't refuse the offer. We were running out of time and options.

The following month, your Appa went to his bank to discuss the mill value and the cost of the current home. To his surprise, he found out that the mill was actually valued at four times the money given by the final buyer. I thought he would go into depression from that moment on. Yet, by grace of God, he continues to be positive. He runs a small storefront selling savory snacks and also offering religious advice.

The boys have suffered the most. They were unable to move on to college. We just didn't have the money. They are both so smart. We still hope that they can follow you to the Western world and study there some day. They deserve so much more. But at this moment, we are simply managing day to day. Music is my solace. I just tend to ignore these concrete walls and the rants of the landlord below. Whenever I feel down, I look at the photo of the grandchildren and feel uplifted. Honestly, what are we to do?"

"But Amma, why didn't you tell me? Perhaps I could have helped with the finances?"

"Seetha, you and Murali are already doing that. It's too much. First you paid for Uma's wedding, then funeral and next you have sent money and gifts periodically to us, too. You have to take care of your own financial stability. You have a young family and you need to save. Plus, we have children yet to marry.

If there is a time that I may need your help, I would ask you then, not now."

Seetha paused, shocked and angry at the news she had just learned.

"I'm frustrate about this. How can you be so calm?" Seetha ranted on, "Who gives away land and businesses without consulting others or obtaining property value information first? I wish you had told me, Amma." She was fuming. Realizing the huge loss that her family was now dealing with and the burden of regret that her father must have been feeling. Not to mention her poor, unfortunate brothers who would surely suffer for not having obtained any further education in this miserable situation. Seetha's mind was now racing, unable to let go of the thousands of thoughts that troubled her overly analytical mind. She arose from the chair, and, pacing, was ready to speak when her mother beat her to it.

"Seetha, I must ask you to give me your word that you will NOT say anything negative to your sister and father. The tide has turned but we will get through it. There is nothing good to come of ill feelings or regret. We simply need to move forward, focus on the positive, and let go of what we cannot change." Ratna's words were wise as expected, and quelled Seetha's rage like an oasis in the desert. Seetha now smiled, hugged her beloved mother and started to unpack, revealing all the wonderful European gifts and chocolates she had brought for her siblings to enjoy for weeks to come.

A few weeks later, Seetha and Murali were back in Himayatnagar, with Baba and Vanamali. Baba was heartened to see his grandchildren, as was Vanamali, who had longed for days with her son and grandchildren. They both pampered the children with new clothes and toys, and enjoyed listening to their British accents, a novelty that was still loved by Indians across the country. Murali helped Baba sort through his office and home mail, and realized quickly how aging his parents actually were. They needed support, and had not tended to their own affairs in the manner in which Murali had grown accustomed to. One morning, Murali and Baba returned from the post office and Baba opened a certified mail. He paused and then sat down, as if weak at the knees.

"Baba, what's the matter?" Murali inquired. "What does the letter say?"
Baba handed the letter to Murali, who was now standing next to his mother and wife, by the dining table.

"Oh, just another piece of mail. You can throw it away if you like." Baba stated, somewhat surprisingly.

Murali read the opening line quietly, but then chose to read out aloud.

"Dear Ramaswamy, sir, you are officially requested to join the Prime Minister Indira Gandhi at Republic day celebrations in New Delhi. You are to be awarded the medal of bravery and a gift for your twenty-five year anniversary of the Freedom Movement that helped India gain Independence from the British."

"Baba, Congratulations this is fantastic!" Murali exclaimed, handing the letter now to Seetha who was smiling with joy. Vanamali, close to tears on hearing her son's words, asked to repeat what was happening.

"Amma, Baba is being presented an award for his role in the freedom movement at the twenty-five year anniversary celebrations".

"Ayyo, this is wonderful. Are we all able to attend?" she asked innocently.

"Yes, Amma. I will book the tickets today. We have enough time today to go to the travel agency nearby."

Baba, who had been quietly sitting at the table, now spoke.

"It's an honor, but I do not feel what was achieved was what we wanted. There's so much more that India can achieve, yet we are now in a strange freedom that seems far removed from what were the movement's initial goals. I do not know what to make of it." Murali, sensing his father's sentiments, responded.

"Sometimes we do not get what we set out for, and sometimes what we want comes with different agendas and sacrifices. All that I know is that you and Amma gave your life energy towards this movement and deserve some praise. What is wrong about that? I will book the tickets and we will all go with you for this great honor being bestowed upon you." Baba, who was now playing with Maya and Rukmini while listening to his son, consented.

Much to Vanamali's surprise, the once skeptical Baba, received the plaque award from Prime Minister Gandhi with tears in his eyes. It was a beautiful plaque, with Baba's name engraved in gold plate in the right lower corner and a stunning marble center inlay that accented the gold leaf beautifully. Baba's tribute had even managed to appease Vanamali who, remembering all of the sacrifices and sleepless nights she and Baba had had while secretly plotting the Freedom movement, began to shed tears of joy. Oh, how time had changed them, aged them, created worry lines on their foreheads and grey zones when they had only ever seen black and white before. Yet, they had survived the turmoil and that alone was amazing.

Chapter Forty-Nine: Essex, 1977

Seetha opened the door to her new Canvey Island independent home. She was gleaming with joy. Years of hard work had paid off and she and Murali could finally leave the confines of Mopsy and Arun in the old Victorian apartment. As she entered the new home, she reflected on the past few years and sighed.

"I miss having elders around to inaugurate the home. We need to have a home pooja (religious service) but I have no one to direct. What do you suggest?" Seetha asked her husband. "Oh, goodness, you don't need long religious functions to inaugurate the home. Just keep a small idol and we will pray. There's nothing difficult about that."

"But what about calling your parents?" Seetha pushed.

"Yes, we will call them when we are ready. But these things take time, and I do not see how waiting for them is really practical. They are slowing down in age and need a lot of maintenance and assistance with their daily activities. I think we need to just focus on our own children and their needs. It is quite enough having a new home to pay for, but also to worry about the elders is just too much. Let's just take one step at a time."

The couple settled in. Seetha, who had the summer off of work, now began to beautify the house and make curtains and decorations to call it home. Seetha was tucking the children in bed one night when Murali told her he was meeting the neighbors at the local pub for an introductory chat. She consented, reluctantly, knowing she really did not have a choice in the matter. Murali had a firm, stubborn mind, not often conceding to Seetha's plans he did not want it. He was quite willing to let her attend such events on her own, but wanted no part of it. A casual pub dinner was much more up his alley. He looked forward to meeting his new neighbors there but also his best friend Sandeep. Murali was eager to bring Sandeep up to speed on his recent India vacation and all the changes he had observed during his visit.

When Murali arrived at The Orange Tree, Sandeep was already seated at the corner table. Murali approached his good friend, shaking his hand firmly with a big smile.

"So tell me, how are your parents?" Sandeep asked, kindly.

"Oh, they are well, thank you, they are well." Murali described to Sandeep all of ups and downs of the family- the plaque, the aging parents, the property in Bangalore, the frustrations of un-wed siblings for Seetha yet their own personal contributions. Sandeep had always been supportive, and many ventures the two friends had undertaken together had shown Murali that he could speak openly with his buddy without fear or regret. Sandeep, similarly, discussed with Murali his own recent trip to Bihar, India, and his wife's family and life. A few beers later, Sandeep asked Murali when he was going to bring his parents to United Kingdom.

"Surely, you want to sponsor them? I mean, you are all they have now. I'm sure they miss you and the children." Murali called for another round of drinks. When Sandeep declined, Murali only frowned, not understanding what was the big deal. While the bartender was preparing Murali's drink, Sandeep continued to ask about Baba and Vanamali.

"Listen," Murali told his friend. "You don't know my father. He is so attached to India, he only wears khadi cotton and walks to work every day. He has lived and breathed the freedom movement, and is still in a time warp, torn between old India and the modern world. Do you think he wants to come and live in

England? I do not. He wants to visit, see the grandkids, but then rush back to his country."

"But what about your mother? Surely she misses you?" Sandeep asked.

"Yes, yes, Amma hates being away from us. But I do not see any immediate solution. Do you think she can come here and live? I think she would struggle unless she had a lot of things to do. And, I do not need to be worrying about her, and Baba, and their ailments and issues. It's not as if they cared for my infant issues when they were in jail and then out fighting for freedom. I was left on my own, aunt to aunt, house to house. Then they shipped me out to private boarding school the moment I began to understand what is a family. They do not care enough for me. Do you think I want them caring for my kids?" Murali choked up, drowning himself in yet another beer before leaning back against the vinyl booth lining. Sandeep gazed at him, astounded at his childish accusations. He wanted to correct his friend, but held back, knowing that he was under the influence and likely nothing would get through.

"Who cared for me? Who took care of my needs when I was a baby?" Murali kept on repeating until Sandeep changed the topic.

The friends reminisced over their emigration together and young children, new homes and jobs. Life was good. They had accomplished what many immigrants could not, and looked forward to a future full of promise and success.

Seetha waited at home with children tucked in bed, eager to have dinner with her husband in their new home. She had all of Murali's favorite dishes laid out on the table. Potato curry, kidney bean curry, thick lentil dal and rice with papadams. Hours went by as Seetha awaited her husband's return home. There was no knock on the door.

As the sun set, Seetha put a few morsels of food into her hungry mouth, then cleaned up and went up to bed. Her head hit the pillow and she fell into a fitful sleep, tossing and turning as she fought her mind games. She pondered on what the future might hold for her. Murali's cool, logical manner was so distant from the social butterfly that she was. She craved family, friends, and culture. As she lulled into a deep sleep, she struggled with what to expect in her life, alone in a foreign country without another Indian face anywhere in sight, and a husband who sought solace in a beer with friends rather than bear his soul to those who mattered. She wondered what life would have in store for her and her young family. She closed her eyes again and imagined her children, her parents, Baba and his India free from British rule. Yet now, here she lay, in a British house, sister-in-law gone, and no family in sight to guide or counsel her, just her own gumption, willpower and diligence. Decades ago she would never had realized this is where her life would be. "I can do this," she told herself. Wrapping her arms around her body, she cradled herself to sleep.

A fortnight later, Seetha hurried to dress the children prior to the celebrations outside.

"Hurry Rukmini, put on your dress!" Seetha ordered. Meanwhile, Maya was attempting to dress herself and was now stuck half way inside her blue and white maxi-dress, handmade by her mother too.

"Mummy, help!" Maya giggled.

"Come on, the parade will start in a few minutes. Let's finish getting ready and go outside!" Seetha said.

The girls looked radiant. They wore royal blue and white dresses that Seetha had made to match the glorious occasion of

Queen Elizabeth II's silver jubilee celebrations. "Mummy, we are princesses today!" Rukmini exclaimed, as the girls and their mother joined the street party. They were each handed miniature Union Jack flags to hold and wave as the town mayor and officials came in a processional. Later, the neighborhood families each shared mini sandwiches and petit fours and kids danced. The children were joyous. At that moment, Murali returned from work, and joined the street party.

"Daddy, Daddy!" Maya yelled, running into her father's arms. "Can I have one of those mugs? They are so pretty. Please, Daddy!"

Murali smiled at his girls. He picked up a jubilee mug and examined it, turning it around in his hands. The face of Queen Elizabeth II adorned one side, with Her Majesty's crest on the opposite face. The vendor's table was covered with commemorative plates, mugs, pens, chocolates, shot glasses and tiaras. He turned back to see his girls waiting with baited breath for their father to give them the item they wanted. Murali grinned, then handed the man some money.

"I think it's time to head home now," Murali advised, gently picking Maya up, who was exhausted with all of the events of the evening. Seetha held Rukmini's hand as the family walked the short distance home. The parents tucked their girls in bed and headed downstairs for some well-deserved quiet time.

"Oh, I forgot about the girls' goodies!" Seetha exclaimed, picking up the mugs and tiaras from the dining table.

"Oh right! Let me take a look at those," Murali said, reaching for the items as he approached the table. He examined the mugs, yet again, an expression of conflict covering his forehead as if he were trying to swallow a pill which had become dislodged in his food-pipe. He set the mugs down on the mantelpiece.

"What's the matter?" Seetha inquired.

"Nothing much. It's just odd," Murali replied.

"What is?"

"Well. I was just thinking that the force that my Baba worked to kick out of India is now sitting on our mantelpiece right now!" Murali chuckled, with his cool ability to squash his mind's struggles as soon as they surfaced. "Oh well, I suppose we are Brits now!" Murali added as he sat down next to his wife on the settee.

THE END

About the Author

Anjana Barad is a mother of three who resides in Midwest USA with her family. She is a practicing family physician who has been writing since childhood. This novel is her first adventure into the fictional literary world.

Dedication

This novel is dedicated to the memory of Uma Ramaswamy.

I would like to thank the numerous friends who have helped me in this writing journey, with patience, support and guidance. Specifically, my unofficial editors Dr. E.T and Dr. W.D, who provided tremendous input and gave their time freely. Also, my dear husband N.B and children, the three R kids, who believed in my creation and have provided me so much love and support in the process.

www.ingramcontent.com/pod-product-compliance
Lightning Source LLC
Chambersburg PA
CBHW070913260626
47162CB00007B/2660